G000078591

MIRIAM'S
TALISMAN

MIRIAM'S TALISMAN

ELENOR GILL

HarperCollins*Publishers*

The references to Celtic mythology and events in Irish history, although based on researched information, are intended as a background to a fantasy. All the characters, contemporary and historical, are totally fictitious and have no connection with any events, past or present, or any persons, living or dead. Any resemblance to any person, name, place or event is entirely coincidental.

My thanks to Brendon, for his encouragement and practical help. A special thank-you to Tinch Minter and the group back in England. I am, as ever, grateful to the Poverty Bay Pen Pushers for their enduring support.

National Library of New Zealand Cataloguing-in-Publication Data
Gill, Elenor, 1945-
Miriam's talisman / Elenor Gill.
ISBN-13: 978-1-86950-609-4
ISBN-10: 1-86950-609-X
1. Title.
NZ823.3—dc 22

First published 2007

HarperCollins*Publishers (New Zealand) Limited*

P.O. Box 1, Auckland

Copyright © Elenor Gill 2007

Elenor Gill asserts the moral right to be identified as the author of this work.

All rights reserved. No part of this publication may be reproduced, stored in a retrieval system or transmitted in any form or by any means, electronic, mechanical, photocopying, recording or otherwise, without the prior written permission of the publishers.

ISBN (10-digit): 1 86950 609 X

ISBN (13-digit): 978 1 86950 609 4

Cover design by Louise McGeachie

Cover images: Getty Images; Corbis (APL); Shutterstock

Internal text design and typesetting by Springfield West

Printed by Griffin Press, Australia, on 70 gsm Bulky Ivory

AUTUMN
1999

One

MIRIAM WAS DEAD.

I tried saying it over to myself: Miriam's dead — she died — her death occurred at . . . It made a flat, jagged sound that lost more of its meaning each time I said it.

I stood alone on the city street where the morning split the air into shafts of sharp, lemon light. The crowds parted and moved around me. Nearby a man sat on a wall eating a sandwich and reading his newspaper, just as if nothing had happened. The glare of the sun stung my eyes, already red and gritty from lack of sleep. I don't think I had been crying; I didn't believe it enough to cry. I can remember feeling a sort of detachment, as if an invisible mantle separated me from the rest of the world. Everything seemed distant and subdued: the voices of passers-by were muffled, students cycled past on silent wheels, cars droned and purred. A bus rasped a sigh of air brakes as it swished along the kerb, causing the few, early-fallen leaves to skitter across the pavement. I stood, hovering on the edge of the city, holding onto a deep emptiness for fear that something more dreadful would take its place.

So what was I supposed to do next? There were things I ought to do, but I was too exhausted even to think about them. Then suddenly I was aware of the day. She always loved this time of year, the thinning of the summer sun into a paler light, the subtle pungency of decay in the cooling air. But this time she would not be sharing it with me. This was my first day without Miriam, and the first time I saw *him*.

I'm making this sound as if it all happened a long time ago and it feels almost like another lifetime, but in reality it's only been a few weeks. Early September it was, and the leaves had started to turn from gold to flame. Even now the last of their kind, the most determined, are still clinging to the trees. I'm trying hard to keep the image of that day in my mind. I must take all the memories, polish them clean like pebbles, collect them safely in a secret place. But already the picture is fading. I suppose that must be part of it, some sort of enchantment that steals away every memory that would lead me to him.

And I wonder how much, if anything, he'll remember of me.

Just a few steps away there was a small, French-style café and a rich miasma of freshly ground coffee thickened the air. Miniature orange trees in wooden tubs stood on either side of the swinging doors. The fruit must be plastic. Oranges wouldn't grow on an English street, would they? This piece of trivia took on such heightened significance that I found myself walking towards the doorway to investigate. Yes, they were plastic, but the menu in the window was handwritten. At that moment I doubted I could ever eat or drink again, yet I walked inside and sat down, studying the grey and white swirls of the marble tabletop. Coffee was placed in front of me, even though I could not recall ordering anything. I lifted the spoon and traced lines in the creamy foam.

The three of us, that is how it had always been. Miriam is — was — my grandmother, Hannah her daughter and my mother, and then there was me, Chloe. Mother, daughter, child. Three slivers of brittle glass, edging and grinding away at each other. And then there was him, although up until that moment I didn't know he existed. He must have known some of it. And Miriam?

Of course Miriam knew everything. What about Hannah? I'm still not sure how much she was aware of.

I, of course, knew nothing. They'd all made sure of that.

My hand was hurting. I found it grasping the pendant, holding onto it so tightly that red and purple marks were scored across my palm like stigmata. My eyes were hot and sore and I could feel tears pricking the corners, but I was determined not to cry. Grief is a private matter, Hannah would say. My mother never approved of public displays of emotion, would never be seen to lose control. Miriam pitied her for that and many other things. A strange thing to feel for one's own daughter — not love or pride, but pity.

There was a flurry near the door, a swirl of brown and black, a long, dark coat, ebony hair slicked back and caught into a smooth tail, the scraping of a metal chair against a tiled floor.

'You won't mind if I join you.' It was a statement, not a request for permission. I wished he would go away. Instead he sat down opposite me, the hem of his coat sweeping the floor, and leaned his head down sideways to peer up into my face.

'It is, indeed, a beautiful morning. You are Cliohna, aren't you? Though of course you prefer to be called Chloe.'

I swallowed back the tears. My voice came out in a broken whisper. 'Yes. Do I know you?'

'Miriam, I know . . . I knew your grandmother. Miriam.' I looked up into eyes that were more gold than brown, a sweep of black lashes, and black brows arched like wings on a pale forehead. He could have been my age, early twenties, but it was difficult to tell: his age seemed to change from moment to moment. He lowered his eyelids, his mouth pulled taut. Like me, he seemed to be bearing the sorrow of a loss and struggling to maintain a public face.

'I don't know you, do I? I don't think we've ever met.' I knew we hadn't. He wasn't someone to be overlooked. 'You say you knew Miriam?'

He looked directly into my eyes and nodded. 'Yes, I have

known her a long time. A long time.' Then his gaze drifted to the window and he was silent for so long that I thought he'd forgotten about me.

Suddenly, without looking back but in a voice so clear that I was startled, he said, 'You could say that through her I have known you, also.'

'Oh,' I scratched around for something to say. 'Perhaps she spoke about you. I'm afraid I don't remember. I'm sorry, this is embarrassing. You seem to know who I am, but I don't know anything about you.' To be honest, I didn't care who he was; I just hoped he would go away and leave me alone to nurture my misery. I thought that if I maintained a cool politeness it would somehow sustain the distance between us, but this strategy failed.

'My name is . . . It's difficult to pronounce. It would be easier if you called me Iolair. That's what she called me.'

'Iolair? That's easier, is it? What sort of name is that?'

'It's Celtic, like your own Cliohna, from the Gaelic. I know you prefer Chloe, but didn't Miriam sometimes call you Little Wren?'

This was too much, too intimate, this closeness from a total stranger. Who was he to know my name? What else did he know about me? I felt exposed, undefended, a small animal trapped by the intensity of those golden brown eyes. As if he sensed my unease he straightened, pushing backwards in his chair to break the spell.

'I'll have some coffee. Dark and sweet and very strong. That's what's needed at moments like this.' He smiled at me, and before I could help it I had smiled back. He raised a long, slender hand in the slightest of gestures and a waiter, busy at a far table, his back towards us, turned from his task and walked over to our corner. At the time my thoughts were too jumbled to register the significance of this. Nor was I concerned when, having brought a second cup to place next to mine, the waiter failed to place with it the slip of paper for the till. It's only now, knowing what I know, that all the tiny shards of abnormality begin to fall into place.

'You managed to get some sleep.' Again it was a statement.

'Yes, a little.'

I had slept, but fitfully. Paul had pressed some tablets into my hand, insisting that I go home and try to get some rest. I had drifted in and out of dreams filled with images of my grandmother weaving her magical stories, and Hannah, tight-faced and weeping. And there was a bird, a large, brown bird with a vicious beak and talons and the saddest of sad eyes. Its outstretched wings beat against the rushing of wind. Images of Miriam were pierced by its sharp eyes and its strange cry, a scream of pain and despair so real that it woke me several times.

'I didn't think I would sleep,' I said, 'but I managed to catch a few hours. I woke early. There seems to be so much to do and I don't really know where to start. It's all very confusing. I've just come from the undertaker's. What an odd word that is. When I was little I thought they were the people who took you under when you died. You know, under the ground. I'm still not sure why they're called that.' Oh, God, I thought, why am I blathering on like this? I sound like an idiot.

The doors continued to open and close. The room was made hot and humid by the polished chrome machines constantly exhaling gasps of aromatic steam. Iolair sipped his coffee, watching me, unblinking, unerring, forcing me to prattle on.

'The man there was very solemn and respectful. He talked in whispers, and minced around me as if I were an invalid. He reminded me of an old-fashioned butler, the sort you see in a Noël Coward play. He kept asking me all sorts of questions about what sort of funeral it was to be, where it would be held, and how many cars did I want. And I kept saying that I didn't know. At one point I said that I'd have to ask Miriam. I felt so stupid. He kept referring to her as "the deceased" and talking about "the arrangements". I wanted to shout at him, tell him that her name is Miriam and that she's dead and I just have to bury her. He was a kind man and he was only trying to be helpful, and I felt like punching him in the face.'

'There will be a lot of that, I'm afraid — people using the correct words, making the proper gestures. It's all part of the ritual, the process of grieving. You will have to make allowances.'

I picked up the spoon and stirred my unwanted coffee while he took a sip of his, then another, his eyes closing and the tip of his tongue circling his lips.

'You know, this is an excellent blend. Strong on flavour but gentle on the palate. A slightly nutty taste. It's got quite a zing to it. You should drink yours — it will kick some life back into you.'

'I gather you're not one of those people, are you?'

'One of who? Or is it "whom"? I'm never quite sure.'

'People who go through the ritual, say all the correct words. Try to give comfort.'

'Would you like me to? I'm willing to give it a try, although I've not had much practice.'

'No, I couldn't bear that.'

For something to do, I picked up my cup and took a few sips. He was right: the coffee was good. Then I felt guilty about enjoying it.

'You know, I'm not sure what I'm supposed to be feeling.' The line of his eyebrows flicked up in question at my words. 'I mean, I'm all hollow and empty. Waiting for it to start hurting. They say that at first you forget that it's happened, especially first thing in the morning. I had a friend lost her boyfriend in a car accident. She'd wake up looking forward to meeting John for lunch, or thinking she'd get him to look at a faulty plug on her kettle. Silly things like that. Then she would remember that he was dead and it would all come flooding in again. It was like she lost him over and over again each day. I wonder how long it will be before I understand that Miriam has gone?'

'She loved you very much, you know. In a way she could not love Hannah.'

'How would you know? Oh, sorry, I didn't mean to be . . . But you're right. I think it's because I can enter her world, you know, the stuff she writes, the stories and folk tales. Hannah always hated all that. Besides, they've hardly spoken for years.'

'That made things difficult for you.'

'Well, it's not easy. It's like I'm trying to be two different people. There, see. I'm doing it already. Talking as if Miriam were still here. I'll have to get used to saying *was*. It *was* difficult. She *did* love me.'

The stranger said nothing. He leaned across the table and covered my hand with his. A sudden rush of salt-hot tears gushed down my face. I rummaged in my pocket for some tissues, trying to disown the helpless sobs and gulps that shook my body. A few people fidgeted, embarrassed, and politely turned away. It was easier to study the pattern of fine blue veins that traced his wrist bone and the delicate curve of the thumb. He waited, still and silent, until the storm had subsided. I began to apologise and search for more tissues.

It was as I bent down to retrieve my bag that my jacket fell open and the pendant swung forward, clinking against the rim of my cup. Iolair jolted violently, as if a surge of energy had coursed through him. He stared at the silver ornament and for a moment stopped breathing, his body held rigid.

'It suits you well, the talisman.'

'Talisman? Is that what it is? I'm not sure what that means. It was Miriam's.'

'Yes, I know. She always wore it. And now you seem to be in possession of it.' His fingers gripped the rim of the marble table. 'An intriguing design. Celtic obviously. Do you know anything about it?'

'No, only that she wore it constantly. She gave it to me last night.'

'Did she, indeed?' His voice fell to a whisper. 'Did she?' His arm reached out. 'May I?' Slim fingertips took hold of the silver shape, tracing the interwoven lines and knots of the pattern. His hands were shaking. How pale they were, almost silvery blue, long and tapered with a delicate webbing of skin between each finger. 'I would like to see it more closely. Would you mind just slipping it off for a moment?'

It was a reasonable request, a harmless curiosity, and I responded accordingly. Or was it the habit of obedience? 'Do as you're told, there's a good girl.' I took the chain in both hands, about to lift it over my head. Then something held me back, something Miriam had said as she gave it to me. I thought at the time she must be delirious and I should humour her, but I had given my word. It was a promise, the last one I ever made her. I hesitated, then let go of the chain, allowing it to fall back into place.

'No. No, I'm sorry, but I'd rather not if you don't mind. It's very special. I don't want to take it off, well not yet anyway.'

He sighed heavily. 'Of course not. How insensitive. I should never have asked, I apologise. I know how very precious it must be to you.'

'She told me never to part with it. As you say, she always wore it. Perhaps I will too.'

'Perhaps.' He looked suddenly weary and defeated, slumping back into the chair, his head thrown back.

I thought of the bird I had seen in my dreams, its cry of despair. I watched the angular line of his throat rise and fall as he struggled to hold down his own distress. Why should Miriam have meant so much to him? We had become very close, my grandmother and I, over the last few years. It was strange that she had not spoken to me of this man.

He looked at me again and his expression softened into a gentle smile. 'I have intruded upon you long enough.' His departure was as abrupt as his arrival, and for a moment I almost asked him to stay. But then didn't. 'We shall meet again soon, Little Wren.' He stood and turned from his chair, and his long black coat swirled around him like a cloak. At the door he turned and looked back to me. 'Try talking to Greg Uson. I'm sure he can help.' Then he was gone.

The café subsided back into normality, and all the mundane noises of dampened conversation and clinking china sank in to fill the spaces where he had been. The only evidence of his presence was a half-finished cup of coffee.

After a few moments, I began to wonder if he had ever been there at all.

Two

GREG USON WAS the obvious person to talk to, so why the hell hadn't I thought of him myself? Within half an hour I was sitting on the leather chesterfield in the outer office, waiting for him.

I've known him forever. He's not exactly my uncle. One of the strange things about our family is how we call each other by our first names (or perhaps it's one of the least strange things, now I think about it). Anyway, I'm sure that was all Miriam's doing. David and I have always called our mother Hannah behind her back, following Miriam's example, although Hannah would have been furious when we were young. Now we use her given name most of the time. Everyone called Miriam by her first name. She made it clear that that was who she was and that she didn't require unnecessary labels. Yet, though we're not related, we all call Greg Uson our 'Uncle Greg'. He'd always been there for us, and in the old days he used to come to our house often. I'd been coming to this office for as long as I could remember, though not so much in the past few years, and I realised, as I entered the outer room, that I'd kind of lost touch with him.

I could recall coming into this room when I was small and sitting on that same sofa, hoping my father, Richard, could snatch a few moments from business to speak to me. I'd had to struggle on and off the huge, leather monster. I would perch on the edge, afraid that if I sat back my bottom would slip forward and I would slide down into a heap on the floor. My legs dangled in mid-air, the heels of my prized Nike trainers drumming against the padding. In a way I measured my growth and maturity by my ability to master this leviathan of the furniture world.

The room was as I remembered it, with its monumental oak desks and moulded ceilings, everything dark and heavy. I suppose it said something about the nature of the legal profession, impressive and imposing. Nothing had changed. The books were still there, lining an entire wall, as intimidating as they had seemed when I was small. They were far too large for me to hold then, and I knew it would be pointless my trying to read, let alone to understand, the thin, filmy pages of minute type. I would wait patiently for my father to appear. I could read the gold writing through the glass of the outer door. It was back to front and inside out, but I knew the names and was able to trace the letters slowly from right to left. *James, Uson and Blackthorn, Solicitors*, it used to read in those days, Blackthorn being my father, of course. Now the letters spell out *James, Uson and Bendage*.

That morning I arrived unannounced, but the secretary, whom I hadn't met before, seemed to be expecting me and called Uncle Greg on the intercom.

'Miss Blackthorn has arrived, Mr Uson. Will you see her now?'

'Yes, tell her I'll be right out.' His voice spat and crackled through the desk speaker.

The secretary was a middle-aged woman, rather plain and very businesslike. The firm had obviously learned its lesson about employing pretty young secretaries. The woman who presided over the outer office when I was young was very pretty. She had short, curly blonde hair and wore lots of make-up, meticulously applied, like one of those models in Hannah's magazines. She'd always seemed delighted to see me, and would neglect her work while she asked me about school and friends and things I was sure grown-ups weren't really interested in. When I was very small she would search out all the different coloured pens and plain paper so that I could draw pictures to put on the staffroom wall. In the later years, she often helped with my homework.

Eventually my father would appear. 'Ah, Jean, you've been keeping my girl amused. Thank you.'

'No problem, Mr Blackthorn, we've had a good time.' She would smile at him and he would rest his hand on her shoulder while he looked at what we had been doing. I thought she was beautiful and clever and perfect; a sort of angel of shorthand and typing.

Then one day she was gone and so was my father.

It was just after my fifteenth birthday. David, my older brother, was away at university most of the time, so it was just Hannah and me at home. Richard had been spending more and more time at the office and we saw little of him. His workload was increasing, or so he said. I had come home from school to find the house untidy, the breakfast dishes still unwashed, and Hannah silent at the kitchen table, still clutching the letter. She had crumpled and smoothed it out again so many times that the paper had become limp. I took the letter from her and read it myself. Then I handed it back. I too was silent. She read it over and over again for days afterwards. Perhaps she was hoping there was something she'd missed, a message hidden between the lines that would explain what she had done to deserve this.

I think I was more dismayed by Hannah's silence than by my father's leaving. Perhaps I'd never been that close to him, not really. I was Daddy's little girl, of course, and he was our beneficent king, the grand provider of the executive home, the private school and the ballet lessons, to whom we should all be eternally grateful. But it was Hannah who ran our lives and who had raised us. My father was a sort of heroic figure, who always seemed to be working or involved with something outside the home. So I can't say I truly missed him. But the act of abandonment ignites fear in a child, and it was that, rather than his absence, that fuelled my grief.

And I felt partly to blame. Hadn't I loved Jean, worshipped her as Richard did? Hadn't I colluded, however unwittingly, with the two errant lovers? I forced myself to bear my portion of the guilt and made acts of contrition by cleaning the oven and washing the kitchen floor. Of course I never talked to Hannah about Jean. In fact Hannah and I never really talked about Richard's leaving at all, especially the reasons why. She made it clear that she could cope, that we could manage alone.

'We'll show him,' she repeated constantly, although show him what she never said.

But she did show him. We survived, Hannah saw to that. David had already achieved a degree of independence, so Hannah, the lioness, threw her energies into providing for me, her remaining cub. She went back to work. Finding a job was easy enough. She had trained as a legal secretary — that's how she had met Richard in the first place — and she became even more fiercely independent despite all the offers of support that came from friends.

Miriam made some tentative approaches, but was, of course, rejected.

We continued, as a family, to use the same firm of solicitors, and Uncle Greg was superb at looking after our affairs. I think he somehow felt responsible for Richard and Jean, and wanted to make amends by protecting our interests. Also Greg was my godfather. Not that our family set much store by religion, even though I had been christened. I think Hannah had it done more to annoy Miriam than anything else. But it did make a bond between us.

I'm not sure, even now, what I really felt about being deserted by my father. I did talk to Miriam about it once. 'Do you think it was wrong, what Richard and Jean did?' I'd asked.

'It depends what you mean by wrong. It certainly hurt many people, and that was bad. But they were in love, or thought they were. Perhaps more people would have been hurt if he had stayed with Hannah. Who can measure one person's pain against another's? Besides, he and Jean needed each other. I'm not sure Hannah needed him.'

I could understand that. I doubted Hannah had ever needed anyone. She could stand on her own.

'But what about David and me, didn't we need him?'

Miriam paused at this and looked into the distance. After a while she spoke slowly. 'Yes, perhaps a child should have a father. It is easy to lose sight of everyone's needs.' I knew she wasn't talking about Richard and us any more. I sensed I was treading on dark and dangerous ground. I decided not to pursue the matter further.

One of the inner doors swept open and Uncle Greg appeared, a huge, square block of a man, solid in his granite grey suit. He scooped me up and hugged me to him.

'Ah, Chloe, you're here! That's a relief! We didn't know where to find you, and Hannah was beginning to get worried.' My nose crushed against his silk shirt, I could smell the muskiness of his aftershave and the dry tang of stale cigar smoke.

'You've spoken to Hannah? You know then? About Miriam.'

'Yes, she rang me first thing this morning with the news. My love, I'm so very, very sorry.' He just held me for a while and I leaned against him, taking comfort from the wall of his body. Then he grasped my shoulders and held me at arm's length.

'You must be exhausted. You look all-in. Is Mrs Beckett making you some tea?' He looked over my head at the secretary. 'Could you rustle up something, Susan? Perhaps a sandwich?'

'Oh no, please, I don't want anything, really.' The office was only a short drive from the café, and the bittersweet taste of the coffee was still with me; a remnant of something I wanted to hold on to, to savour a little while longer.

'Well, come into my office and we can sort things out. Susan, would you please ring Mrs Blackthorn and let her know that Chloe is with me now.'

I sank into a deep armchair as he closed the office door, then took up his customary seat behind his desk. He would take charge now, become the consultant — and I would lay my problems out in front of him and he would pronounce the words that would make everything all right again. This is how it had always been between Uncle Greg and us three women. He was the wise counsellor who petted me, coaxed sense from Miriam, and allowed Hannah's rasping demands to wash over him.

'If you promise not to tell Mrs Beckett,' he whispered, 'I might be able to find us a drop of brandy.'

'Brandy? Uncle Greg, it's not even lunchtime.'

'These are extraordinary times, Chloe. We're allowed to bend the rules.'

Despite my protests he forced a tumbler into my hand. Still protesting, I took a sip, gasped and choked as the spirit sent a burst of fire down my throat.

'I heard your studies went well. A degree course, wasn't it?'

'Yes. Computers, of course. And I managed to land a plum job at one of the science park laboratories. It's a big American company, very dynamic. But I expect Hannah's told you all about it?'

'She's very proud of you, you know.'

'Yes, I know.' I felt as if I'd been reprimanded — not an uncommon reaction for me then.

'I gather you were with your grandmother when she died.'

'Yes. Hannah's told you?'

'She did, but I'd like to hear your version.'

Dear old Uncle Greg. It was his way of giving me an opening to unload something of yesterday's nightmare. In that old, familiar sanctuary I began to relax a little, helped, no doubt, by the warmth of the brandy. I was ready to talk.

'Yes, I was with her. I went to see her after I'd finished work. You know how I'd often call in before the weekend to see if she needed anything. Well, that was my excuse: I really wanted to see if she'd made any plans that I wouldn't want to be left out of. Usually I'd find her at the table, wading through piles of scattered papers or rearranging her book collection. Though I wouldn't have been surprised to have found her outside. It had been a sunny day and she might well have been working in the garden. Clearing away the debris after the summer riot, she called it. Instead she was sitting in her armchair. She was very still and quiet. Said she felt a cold coming on and could I light the fire for her, but when I felt her forehead she was burning up. So I called the doctor.

'Miriam was furious, as you'd expect, and she swore at me all the way in the ambulance. And then they took her away and wrapped her in a white gown. The next time I saw her she was in a high metal bed with machines and tubes and flashing lights. She looked so small and fragile. I hadn't realised until then that she was an old woman. I think that frightened me more than anything — that she could have grown old without me noticing. I insisted on being with her, but I knew I was in the way. Thank God, Paul was there.'

'Paul? Do I know Paul?'

'Oh, no, of course you don't. It's so long since I've seen you, Uncle Greg — such a lot to catch up on. Paul's my boyfriend. Well, we're engaged actually.' I felt uncomfortable as I said it, like a child pretending to be an adult.

'Ah yes, Hannah did tell me. Quite a surprise, our young Chloe planning to get married. I keep forgetting you're not a teenager any more. And how did Hannah take the news?'

'Oh, she's very pleased. She and Paul are great friends.'

'Are they, indeed? And what about Miriam? She didn't mention it when we last talked.'

'Well, I don't think she took it very seriously.'

'So, Paul's the reason you're not living at home with Hannah?'

'Oh, no, I'd moved out before I met him. I'm sharing with some friends in town. Paul's a junior doctor at Addenbrooke's Hospital. He works impossible hours, so there's not much point in us living together at this stage. Besides, he needs to be close to the hospital.'

Greg raised his eyebrows, but allowed me to continue. 'We won't be getting married until he's fully qualified.'

'Of course not. Very sensible.'

'Fortunately he was on duty when they admitted Miriam, so I got the nurse to contact him and he came and talked to the consultant with me. Pneumonia, they said. And her heart was already weakened from attacks of angina. Something she'd neglected to mention, naturally. I'd wondered what the little white tablets were for. She said she had indigestion. Paul called Hannah and she came straight away, although I thought at first she might not. But you know Hannah. She would always do the right thing regardless of how she felt about Miriam.'

'I gather she was surprised to find you there already.'

'Miriam and I had grown very close recently. I didn't think there was any point in discussing it with my mother. Actually, I'm being unfair. Hannah's been great through all this. A tower of strength, as they say.'

'Yes. I can imagine.'

'But I think it was more for me than for Miriam. I refused to leave her, so Hannah ran around and organised things, made all the phone calls and tried to look after me. Paul was on duty most of the time, of course, but he did what he could. I just tried to hold on to Miriam as long as possible. She kept drifting in and out of consciousness. She tried to talk a little, but it made no sense. Then late last night she just . . . stopped. They tried to resuscitate her. I think that was the worst part.'

As I talked, I became aware of my hand moving to my throat and my fingers following the line of the chain as they sought to touch the pendant. A talisman, the man had called it. Wasn't that some kind of good-luck charm? My fingers traced its outlines and I became aware that Greg was watching me.

'I noticed you were wearing it when you came in,' he said. 'I've never seen her without it.'

'She gave it to me. It was the last thing she did.'

'It's an unusual ornament. It has a strange sheen about it. Even in a dull light it seems to glow. I often meant to ask her about it, but somehow I never did.' As he said that, I realised that I'd never asked her about it either, even though it had fascinated me for as long as I could remember.

'Uncle Greg, did Miriam ever mention a young man to you?' I described him briefly. 'His name is Iolair.'

'What was the name again?'

'Iolair. It's odd, isn't it? Celtic, apparently.'

'Yes, that figures. No, I don't recall the name. Who is he?'

'Just someone I came across recently. He seems to have known Miriam, but I'd never seen him before and I don't remember her ever mentioning him.'

'She had a lot of friends. We couldn't know them all.'

'No, of course not. I was just curious about him, that's all.' Strange, it was Iolair who had sent me to Greg. Perhaps there was some reason Miriam had wanted their association kept quiet. Anxious now to avoid unnecessary explanations, I pretended to change the subject.

'What I really came to see you about was the funeral. I insisted that I would arrange everything. I suppose I needed to feel I was doing something, and that was the only thing left to do. Hannah tried to take over, of course, but I managed to stand my ground. Only now I realise I don't have a clue how to go about it. I wondered if you had any idea what Miriam would have wanted.'

'But of course. That's why I was trying to contact you earlier. There's no need for you to worry. It's all arranged. Miriam saw to everything.'

'*Miriam* did?'

Uncle Greg rose and crossed the room to one of the old wooden filing cabinets, returning with an armful of folders and envelopes, which he spilled onto the desk. 'Now of course we can leave all this other stuff until another time — there's nothing that needs urgent attention. However, I do have . . . somewhere among this lot . . . Ah, here it is. Funeral arrangements.' He handed me a large envelope and I studied the lettering, written in Miriam's ornate script:

> *For Cliohna Blackthorn,*
> *Instructions for the burial rites of Miriam Katherine Shaw*

I stared at it for a long time, until Greg whispered, 'I think you're supposed to open it.'

'Yes, of course.' The flap was secured with old-fashioned red sealing wax, the sort of dramatic touch that could only have been Miriam's doing. I levered the wax off with a paperknife, then up-ended the package. Out slid a sheaf of papers, some handwritten and some printed on various headed notepapers, along with several cassette tapes and a book of poetry.

'What's all this?'

Greg sorted through the papers, then handed me a page in Miriam's handwriting. 'I suggest you start with this one.'

'Good God, it's instructions for the service. And a list of who to invite. What are all these notes in the margin? Oh, I see, that's people who should be invited to speak. Look, there are even some suggestions for readings — that must be what the poetry book's for. Yes, look, Yeats and Tennyson. She says something about her doing a reading from *Beowulf.*'

'Yes, it's on one of those tapes. She wants that played back as part of the proceedings.'

'Good God. Look, she's even given us a list of who *not* to invite. Hey, listen to this: "Don't let Hannah recruit her local vicar, I don't want some Christian upstart chanting over my bones." That's Miriam all right.'

'These other tapes are music: Mozart and Rachmaninov and some traditional Irish harp tunes.'

'Yes, there's a list of music here. And it says, "I don't want anyone singing. Nothing worse than a room full of people singing hymns they don't believe to a tune they don't know in a key their voices were never designed to reach." ' We were both laughing by then.

I shuffled through the other pages. 'Where is this event supposed to be held?'

'Ah, that's this one,' he said, handing me a letter embossed with the crest of King's College, Cambridge. It confirmed the use of their Great Hall for the pre-burial service.

'This is amazing, Uncle Greg. I called in at an undertaker's this morning — you know, the one on Station Road — but it all made no sense, so I just left it.'

'That's OK. An undertaker's already been appointed and has received full instructions. They only need a phone call to move into action. Here's their number. And these are the deed papers proving ownership of a cemetery plot. There should be a list of pall-bearers there, as well as the address of a florist and a choice of flowers.'

'Oh, you're joking. This is incredible. What about a reception after? I suppose she's already made the sandwiches.'

'Not quite. Here's an estimate from a caterer for a small gathering at the cottage.'

'And look what she's written on the bottom. "I don't want any of this piddling sherry nonsense. Make sure they serve a full-bodied red wine in large glasses as befits a warrior." '

I continued to search through the documents, hoping there would be a personal note for me, but I found nothing.

'She seems to have thought of everything. It's like she knew.'

'She came to me six months ago and told me she needed my help to make plans.'

'But that's awful, morbid. Fancy making plans for your own burial.'

'Not at all,' he said. 'She was like a kid plotting a surprise party. She really enjoyed stage-managing it all.'

'I wish she could have seen the end of the year. She talked a lot about living in two centuries, but she never made it that far. What a party that would have been.'

'And,' he added quietly, 'she didn't want you to have to deal with any more conflict.'

I touched the talisman and whispered a silent thank-you. Greg waited patiently while I continued to read and sip my brandy.

'Would you like a top-up?' He waved the bottle towards my glass and I was shocked to find that it was empty.

'Oh, God, no thank you. I'm supposed to be driving.'

'OK. So is everything you need there? You know if there's anything else I can do, you only have to let me know. I can take it all off your shoulders if you'd rather.'

'No, no. It's what she wanted and I want to do it. It's just so hard to imagine Miriam being so organised and practical. She seemed to live in a dream most of the time, hardly aware of what the rest of the world was doing.'

'And most of the time that was true. All that eccentric, mystical stuff. But underneath lurked a hard-nosed and very astute businesswoman. She was very wealthy, you know. She made a lot of money from her books, of course, both here and in the States. And she managed to invest it very wisely, though her methods may have been a bit off the wall.' He smiled and shook his head. 'Sometimes she'd buy shares because she liked the design on the company's notepaper. But they always came through. And of course the cottage was an excellent investment, and she was forever buying things at auctions. All in all, the estate amounts to quite a sizeable sum. But of course we can deal with all that another time. Perhaps after the funeral you could come in and I'll go over everything with you.'

'Why me? Surely Hannah would be the best person to talk to?'

'Oh, my God, you don't know, do you? Do you mean she didn't explain it to you?'

'Explain what? Uncle Greg?' I tensed: something bad was coming and I didn't know if I could cope with any more.

'It's yours, my dear. All of it. Apart from a few token gifts to friends, she left everything to you.'

I had been betrayed. I stumbled out of Uncle Greg's office and onto the pavement, desperately clutching the brown envelope and trembling with rage. Little more than an hour had passed since I had arrived. The sunlight washing the midday street had barely shifted its shadows. But for me, for the second time in less than twenty-four hours, the world had jolted on its axis and nothing would ever be the same. I suppose it's laughable really, but at the time I was furious. There I was, stomping along the road, telling her all about it.

'Why? Why me? I thought we were special? I didn't want this. I don't need your bloody money. I don't need anything from you.' I'm sure I was muttering out loud and completely oblivious of passers-by. 'And what am I supposed to do with it all? Why didn't you give it to Hannah?' I fumbled with the car keys, dropped them. 'Oh, my God. Hannah. What the hell is she going to say? She'll hit the roof. How could you do this to me? No, Miriam, I'm not having this!'

And it couldn't wait. I'd have to have it out with her immediately. I scrambled into the driving seat, wrenched the engine into life and swerved off in the direction of Miriam's cottage.

Three

I WILLED THE CAR forward, foot down hard to the floor, knuckles straining white on the steering wheel.

'Quitter!' I muttered. 'Deserter!' Anger rolled and coiled inside me. How dare she land me with all her worldly goods and then just run out on me?

'I never wanted this,' I told the dashboard. 'I can't do it on my own.'

But, strangely, some small part of my mind looked on, observing with detached interest, as if I were playing out some pre-determined role. But then I was used to playing a part.

Fortunately, by the second set of lights a steady stream of traffic had forced the car below the legal speed limit and my fury had subsided into self-pity. And by then, of course, common sense had kicked in and I had realised that the cottage would be empty. But I went there anyway; there was nowhere else I could run to.

So I drove on and out of town, until the houses parted and opened onto fields, black and stubbled from the recent harvest. Cambridge, though a city, is small and huddled at one corner of the fenlands. The suburb where Hannah still lives and where I was brought up has long since been absorbed by the amoebic spread of development, and now it's a jumble of Victorian brick dwellings peppered with modern houses, but all neat and presentable. Beyond this, one has to pass through flat, open fields to reach the circlet of villages that surround the city, yet somehow retain their separation, like maiden aunts pulling tight their skirts. It is a landscape of skies, of grey clouds, raw winds and crouching hedgerows; whole counties reclaimed from the bogs, drained and ploughed and as medieval as the workers who dug its ditches.

Miriam's cottage is in the village of Grantchester. Where else? The place is suspended in time, just like its church clock that, in the famous poem, 'stands at ten to three'. The clock's still there and there's honey still for tea, taken beneath the apple trees in the same Orchard Tea Gardens where Rupert Brooke and his circle reclined in deckchairs to share their latest stanzas.

I was about fifteen when I started going there. Even then I was usually in a state of high emotional intoxication, as you mostly are when you're fifteen. There was always some adolescent crisis, an outraged ego to be soothed, some dark sin to confess. Miriam would understand. Sometimes it was a grand achievement that I was bursting to share with someone. Who else was there? Whenever I needed to unburden my soul or to seek wise counsel I would head for Miriam's cottage. I've travelled the road to Grantchester so many times over the years that I know every curve and bridge, every crack in the footpath where oak tree roots bulge like blisters, every whitewashed wall that teeters along the grass verge.

I remember the first time I went there on my own. It wasn't long after my father had left. I can't even remember now what awful event it was that sent me running to my grandmother. Some argument with my best friend, I think, probably resolved the next day, but at that moment I had hated her and was never going to speak to her again. Ever! I rushed from the school gates, knowing that Hannah would not be home for several hours and I needed to justify my outrage to someone. I had plenty of other girlfriends only too eager to take sides. There were neighbours, family friends, no end of places to run to and shoulders to cry on. So why Miriam? I've always put it down to impulse but, with what I know now, I'm no longer sure.

I had to cycle several miles from my city school and along the Grantchester road, but on a warm day in late summer, on the swiftest of bicycles and spurred on by a tragedy to rival those of ancient Greece, the distance was eaten up in minutes.

I didn't stop to think if she would be there, or of the reception I might get by just turning up out of the blue. I hadn't seen Miriam for several months, and then only briefly and very formally. This was 'post-rift', of course. My early years were divided into the 'pre-rift' and 'post-rift' eras. There was a time when Miriam had been an everyday part of our lives, although even then I was aware of a coolness between her and my mother. This seemed to centre on me and, as children do, I gained a sense of power from being in control of two opposing adult forces. Then, on my ninth birthday, I caused those underlying currents to erupt into the full confrontation that was to divide our family. Since then, there had been visits from Miriam at Christmas and birthdays, but those were brief and tense — an exchange of gifts and civilities and a regretful departure. We never visited her. When Richard abandoned us, I had hoped that Hannah might look to Miriam for support. But she didn't. Of course I was aware that my mother would be furious if she knew where I was heading, but I wasn't going to let *that* stop me.

I slowed down when the road reached the edge of the village, panicked by the sudden fear that I might not be able to find the house. I started to think of turning back. Then suddenly there it was, emerging from a tangle of willow trees and beech hedges. It's a sprawling old building of crumbly red brick and tiles, and a dishevelled thatch, a home that passes from generation to generation, loved and unkempt. The garden is still as it was then, wild and rambling, attempting escape by scrambling over broken walls. I skidded to a halt amid a screech of brake rubber and the pneumatic pumping of my own lungs. Then I became aware of other sounds: the rustle of willow leaves, birds squabbling over hedgerow berries and the rasp of grasshoppers.

I leaned my bicycle against a bush and crept up the garden path, fearing Miriam would not be at home or that she would be angry at my sudden appearance. Before I was halfway to the door, it opened and she stood there smiling, her arms open, as if I were expected and she impatient for my arrival. And then we were both hugging and tearful either side of the threshold.

'Come in, girl, come in. Let me look at you. Oh, you've grown so tall. And so pretty. Come along, I'm gathering apples — you can give me a hand. They've been abundant this year and they're ripe early.'

Somehow I found myself in the orchard. We collected fruit fallen among the long grass, and she told me the country names of the wild flowers. Afternoon sunshine was hot on my back and wasps rose in angry formations when we stole away their feast. She never asked why I had come or if Hannah knew where I was. We both knew that she didn't, and from that moment we entered into an unspoken conspiracy.

We took the fruit into her kitchen and she brewed up some tea, a strange, soothing blend that was both bitter and sweet.

'We must make apple pie in honour of the occasion!' she said. I was always startled by her accent. She seemed so utterly English that I always forgot that she was born and raised in America. 'Here, you can peel and core the apples while I make the pastry.'

Before I knew what was happening, I was set to work at the kitchen table. Things weren't going the way I'd intended, but somehow this was more comfortable and I went along with it.

'The apple is quite a special fruit, you know.' Miriam tipped flour into the pan of an old-fashioned kitchen scale. 'It has all kinds of mystical associations. Did you know that?'

I shook my head.

'Well, in many countries people believe that each tree has its

32

own elemental, a sort of guardian spirit, that could bestow magical powers on anyone who ate the fruit. In Ireland the apple tree was considered to be sacred. They thought that if anyone harmed the tree the gods would be angry. There's a poem called "The Triads of Ireland".

> *Three unbreathing things,*
> *Paid for only with breathing things,*
> *An apple tree, a hazel bush, a sacred grove.*

'Do you know what that means?'

Another shake of my head, fearful she might stop. I'd no idea what she was talking about but I was bewitched by the sound of her voice.

'It means that if they cut down an apple tree they would have to make a sacrifice of a living animal to recompense the gods. Otherwise some terrible disaster would befall them. It would have been a goat or a sheep. Some believe that the Druids made human sacrifices, but I'm not too convinced about that.'

The pie was made and most of it eaten. We talked for ages; at least she talked and mostly I listened as she wove magical tales in and out of the conversation. I had stumbled upon another world, wedded to another time. The trials and tragedies of everyday life became inconsequential there. I never did get around to telling her why I'd come.

And that was the first visit.

I made some excuse for being late home, and that was the first lie. The first of many. At the beginning, the visits were infrequent and clumsily camouflaged, but as I began to see Miriam more, the excuses became increasingly elaborate and fell easily from my tongue. 'I'm staying after school for netball practice.' 'Sorry I'm late, went round to Julia's to go over maths revision.' I knew which lies would appeal to my mother and I tried my hardest to please her with them. Of course it became easier as I grew older and less obliged to explain my whereabouts. But I still did not tell. When I was twenty I moved in with my friend, Angie, and a succession of 'third girl to share central city terrace'. There was no longer any need to lie, but by then it had become such a habit I saw no reason to stop.

I parked the car and walked up to Miriam's door, the same as all the other times; only this time I could feel the emptiness wrapping itself around the place, the silence as palpable as a pall. It was only the day before that I'd found her ill, yet already the rooms were cold and smelt slightly musty, as if they were becoming accustomed to their abandonment. I don't know why, but I was surprised to find everything else just as we'd left it.

I threw my bag and coat down on the dining table, scattering the eternal piles of work notes. Sunlight poured through the leaded window, setting dust motes dancing in their own spotlight. How I loved this room, the rich shambles of it all. Things piled on other things or clustered in groups with no rhyme or reason other than they looked comfortable together. Shells and stones and pictures, china whole and broken, new things and old things, worthless and priceless. Their quality and value didn't matter, only that they were pleasing to the eye and a joy to the spirit. I could not bear the responsibility of their being mine. I circled the space, fingering objects that I knew well and loved, and the touch was almost painful.

Had he ever been there, the man I'd met in the café? Where would he have sat? Not next to the inglenook, no, surely she would not let him use her favourite chair. I was allowed to sit there sometimes, but no one else. Perhaps the sofa, leaning back into the cushions, his long fingers stretched out to catch the warmth from the fire. Or maybe he sat at the table. That must have been it: he had to be a student or a fellow researcher. He would have sat next to her, making notes from her handwritten pages, their heads bent together over some minor point of Gaelic diction. Perhaps he had come seeking information from her collection of books, looked something up, borrowed one even.

The line of bookcases covered one wall, shelves bowed under the weight of volumes bound in dark, dilapidated leather. Most were in English, but some were in other languages; many were in Gaelic, which I recognised but could not read. Then there was that special row of shiny hardbacks in dark green with gold lettering: *History and Legends of Ancient Ireland* by Miriam Shaw, *Celtic Gods and Kings* by Miriam Shaw, *A Strange and Mystic Land* by Miriam Shaw . . . Eight of them in all, lined up in order of age, the last and latest supported by a curled ram's horn set in silver.

Many hours I had sat, cocooned in the big armchair, dipping into these books and reading snatches of mystical tales, myths and legends, while Miriam worked at her table. Better still were the times when she would recount these stories to me herself. When I was a child I took in every word of her magical tales of kings and strange beasts and fairies and magic spells. I relived every image until they became part of my conscious perception of the world. Even as a young woman I never tired of listening, although the nature of the stories had changed. She began to tell me of the enchantment of love and birth and death. I learned that there were different kinds of pain from that inflicted by the sword. Hungry for every word, I neither believed nor doubted. Never once in all those years did I think to ask how much of it, if any, was true.

I found myself heading for the back of the house, and walked through to the little sun-drenched room that had already been made mine. As I opened the door, there she was, smiling down at me from the stillness of the canvas. I thanked God the portrait was almost finished and I would be able to complete it without her. How different this woman looked from the Miriam I had held the day before. Everyone says that I look like her, and I can understand that, but I am also aware of the differences. The high cheekbones that gave her classical beauty, on me are exaggerated into an elfin face. Her hair was still thick and silky and, although recently silver grey, it had once fallen in waves of dark amber. Mine is a lighter red and corkscrews into curls. But we have the same eyes — peridot green, like water ice. Her eyes looked down at me then, bright and clear, and her skin was smooth and taut. Yet she was over seventy. It was outrageous, the way she defied the passage of time.

The room had been a present on my sixteenth birthday. When I had first arrived I thought she had forgotten. As usual I found her busy at the dining table, that huge circle of polished wood that could rival King Arthur's.

'Oh, it's you, girl.' I had my own key and had let myself in. 'Well, come on through. Is that the time already? I was so involved in this translation. Perhaps you could make us some tea?' And she bent over her work again.

I returned from the kitchen with a tray and poured us each a cup, setting hers beside her on the table. I waited for some word, some acknowledgement that this was a special day. Surely she could not have forgotten? She didn't even look at me.

'You must forgive me, dear, I just have to finish this while my mind is tuned to it.'

I swallowed my disappointment and reached for my sketchpad and pencils.

Art was my secret passion. More secrets — although I don't hold myself responsible for this one. School was a pleasure ride, as, fortunately, most subjects came easily to me and my grades were usually good. I excelled at maths: often the answers would pop into my head before I'd hardly had time to read the questions. This guaranteed me top marks on school reports, although I often suffered pangs of guilt because I had put in so little effort to gain so much praise. Oh, and Hannah was so proud of me.

'My Chloe just seems to have a natural talent for figures' she would croon. 'Such an important requirement these days, of course. Perhaps accountancy, who knows?' She glowed with pride at her offspring's achievement, and I, basking in the warmth and safety of her approval, knew exactly how to fuel the fire.

However, there were other lessons I did not bother to mention. The school art studio was my Utopia, where I worked hard in and out of class time and earned the praise of my art teacher. But at home those high grades were dismissed with a shrug. It was a pastime, a nice hobby. Hannah thought her daughter fortunate to have something to amuse herself on rainy days, but art was hardly something to take into account when considering a future career.

At my grandmother's cottage there were subjects to draw in every inch and corner, a myriad of shapes and textures and patterns of light. I worked at my sketchpad every moment I could. Miriam studied my work carefully. A few of the sketches quietly disappeared from my folder to reappear on her wall, mounted and framed.

'Look out, girl! You're spilling tea over my notes! There's just not enough room for us both to work at this table. You'd better move your drawing somewhere else.'

I was shocked. I had never heard an unkind word from Miriam before.

'Come along here, I'll find you a space where you won't be in my way.'

Too startled to speak, I was herded through the house to the back storage room.

'In there,' she said, whisking the door open and pushing me inside. 'See if you can make use of this.'

I stumbled through, bewildered. This was not the same room. Where were the piles of dusty furniture, the boxes and packing cases? The heavy, drawn curtains were gone and sunlight streamed onto a bare wooden floor and freshly painted walls. In the centre of the room stood an easel set with a clean white canvas. I moved forward, not daring to hope. My fingers traced the edge of the huge white square, and I saw there were other canvases of varying sizes stacked against a wall. I turned to her.

'Is this for me?'

She nodded.

'For me to paint?'

Another nod and a beaming smile.

'I've always wanted to try oils. I'm not sure how.'

'There are some books that might help.'

She pointed to a table piled high with brown cardboard cartons. Yes, there were books, smooth and glossy with coloured illustrations. I flipped through the pages, breathing in the smell of new print, then picked up one of the cartons.

'Are these paints?'

'Why don't you open and see?'

And I prised open box after box, the white metal tubes tumbling onto the table.

'The man in the shop said you would need those too.'

She indicated a shelf laden with bottles and cans, linseed oil and turpentine, adhesives and varnishes. And there was a big earthenware jar crammed with brushes, so many brushes, all different shapes and sizes. I lifted one out and ran the golden tufts down my cheek.

'I had the plumber install that big old butler sink that was in the garden. He's put in hot water so you won't go making a mess in my kitchen. Oh, and I don't want you neglecting your drawing.' She guided me round to a desk set to catch the light from the window. There was a drawing board, a real drawing board with adjustable angles.

'You'd better look in the drawers, too.'

I pulled them open, one after another. 'Oh, pastels! And watercolours! Exactly the right pencils! How did you know which pencils?'

'I do observe things, you know. Besides, you're always leaving them lying about. However, I confess I had to ask the assistant about paper. I hadn't realised there were so many kinds. He was very helpful.'

'Helpful? I'm not surprised. You must have bought up half the shop. And it's mine? It's really all for me?' For a long time I stammered incoherently. I didn't know where to begin to thank her.

'You have a talent, girl. Someone should recognise it.'

So, the months went by, and turned into years. The visits fell into a regular rhythm.

It's amazing how you can choose not to see things when you're standing in the middle of them. But that's how it was. I really couldn't, or wouldn't, see that the whole set-up was wrong. My life was gradually split in half as if I had been torn in two by the rent between my mother and grandmother. I became two separate people, one for Hannah and one for Miriam. I suppose I became so adept a chameleon that I fooled myself. Even with Miriam's portrait looking down at me and her death echoing through the empty rooms, I still couldn't see it.

And I became really good at acting out the parts, switching roles on demand. At home I would study, listening with serious intent as Hannah talked of college and careers. At the cottage I would paint to the sounds of Mozart. My bedroom at home would be scattered with teenage magazines and editions of books carefully selected as being suitable for a growing girl. I rarely read them. *The Lord of the Rings* and *The Once and Future King* lay concealed in the depths of my school bag. I learned to love music and nature and form and texture. Hannah was so relieved to see her daughter growing up into a normal, healthy, co-operative teenager that I tried even harder to please her. Yet all that gave my life meaning, I found with Miriam.

The portrait was to be a way of saying thank you, but she didn't wait long enough for me to finish. Still, there she was, smiling, her eyes shining and the talisman at her throat. I became aware of the heaviness of the same ornament around my own neck and touched it gently.

Then I turned and left the room, closing the door behind me.

There were things to attend to. The bed needed stripping. I remade it with clean sheets, in readiness for I knew not what. Then I loaded discarded clothes into the washing machine and its rhythmic drone broke the spell of silence. Half-empty teacups had acquired a blue surface scum that threatened to grow mould very soon. At the sink I immersed my hands in hot soapy water and gazed out across the garden. The orchard would have to be attended to. Apples were rotting on the ground and wasps were swarming. A pity Miriam didn't have a gardener.

Or did she? I sometimes thought I caught sight of someone in the garden. Certainly there were times when I thought she wasn't alone. Oh, I don't mean visitors — there were always plenty of those: friends from the university, historians or students who had begged an interview for their research project. No, sometimes I had the impression that there was someone else, that she had been expecting me, despite my arriving unannounced, and that someone had just left the room as I came in. There was never any physical evidence, just a trace of something in the atmosphere, or in Miriam, that told of a hasty retreat, an unfinished conversation hanging in the air. As with so many other things, I never asked, I never said.

Though I did tell them about the bird.

It was many years ago. I must have been about seven or eight, I think. Anyway it was during the 'pre-rift' era when Hannah would sometimes take me to visit Miriam. I loved these visits. The cottage seemed dark and mysterious, full of secret treasures, and the overgrown garden part of an enchanted forest. On several occasions I had caught a glimpse of something, a rustle in the trees, a shaking of branches, a flash of brown among the leaves. Strangely, I had never felt afraid.

Some of the memories are fading faster than others, and I'm trying to hold on to what I can. But that day I can remember clearly. And I know I saw something.

I've been sent out to play while the grown-ups talk. They think I would overhear things I'm not supposed to know about. Actually I don't care at all. It's all boring stuff and I'd have to sit still and not interrupt. Anyway it's too sunny to be indoors. I'm going to run down to the orchard and climb my favourite tree. Nobody can see me up there, but I can just see the river if I get high enough. Last summer I spent whole afternoons up here. I brought my book to read and ate dozens of apples. Miriam says it's too early for apples. Most of them are still green, but I can see one that's turning red. It's right on the end of the branch, as if it's leaning to catch the sun. If I inch out very carefully and stretch my arm as far as it will go I might be able to reach it.

I can feel the tree give beneath my weight. It's a bit wobbly. Just an inch more. Oh no! The branch suddenly dips. I'm slipping sideways. I can't catch hold. I grasp at leaves. They come away in my hand. Twigs snap as I fall. I try not to, but there's a scream, which goes on and on, even when I bite my lip. No, it's not me. It can't be. Branches crash. A sudden rushing of air. As I tumble over and over I catch sight of it. Big enough to block out the sun. Only a glimpse but enough to see wings spread open wide, feathers like fingers. Its hooked beak is gaping open as it screeches an alarm.

I land with a thump on the grass and manage not to yell. But it's gone. Miriam is running from the house with Hannah close behind her.

'What is it? What's wrong?' That's Hannah shouting.

'Cliohna! I think she's had an accident.'

I'd better show them I'm all right, even though I'm bound to get told off. I scramble to my feet and run out from the trees, desperately wiping at scratches and slimy moss.

'I just slipped, that's all. But there was this bird. It was enormous, and it had huge talons and I'm sure it was an eagle.'

'Nonsense, Chloe, and look at your T-shirt.'

'But it was. I did see it. It was brown and it had a big, black beak.'

Then Miriam pushes forward and she's bending down and grabbing my shoulders. Her face looks a funny grey colour and her hands are shaking.

'An eagle? You say you saw an eagle? What colour were its eyes?'

'Oh, for God's sake, Miriam, don't encourage her. You've filled her head with enough rubbish without telling her there are eagles in your garden.'

'But Mum, there was. I saw it.'

'I don't want to hear another word of this, do you hear?'

Hannah grabs my hand and she's dragging me towards the kitchen. I'm going to have my imagination scrubbed with a soapy flannel and sealed with a plaster.

Miriam is left behind among the trees.

I looked out at the same apple tree, catching the memory, replaying it. Then I forced my attention back to the washing up. The kitchen clean and tidy, I wandered back into the sitting room and fell into an armchair, the one in which I had found her only the day before. She had wrapped herself in a voluminous mohair cardigan which was still there. I snuggled inside it and drank in her own distinctive perfume of jasmine oil and spices. Clutching the talisman I closed my eyes and sank down into a blessed darkness. I seemed to be back in the café again. The man, Iolair, was there. He was trying to tell me something, but although his mouth shaped the words all I could hear was the screeching of a bird. And then it seemed to be outside the window, scrabbling on the sill and beating its wings against the glass.

I awoke with a start to find that several hours had passed and sunlight had deserted the room. The exhaustion of the past twenty-four hours had caught up with me. What I needed was a good night's sleep. And then there would be another day, and how would I survive that? Oh, God, I'd have to talk to Hannah about the instructions in Miriam's will. I felt sick at the thought.

I also realised that I hadn't let Paul know where I was, and by now he would be worried about me. In fact, until that moment, I'd forgotten all about him.

Four

I TURNED ON TO the main road into town. The sun was setting, and deepening shadows softened the rows of old houses. I drove carefully this time, aware that my judgement was unreliable and trusting Fifi to guide me home. She knew that road as well as I did. The little house I shared with the other girls stood perched on the pavement in one of the narrow side streets. Built cheaply in the eighteen-hundreds as homes for the university's domestic staff, the terraces had become fashionable city dwellings, painted up and preened like rows of pretty dolls' houses, all sparkling in the yellow light of the street lamps. I drew Fifi into a space at the kerb and sat there for a moment, realising I couldn't put it off much longer.

Fifi was another gift from Miriam.

It was just after I had started my first job and had managed to pass the driving test at the second attempt. After years of student deprivation and a succession of increasingly dilapidated bicycles, I decided I deserved a car. So I cleaned out my piggy bank, a lifetime's accumulation of saved pocket money and birthday donations, and took out a small loan. All right, so the car I chose had a few rust patches on the bodywork and it vibrated if it went over fifty. Still, it had six months' road tax and the small engine would go a long way on a litre of petrol. And it would be mine. I'd be a working woman with my own wheels, and next year I could trade it in for a newer model. The salesman was a friend of a friend and said I could take it for a test run. So, of course, I drove it to the cottage.

And there was Miriam outside on the grass verge, all smug and smiling and leaning against another car. This one was bright red, shining and new from the showroom. I protested for at least ten minutes before I caved in and agreed to keep it. She was French and looked so brazen that she had to have a name to flirt with, so Fifi it was. We christened her with champagne. Then I took her to show Hannah.

'Guess what?' I said. 'They've given me a company car. Sort of perk.'

'That's wonderful. And you were just talking about buying a car. They must really value the work you've been doing. A promotion next, you'll see.'

What's another lie? Fifi was the best present I'd ever had and I wasn't going to let Hannah spoil it for me. Besides, it wasn't deceiving her that was making me feel uncomfortable. Something else didn't feel right.

'Is that you, Chloe?'

Angie's voice sang out to me from the kitchen. Then she came through into the hall and was so solid and ordinary that I clung to her.

'God, you look awful! Where have you been all day? You might have let us know — we've all been worried sick. Oh, you poor thing. It must have been awful for you. And your hands are frozen.' Angie works with animals, a veterinary nurse, so she's accustomed to maintaining a one-sided conversation with her charges. For once I was thankful, as I didn't feel much like accounting for my actions.

She disappeared into the kitchen and there was a blast of cold air as the back door opened. 'It's OK. She's here!' The door slammed and she returned. 'Come into the lounge. We're trying to light a fire. When was the last time you ate? I bet you've had nothing all day. I'll go and put the kettle on.'

I sank down beside the little tiled fireplace and stretched my hands over the few flames that were struggling for life among a pyramid of logs. The house was warm anyway, but we loved the idea of a real fire, even if the reality never quite lived up to our expectations. When Angie and I moved in we promised each other that we would light real fires and buy a toasting fork and make buttered toast on Sundays. The squashed little rooms were crammed with dusty bargains from charity shops and car boot sales. But it was our home.

There was another cold draught and a slam, then Paul hurried into the room, his arms laden with sawn wood.

'Rabbit, where the hell have you been?'

Paul often called me Rabbit. A pet name, he said. Angie thought that was funny. Usually I found it endearing, but just then it jarred me to the bone.

'Oh, I went to see Greg Uson. We had to sort out some stuff, you know, for the funeral.'

'Yes, Hannah said you were at the solicitor's, but I rang there and they told me you'd left hours ago.'

'I'm sorry. I didn't realise you'd be here. I didn't think.'

'Of course I'm here. I've been waiting for ages. Are you all right?'

I began to feel defensive. 'Yes. Why shouldn't I be all right? I'm fine.' Was this what I had been avoiding?

'Well, we didn't know what to think. Where have you been all day?'

'I went to the cottage, that's all. I fell asleep.'

'What were you doing there?'

'I went to see Miriam.' I didn't know how else to explain and I wasn't sure if I wanted to.

Paul hesitated and drew a deep breath. 'Look, you've been under a tremendous strain. You'll be able to think more clearly after a good night's rest.'

I thought I was thinking clearly, but I couldn't summon up the energy to protest. I looked up and saw the concern in his eyes. His face was always so wide open. I leaned into the hardness of his shoulder and allowed my body to wilt. When I was with him I didn't feel I had to play a part, or so I told myself. There was certainly no need to lie. Well, not very often. Only when I wanted to keep something to myself.

At that moment I wanted things to be right between us, so I said, 'I could do with a hot bath and something to eat.'

'No sooner said than done, my lady.' And he hoisted me up in his arms and carried me up the stairs. I felt giddy and screamed with laughter as he whirled me around. I was startled. I hadn't expected to be able to laugh. Angie came out from the kitchen to see what all the noise was about. 'Angie, could you rustle up some food? I think she needs some TLC.'

'I was just making some soup and sandwiches — be ready in about ten minutes.'

Paul filled the bath with an assortment of oils and foams and the scented steam made my head swim. My clothes lay strewn on the bathroom floor where he had helped me undress. I lay back, eyes closed, while he soothed my shoulders and sponged water to trickle down my face. I tried to recount the events of the day, especially the conversation with Greg about Miriam's will.

'You mean everything is yours, the cottage as well as the money?'

'Yes, I think so. We didn't really talk about it much. He wants me to go back after the funeral.'

'Hey, what's this round your neck?'

'It's something Miriam gave me. A sort of talisman, I think. No, don't take it off. It was rather special to her.' I did not mention the man in the café. It wasn't important.

'Oh, OK. Hungry?' Paul put his head around the bathroom door and shouted over the banisters, 'I think we're ready for that soup now.'

'Coming right up!'

I was towel dried and dressed in a voluminous old T-shirt, then tucked into bed. Angie's feet thumped up the stairs and she appeared with a tray. She has a tendency to thump about everywhere. Her hands and feet are large, and she is always too busy to worry about being graceful. She seems to be completely unconscious of her appearance, yet, somehow, she manages to be beautiful. We're so unalike, I don't know how we ever became friends.

'Have you heard?' said Paul, taking the tray from her. 'I'm going to marry an heiress.'

'What's this?'

'Apparently Cliohna's been left a lot of money.' They stood either side of the bed, dissecting my life and prospects while I tore into the pile of bread and cheese, dipping it into the bowl of rich tomato and coriander. God, it tasted good! I was ravenous. I was deaf to their conversation until I realised they were debating whether or not I should have some more sleeping pills.

'Look, she needs a good sleep. She's exhausted, emotionally as well as physically.' That was Paul.

'Yes, I agree, but I don't think popping pills into her is going to help. She needs some natural sleep.'

At this point I decided to rejoin the discussion and came down firmly on Angie's side. The tablets I'd taken the previous night had left me tired and confused. 'What I could really do with is a drink. Scotch, I think. If we have any.'

'That's the last thing you need. Alcohol doesn't really help you sleep.'

'Paul, I would like a drink.'

'It's a bad habit to get into.'

'One small glass of scotch isn't going to turn me into an alcoholic.'

And then for some reason I dissolved into tears again. Paul shook his head in patient despair, then rocked me gently while Angie took away the tray and returned a few minutes later with a cup of tea. She winked at me over Paul's head as she placed it on the bedside table. I took a sip and whisky bit into the back of my throat. A small victory.

'I'm going to have to go.' Paul stood up, rolling down his sleeves and buttoning the cuffs. 'I'm on duty in half an hour. I'll try to get back in the morning.'

'No, don't bother. I'll have to go and see Hannah. I'll ring you later.'

'OK, Rabbit, try and get some rest.' He brushed my unruly hair back and kissed my forehead. 'Take care of her, won't you, Angie?'

Angie sat on the bed and we listened as the front door slammed downstairs. The house was filled with silent echoes. I sipped my tea and whisky as if I were an invalid, and it was a while before either of us spoke.

Eventually Angie whispered. 'Was it awful? Last night, I mean. Miriam.'

I sniffed and nodded. 'It's scary, you know. The way it changes everything. I feel as if something has happened to me too. It's like something has been torn out of me and I'm left with a big gaping hole. I can't imagine what it's going to be like without her. I'm not even sure I really believe it yet. I keep hoping that it's all been a mistake, that the hospital's going to call and tell me she's really all right.'

'What can I do? I don't know how to help. I know nothing I say will make it any better. But I promise I'll be here. I'll do anything I can.'

We both fell into silence again. Angie held my hand while I finished my drink, just as I had held Miriam's. After a while I put the cup down.

'Angie, what do you think of Paul?'

'In what way?'

'Well, do you think I'm doing the right thing?'

'What, marrying him, you mean? How should I know? I'm the last person to give advice about someone's love life. I can't keep a bloke five minutes. Too fussy. Now ask me about choosing a dog and I might be able to help you. How about a retriever? Actually Paul does remind me of a retriever.' This sent us both off into gales of laughter. I think the scotch was working.

'Hey, you don't think he's after your money, do you?' she said.

'Course not. Don't be daft. It's just . . . you have to be sure, don't you? Not just about him, but about myself, too. At the moment I'm not even sure who I am.'

'That's hardly surprising with everything that's happened. How long have you known him now? Must be about a year since Cindy's party.'

'Yes, I suppose it must be. It just all seems to have happened so fast. Remember how I'd barely met him when he was claiming he was in love with me and deciding we should get married? Before I knew what was happening, it was all settled.'

'Are you saying that's not what you want?'

'No, of course it's what I want. Paul's very kind and thoughtful. He'll make a wonderful doctor.'

'Why, are you planning on getting sick?'

'No, silly. No, it's just . . . well, it's me really. He's very open and straightforward, that's what I like about him. I thought that I could share in it. As if being paired off with someone would allow you automatic access to his finer qualities, like holding a joint bank account. But it doesn't seem to be working out like that. Instead I seem to be tying myself into even more complicated knots and end up feeling guilty whenever I'm with him.'

'Sounds to me as if you need more time to sort yourself out. There's no rush, is there? You're already in the middle of one emotional crisis, not the best time to be making lifelong decisions. Wait till things settle down again, then you two need to do some talking. But not now.'

'Yes, you're probably right.'

She stood up and moved to the light switch.

'What you need now is some sleep.'

Alone in the dark I snuggled down into the warmth of the quilt and at last felt that heaviness which presages a natural, deep sleep. I became aware of a dull throbbing in my hand, the one that gripped the talisman, as my own heartbeat was amplified and echoed back to me. It was a slow, steady rhythm and my fingers tingled slightly on the cool metal. It must be nearly twenty-four hours now that I had worn it. I was back in that sterile room with its chipped plaster walls and all-invasive hospital stench.

I sit by her bedside, our hands entwined and laid to rest upon stiff, white cotton. She drifts in and out of sleep. I try to talk in the hope that she can hear and understand, but I'm sure only the empty walls are listening and, although I must keep trying, I only feel foolish. Now she is muttering, tossing her head from side to side, her fingers rigid and clasping at air. Her breathing is laboured, despite the oxygen mask. I stroke her forehead and whisper.

'Hush, hush now.'

Her voice is louder, but still I can't make any sense of the words. It's as if she's talking with someone else, a private conversation wavering on the edge of argument, one from which I'm excluded. There's no one else in the room. She must be delirious and I don't know how to console her.

'Hush now. Hannah's been here with you. She'll be back soon. We're all taking care of you. Paul's helping. He knows what to do.'

She shakes her head violently and pushes me away, but now she's looking at me. When she speaks I can hear her clearly.

'You don't know what love is, child. You know nothing of it.'

Suddenly she finds strength and I'm dismayed as she struggles to pull herself upright. The little mask on her face slips sideways and one of the tubes in her hand flies adrift as she gropes for the chain around her neck. Red lights flash on the machine next to the bed and an alarm sounds somewhere outside the room. But Miriam clasps my wrist, her nails tearing into my skin.

'You must take it,' she gasps. 'Take it now.'

'I don't understand. Please lie still. Nurse! Nurse! Please help me!'

'Listen to me. You have to take it now. Put it on. Now, while we still have time.'

She is tugging at the chain. There is a rush of movement as the door swings open and a nurse is at the bedside.

'Take it, will you! Put it on!'

And I do. I take it. Just to pacify her, I tell myself. But it's more than that. Light dances off the knots and twists of bright silver and I need to put my hands over it. While the nurse holds Miriam's hand and juggles with the tubes and needles, I slip the chain from Miriam and lift it over my own head.

'Never take it off.'

'You must lie down. You have to rest.' I clasp her free hand.

'Never give it back. Promise me!'

'Yes, yes, I promise. Please, you must lie still.'

And then there's another nurse and they are lifting her gently back into place and uttering soothing words. Her mouth is again covered, so I can't be sure. But she repeats it over and over again.

'If you give it back, you will lose him . . . you will lose him.'

In the warmth of my bed, the talisman throbbed in my hand, still echoing my heartbeat as if it held her life within it. I clung to it as I sank down into sleep, and as I drifted away my heart kept time with the gentle, constant rhythm of beating wings.

Five

WHEN I WAS VERY YOUNG someone gave me a kaleidoscope. A birthday present, I think it was, just a little something extra. But I was . . . what? 'Enthralled' would be a good word. I would sit for hours, turning the kaleidoscope slowly, slowly, holding it up towards the light. The picture made by the little spangles and slivers of coloured glass was like a stained-glass window, only the image was whatever I imagined it to be. And only I could see it. And it existed for only that moment. Because as soon as the tube was moved, all the pieces slid about and the pattern disintegrated, only to be replaced by a new and maybe even more glorious configuration. My brother said that the mathematical odds of the same pattern forming twice were nearly impossible. I would try to see pictures so that I could paint them later — fairy castles and mosaic floors and jewelled crowns. But, just when I thought I knew the shape, something would jog the tube and the coloured splinters would shift, so very slightly, and everything would change.

And that's what it's been like ever since Miriam died. The world I had known keeps shifting and changing. One brightly coloured word, one sliver of fact, and everything slides sideways and it all looks different. It's only been a few weeks; I can almost count the days. And every day something else has shifted and changed and the past is no longer what I thought it was. I don't know what's real any more.

The next morning I woke late, thick and groggy with sleep. For a moment I couldn't remember what had happened the day before. Then suddenly it slammed into me: the hospital, Miriam, the cottage. It was like being hit by a truck.

I knew it wouldn't be long before my mother came looking for me, so I thought I'd get it over with and telephone her first. She said to come around, she'd make us some lunch. I said OK, I'd be there at eleven. It was ten minutes to, and already the aroma of fresh coffee hung in the porch. Was Hannah as nervous about this meeting as I was? Apparently we were both eager to get it over and done with. I knew that preparations would have been made in anticipation of my arrival. A tray would be set with matching cups, milk jug and sugar bowl (even though neither of us took sugar), and a plate of biscuits, neatly arranged on a white china plate where they would remain uneaten. Lunch would have been prepared in advance, and all kitchen surfaces would have been wiped clean and the cloth folded into four and draped over the taps.

Distorted by the glass panel, Hannah came towards me, a dark and undulating shape that took form as she walked down the hall. The front door opened and Hannah stepped back to allow me in. There was an awkward pause while we both worked out how to embrace. Somehow the protocol of bereavement demanded we should share this unaccustomed intimacy. It was stiff and formal. I felt thankful once it was over and I could follow her down the hall.

'I was so relieved when you phoned,' she said. 'We were all worried about you yesterday. No one seemed to know where you were.'

I was about to apologise, which was my usual response to any uncomfortable situation. This time I held back. Perhaps Miriam's death had created a watershed in our relationship and one of us had to change. I was going to say nothing. Then I noticed how pale her face was, her eyes red and swollen. She had been crying. I had been so absorbed in my own grief that I had forgotten the enormity of hers. I suddenly felt I should be protecting her.

'I just needed some time on my own. I'm fine, really.'

'Well, I'm sure this whole business has been a strain on us all.'

Whole business, I thought, whole business? That's the way you describe the death of your mother? I followed her through to the sitting room. She was wearing black, a neatly cut suit, probably one she wore at the office, but it was discreet and appropriate for the circumstances. I had given no thought to wearing mourning and immediately felt self-conscious in my old denim jeans. I had slipped the piece of silver jewellery inside my sweatshirt. This was going to be difficult enough without flaunting Miriam's generosity.

'I rang Dad this morning,' I said, 'told him what's happened. I didn't know if he would want to attend the funeral. Of course it's a long way for them to come. Still, I thought he should be asked. It was the right thing to do, wasn't it?'

'Yes, it was the right thing to do. But of course he won't come, not all the way from Cornwall. Or if he does let's hope he doesn't bring that woman with him. David arrived this morning. He'll be around for a few days. He's staying with friends in town, but I asked him to join us for lunch.'

My heart sank. I'd wanted to choose the right moment, hoped that we would have time to talk later, but I would have to do it now, before David arrived, before I was outnumbered.

Hannah lit a cigarette. Clutching a small cut-glass ashtray, she perched upon the arm of a chair. Her hair was sleeked back into a tight bun, her nails varnished red and immaculate. A spot of matching lipstick had coloured her tooth where she chewed her bottom lip.

'Look,' she said, 'I know you wanted to deal with all the arrangements, but it really isn't necessary. At least let me help.'

'No, it's all right, honest. Besides, it's all taken care of. Miriam had already organised everything. She left me instructions. I would like to make sure it's all done as she wanted.'

'Had she indeed? A lot of pagan nonsense, no doubt. Ah, well, I expect I'll have enough to do afterwards. I can imagine the state of that cottage. I won't be able to put it on the market until all the stuff's been removed. It's going to take me ages to sort though it all.'

I could feel a tightness rising in my throat. 'Have you spoken to Uncle Greg yet?'

'No. Well, only to let him know what's happened. That was yesterday morning. But there's no hurry. I'll go and see him after the funeral and we can sort out all the legal stuff.'

'It's not quite that simple. Greg explained to me about Miriam's will—'

'Well, of course she would have left you something. I gather you two have been quite friendly recently. Just take anything you want. I'm sure there's nothing there that I would want to keep.'

'No, that's not what I meant—'

'And there'll be items for her friends. Keepsakes, you know, perhaps some of the books. For the rest, I think I'll get one of those house clearance firms in. Not that they give anything like the true value, but at least it would save me having to sort through all that junk—'

'Mum, will you listen!'

I can't remember the last time I had raised my voice to her, or called her 'Mum' for that matter. Her back stiffened. She stared at me, her hand frozen halfway to her mouth. More of the lipstick was printed around the filter of her cigarette. My eyes sought her coffee cup and the red print on the rim. I wondered how many cigarettes and cups of coffee it would take to remove it all. She was still waiting.

'I'm sorry, I didn't mean to shout. But you must listen. There's something you have to know.' And still she did not move.

'It's the will.' Deep breath. 'It seems she left it to me. The house, I mean. And all her things.'

There, it was out.

Hannah's hand completed its journey. She inhaled smoke and softly breathed out again. Then she ground the remains of the cigarette into the ashtray.

'I see.' That was all she said, and there was a long silence. 'And how long have you known about this?'

'Only since yesterday.'

'But you've been seeing each other, haven't you?'

'Well, yes, but I didn't want—'

'And how long has that been going on?'

'Not very long,' I muttered. Oh, God, what was I to be accused of? I waited for the tirade. Instead, Hannah stood up and walked to the window. She spoke quietly, almost, I thought, speaking to herself.

'What the devil is she up to?'

'What do you mean? I haven't done anything.'

'No, not you. Miriam. It's Miriam. Of course it's Miriam. She's plotting something. What has been going on between you two? What's she been saying to you?'

'Saying to me? Nothing. I don't understand.'

There was a scrunch of gravel on the driveway as the shadow of a car darkened the window. It was my brother, David. A family reunion. A short reprieve.

Lunch was a slow and painful process. David sat at the head of the table, Hannah and I opposite each other. She told him about my legacy and they discussed this new development in terms of property and investment. I said little and concentrated on eating, not daring to reject the food that had been so painstakingly prepared. I forced every mouthful down, fearing it would choke me.

David had altered in the few months since I had seen him last. His face had filled out, broadened. He wasn't yet thirty, but already his hairline was receding. How alike they were, Richard and David, father and son. My brother and mother spoke together of things I would not understand, and I was a child again, eating my dinner like a good girl and listening to the grown-ups talk.

Yes, there was definitely Richard there in David, and something else. Someone else? Someone familiar? Then it rushed over me like a cold sea-breaker. Paul! I could see Paul. It could have been him sitting there, the head of the family, talking with Hannah, recounting the events of the day, explaining the latest management move, plotting the next step in his dazzling career. He would draw circles in the air with his knife to emphasise a point, just as David did and just as Richard did. They all three had large and strong hands which they used to build blocks and bridges in the air. Unlike those long, slender fingers. Unlike the cool, pale hand that had covered mine. Yellow eyes fringed with dark lashes and arched brows like tapering wings. My hand crept to the place where the talisman lay, warm and secret against my skin.

'Chloe? Chloe?'

'Yes?'

'I said, what do you think about Spain?'

'For what? Sorry, I wasn't listening.'

'No, you were miles away. Hannah's right, you look tired. These past few days must have taken a lot out of you.'

'No, I'm fine, really.'

But they exchanged a look, a conspiratorial look that told each other all about me. I was, of course, excluded. They continued talking, and after a few feeble efforts I lapsed back into my silence.

I became aware of the house around me, the house that had once been my home. It felt cold and alien. My room was there, upstairs above me, a room filled with all the days and nights of earliest memory. The bed I had slept in, all clean and smooth, never to be intruded upon again. Small ornaments that I had rejected, now neatly aligned on the window ledge, the curtains behind them never closed. I had taken all I needed with me when I moved out; all the rest had been outgrown. Left behind was the jetsam of a discarded life rearranged into a satisfactory pattern by Hannah, a tableau to which I would never return. I suddenly felt the weight of all this on the ceiling directly above me. At any moment my entire childhood could come crashing down upon my head.

I needed to escape and rose to my feet, desperately grabbing at the discarded cutlery and scraping bits of food from one plate onto another.

'It's all right, Chloe, I'll do that.' Hannah's voice was concerned, commanding.

'Please, you must let me help. It was a lovely meal. Let me wash up.'

But she took the pile of plates from my hands.

'You two have seen so little of each other. You must have lots of catching up to do. David, why don't you show Chloe your new car?'

Another look was exchanged. Then David had his arm around my shoulder and was leading me to the front door and out to where our cars were parked. I remember complimenting him on the shiny blue paintwork and the wire wheels. Fifi, all coy, was crouched beside the newcomer.

'Got it at a good price. Only ten thousand on the clock. Jump in, get the feel of her.'

I slid into the passenger seat. Inside, the car still smelled of new leather.

When we were children, David and I were always arguing. Nowadays, on the rare occasions we meet up, we've learned to rub along together. But it's no more than that. As we both knew, this was an excuse to get me on my own. No doubt he was already under instructions to talk to me about Miriam, let alone the legacy. I thought I might gain some small advantage if I started first.

'God, I feel awful about all this. I truly had no idea. I never wanted Miriam's house or anything else.'

'Well, it can hardly be a surprise, can it? You always were her favourite. Her Little Wren. And she certainly wouldn't have left anything to me, would she? But you might spare a thought for Hannah.'

'Yes, of course I'm thinking of Hannah. I can understand how disappointed she must feel. Apparently there's a lot of money involved.'

'No, I don't think you understand at all.' His voice became louder, his brow buckled by a deep frown. 'The money's got nothing to do with it. Can't you see how hurt she is? I never expected anything from our grandmother — after all she hardly knew I existed. But for Hannah this is the ultimate rejection, isn't it? The final twist of the knife.'

'Oh, now, that's not fair. Surely it was the other way around? It was Hannah who refused to see her mother. She seemed to loathe everything about Miriam, everything she did, everything she stood for. She was always criticising her work, ridiculing her beliefs, her way of life, everything. It was Hannah who kept us apart for all those years. Sometimes she behaved as if she thought we'd be contaminated by her.'

'Yes, that's exactly what she thought. Hannah was afraid, can't you see that?'

'Afraid? Of what, for heaven's sake?'

'Afraid for you. Afraid of losing you. And now it seems you've been playing one off against the other for some time, so don't pretend you don't understand how things were.'

'What do you mean?'

David didn't answer. He shook his head and turned away from me.

'Please, David. I really don't understand any of this. What's Hannah been telling you?'

He breathed deeply and bit his lip before he spoke. 'OK. Hannah was convinced that Miriam was trying to take you away from her. It's something she's believed for a long time. I always thought she was being paranoid, but from what's been happening here — you being all chummy with Miriam behind Hannah's back, all the secrecy, and now the legacy — it seems she was right.'

Was I really hearing this? I turned around in the seat to face him, clutching the dashboard.

'Hannah didn't think any such thing, David! That's complete rubbish!'

'Is it? Isn't that exactly what's happened? Why were you at the hospital with Miriam? How long have you been seeing her? Just what's been going on between you two? Why would she leave the instructions for her funeral for you? And why all the secrecy?'

The world tilted, the kaleidoscope turned and all the little pieces of coloured glass slid sideways. I hadn't seen this pattern before. All the secret visits. All the lies and excuses. All the magical stories. The fairy-tale gifts. I owed everything to Miriam. She had taken me, claimed me as her own. That's not how I meant it to be, but it was exactly what had happened.

I needed to tell David, and it spilled out in a rush and a tumble of broken words. All of it. He listened in silence. And then I told him about how I had found her ill and called the doctor. He reached out and touched my hand.

'Oh God, David, what have I done?'

'I suppose it wasn't entirely your fault, was it? You said you were only fifteen when it started. Miriam was the adult. She should have known better. Besides, you always were more her child than Hannah's, weren't you?'

'What's that supposed to mean?'

'What I say. It was always the two of you.'

'No it wasn't. We were her family. She used to visit all of us.'

'Like hell she did.'

'No, look, you've got it all wrong.'

'I know I was only small at the time, but I'm sure I don't remember seeing much of her until you arrived. She was just this woman who appeared occasionally at the house. She barely spoke to me. And sometimes we would visit her at the cottage. I used to love it there. The garden and all those trees to climb. And then you were born.'

'Yes, and then what?'

'OK, so I suppose I was jealous. Big brother, new baby sister getting all the attention — you know the sort of thing. No, it wasn't just that. It seemed that she was always there. Always hanging over your cot. Always bringing you presents. She would waltz through the door singing, "How's my Little Wren today?" She would just walk straight past me. I can remember her skirts trailing over my head, in her rush to get at you.' David had turned away from me again. He wouldn't look at my face. His hand clenched the steering wheel. 'Then there were the stories. She would sit you on her knee and read to you. And you all snuggled into her lap, your heads touching. I would sit on the floor and listen for a while, then go back to whatever I'd been doing. It was all little girl stuff.'

'What about Hannah? Surely she would have said something?'

'No, she didn't say or do anything as far as I know. But I suppose, even then, I could sense how uneasy she felt. Occasionally she'd protest about all that make-believe rubbish Miriam came out with, but that's all. Then there was that big bust-up, and she put a stop to it. After that we hardly ever saw our grandmother, did we?'

I thought about it for a moment.

'Yes, I remember those arguments. Hannah saying, "Stop filling her head with all that nonsense, she's difficult enough as it is." Was I a difficult child?'

'You were certainly odd! Always off in a world of your own. Talking about dragons and wizards.' His face had relaxed a little. He even managed a faint smile. 'You'd go on as if they really existed — anyone would think our garden was overrun with mythical beasts.'

'Yes, but all children play at make-believe. I just had a lively imagination. Something that—' I nearly said that was something David didn't have. Instead I said, 'Something that our mother couldn't understand.'

'No, it was more than that. I think Hannah was genuinely worried about you and your daydreaming. And I'm sure she blamed Miriam. It was as if you couldn't tell the difference between reality and play. Sometimes you insisted that you'd seen things that weren't there, or even people. Many a time I've seen her reduced to tears.'

As I listened to David, I began to remember. Hannah, her voice raised, almost hysterical, telling me I was lying. And me, stubborn, controlled, calmly insisting that I was right. I took a wicked, almost sadistic pleasure in my power to cause her distress. What had happened to that arrogant, stroppy, little girl? When had I become so furtive? When had I started apologising? David was still talking.

'Miriam was always pretty cool about it, you know. Hannah would get really wound up and Miriam would say, "Her mind needs to grow as well as her body." Only one time I ever saw her get angry. I must have been about five at the time, but I remember it very clearly. It was something Richard said. You were only a few weeks old and they were all leaning over your crib trying to decipher your genetic code. You know how they do with babies: he's got his mother's eyes and Aunt Ethel's chin, that sort of thing. Well, they'd decided that, apart from the red hair, you didn't look like anyone. Dad was joking, "No, don't think she belongs to this family. She's so small. What with those rosy cheeks and the little pointed chin, I think she's a changeling. The fairies must have left her." Well, the old girl went absolutely ballistic! Kept saying something about Chey being ancient and noble.'

'Chey? Who's Chey?'

'God only knows, but I'm sure that's what she said.'

'Or perhaps she said the Sidhe. It's one of those Gaelic words, doesn't look anything like it's pronounced. You say it like the "shee" in banshee. Yes, that's probably what it was. From what I know of Celtic mythology, the Sidhe are the fairies. They were supposed to be an ancient and noble race, very powerful beings. Still, I don't understand why she should have been so upset.'

'Well, she went on about it for ages. Kept saying we shouldn't mock this Sidhe, or whatever. Said they would take revenge. She got really upset, and in the end Richard had to apologise to calm her down.'

We both sat quietly for a while. Then I said, 'She talked about her sometimes, you know. Miriam, she talked about Hannah. About how she was as a child. Nothing like me, apparently. There never has been any closeness between them. I'm sure Miriam did feel some motherly affection for her daughter, but it seems they've been locked in a state of conflict ever since Hannah was young. There was no point of contact, you see. Their natures were too dissimilar for them ever to grow close.'

'They're different all right,' David agreed. 'It's hard to believe they're even related. Well, look at them — Miriam in her shambling, old cottage with her books and her research students, and Hannah in her mock-Georgian semi, holding court at Tupperware parties. I bet she does, doesn't she?'

'Does what?'

'Hold Tupperware parties.'

'I've no idea, but I wouldn't put it past her. Can you just imagine it? Miriam always said that she was a difficult teenager. While her friends had dropped out, Hannah had rebelled by going straight.'

By now the tension had dissolved and we were both laughing. Then we fell silent again.

'You'll be there at the funeral, won't you, David? You'll look after Hannah? I don't think I'll be any help to her. You understand her better than I do. In a way she's right, you know: I *am* Miriam's child.'

'Yes, I'll be there.' He was silent for a moment, pretending to listen to the house. 'Do you think it's safe to go back indoors now?'

'Yes, I think she's had time to finish the washing up.'

I sat on the rug in front of the cold fireplace, hugging my cup of coffee. Hannah leaned back in her armchair and allowed her feet to slip out of her shoes. Her eyes were closed. David had departed in a shower of sprayed gravel, eager to meet up with Cambridge friends and flaunt his new set of wheels. There was a quietness between us that wasn't comfortable, yet it was safer than any words. But I knew something had to be said.

'Look, I'm sure it's not too late to sort this out. We can get it put right. We'll go and see Uncle Greg. I'm sure he'd know how to get the will changed.'

Hannah opened her eyes and smiled sadly. 'No, of course not. It's not the money or the house that worries me, it's . . . well, it's yours now and I'm happy that you should have it. It's just a pity that David was overlooked — he deserved something from her. But I'm not surprised she left nothing to me.'

'Oh, no. It was surely some kind of mistake. She didn't think it through properly. It was just an impulse. You know how generous she was!'

'Generous? Miriam? Generous? Chloe, my mother was the most selfish, self-centred bitch I've ever known.'

I felt as if I'd been punched in the chest, the breath knocked out of me. I sat there on the floor, paralysed with disbelief, while Hannah sat up and searched for another cigarette. Eventually, unable to bear the sudden barrier of bitterness that had sprung up around her, I stumbled for words.

'Perhaps we both knew her differently.' It was a weak, ineffectual statement, meaningless. The silence continued. Then I found another path. 'What was she like? When you were a child, what was it like living with her? You never talk about it. Can you remember Ireland?'

Hannah blew smoke into the room and tapped her cigarette carefully on the side of the ashtray.

'It's difficult. Such a long time ago. It was another world, well two worlds really. There was America before that.'

'You can remember America, then?'

'Well, not very much of it. I was very small when we left and it must have been so different from the life we had in Ireland. There are just odd things, you know — favourite toys, playing in the garden. There was a swing and a slide, painted bright yellow. A special Christmas present. All the children in the neighbourhood were envious. I didn't have to go to the park, you see, I had my own fairground in the garden. And the sunshine, oh it was so warm! The summers were long. Even in winter, in the snow, it seemed warmer there. I suppose the greatest difference was that my parents were together.'

I watched as Hannah's face relaxed and the faint lines of a smile crinkled her eyes. This was something new. Hannah hardly ever acknowledged the existence of her father. I tried to catch the moment.

'Were they happy there?'

'Yes, I suppose they were. Miriam shared in Harold's work. They would sit for hours at the table, their heads pressed close together, engrossed in some small object. Sometimes they would call me to them, gather me into their circle. They would place a shard of pottery or a polished stone in my hands and I'd hold it as if it were a precious jewel. They would explain about its history and about the people who made it. I couldn't understand all of what they were saying, of course, but I knew it was an honour, being allowed to share in their knowledge. It made me important, just as I knew my father and his work were important. "Feel it, Hannah," he would say. "Feel the lifeblood of our ancestors. Feel it stretching back across the centuries. Feel the weight of time in your hand." Then they would hold their breath, as if listening to some ancient voice and I would cup my hands around the treasure and try to listen, too.' She drew heavily on her cigarette. 'But, of course, it was just some sort of game they had got into playing together. Those things were just bits of broken ornaments and old stones.'

'But what about Ireland? Was it the same there?'

'Yes, I suppose it was at first. Then my father left and it was just Miriam and me.'

'Did she ever say why he left? Surely he didn't just abandon you both?'

Hannah shook her head. 'I don't know all of it. They argued a lot towards the end. She drove him away. But she was determined to stay on. God, how I hated that place.'

'Why? I thought Ireland was beautiful. I always imagined you were happy there. That's why you hated the cottage so much.'

'Oh, yes, I'm sure it's beautiful if you're a tourist. They don't have to live there. I can't really remember our house in Boston, but I know it was a palace compared with that hovel Miriam insisted we inhabited in Ireland. And then there was the mud. It always rained. Rain upon rain, until I thought it would never end. It was a land of mud. Everywhere was covered in a thick layer of it. When it dried, it turned to dusty grit that found its way into everything. I always felt dirty. Our house had stone floors with grime between the flags. No bathroom, just that awful tin tub in front of the fire. Only once a week I was allowed to feel clean. And then I had to help bail it out with a tin jug. We would pour it out by the back door and it flowed down the garden, turning the path into yet another river of mud. There was no end to it.'

'Surely not everyone lived like that?'

'They were all incredibly poor, the whole country. We must have seemed rich to most of the village people, but that only made it worse. They hated us for it, you see.'

'I always imagined the Irish were so friendly.'

'The adults were, I suppose, at least on the surface. But we were different, outsiders. The people lived in tight, enclosed groups, huddled together. They would never really let us in. And of course the very nature of Miriam's writing would make them suspicious. She was humoured and tolerated, but I don't think she was ever liked.'

'But didn't you make friends? Surely there were children of your own age?'

'Ah, yes, there were children. That was the worst part, I think, the other children. At first it was just that we were American. It was my accent. They'd gather around me in the playground, tormenting me, calling me the Yankee girl. "Thinks she's a film star," they'd say. "Thinks she's Betty Grable." That was only the start of it. Miriam said to take no notice. They'd soon forget. It would all settle down. But they didn't forget. Then they found other things to use against me.'

'What sort of things?'

Hannah drew hard on her cigarette till it glowed red, holding her breath for what seemed a long time, her eyes closed. Then smoke rushed from her mouth.

'We never went to church, you see. The place thrived on religion and religious hatred — it was their lifeblood, whichever church they went to — and everyone went to church. Everyone except us, that is. We were godless! Pagans, they used to call us. They would follow me home from school, hordes of them, chanting "Pagan" and "Devil worshipper". And they would throw stones and mud. Once someone wrote "Witch's daughter" all over my schoolbook. The nuns blamed me. One of them caned my hand, even though I'm sure she knew I didn't do it. She seemed to take pleasure in it, as if she'd been waiting for an excuse. Nasty, spiteful women, they were, with pinching fingers. So many times I ran away from school. But there would always be someone to catch you and drag you back.'

'But what about Miriam? You told her, didn't you? She would have done something, surely?'

'My mother was busy. She had her work. That was all she had and all she wanted. I spent most of my time alone, dreaming about escape. I used to imagine what it would be like living back in America. There was a church hall in the village, and they had films on every Friday evening and Saturday afternoon. I would be allowed to go. Miriam would take me at first, later I would sneak off on my own. It was the only time I was happy, there in the darkness, watching the people on the screen. They were the real people! For a while I could pretend that I was one of them, wearing nice clothes and living in a proper house, like the one we used to have.'

'What about your father? Did he never come to see you? Surely you could have joined him in America?'

'No, no. I was far too young. He left and I never saw him again.'

'Miriam would never speak about him. When did he die? He couldn't have been very old.'

'I don't know. She never said.' Hannah stubbed out the last of her cigarette. 'Anyway, that's all gone and forgotten now. Eventually she did see sense and we moved here.'

She began to collect up the coffee mugs. I was losing her. I scrambled to my feet, anxious to keep her focused on the past.

'What was that like, moving here, I mean?'

'I've never been so glad to leave anywhere as I was to leave Ireland. I know it wasn't America, but I thought Cambridge was heaven. Real houses, and shops that sold fashionable clothes like I'd seen in the magazines. Somewhere to live that wasn't coated in mud.' She left the room, her voice trailing behind her. 'Mind you, it had to be that awful dump of a cottage, but at least it had hot running water and indoor plumbing. By then I was old enough to go straight into the local high school and I started to make friends. In fact people were impressed when they found out who my mother was. That took some getting used to. But we weren't different here. That's so important, Chloe, to be the same, to fit in. If you try to set yourself apart, you only cause yourself pain.'

I looked around Hannah's neat little house, the ruffled curtains and the display cabinet of crystal glasses that were polished so meticulously. I'd never thought of her as hurt and vulnerable before. I followed her into the kitchen where she was filling the bowl with soapy water and wrestling with the coffee plunger.

'At least Miriam's money will guarantee you a secure future. You and Paul are going to have such a good start, and I'm happy for you both, really I am. And we can begin to make plans for the wedding. There's no reason to put it off now, is there? You'll be able to afford your own home. Once the cottage is cleared and up for sale, you can start looking round for property. You'll be able to afford something really nice, too. I noticed there are some new buildings going up near the science park, three- and four-bedroom detached . . .'

I didn't hear anything else she might have said; my mind had hooked on to three words. Cottage . . . for sale. I felt something rising in my stomach. A heaviness, a pressure, which at first I couldn't identify. I thought it might be anticipation, or maybe just confusion, but then, as it started to tighten, I realised that it was fear.

Six

I WAS EXPECTING RAIN.

I thought it always rained at funerals, death symbolised by all those umbrellas at the graveside like a field of black, decaying mushrooms. But no, there was no rain that day, no abundance of tears to wash the faces of those who could not weep. Instead the morning sprang to life with dazzling sunshine that splintered my eyes and dripped from the trees like breakfast honey.

I had arrived at the cottage early, thinking there would be a lot to do. As it turned out, there wasn't. The little band of caterers arrived and commandeered the kitchen. They asked me to clear the dining table of Miriam's papers, but I forbade them to touch anything, and they were forced to set up a trestle table and spread it with a white, starch-glazed cloth. It looked like a huge wedding cake awaiting decoration. Clearly put out by my refusal to co-operate, the caterers, too, became glazed and starchy, indicating that I was in the way.

So, I had nothing to do and nowhere to go. I wandered through the garden, snapping the dew from spider's webs and stirring up newly fallen leaves. The bright flowers of summer were all but over, making way for the subtler hues of amber-tinged foliage and yellowing grasses. I decided to gather some and arrange them in vases in the house. They would make a pleasing contrast to the garish carpet of reds, pinks and purples that had been creeping up either side of the front path since early morning. People had entered the gate in reverent silence, then slipped away unnoticed, leaving flowers swathed in crackling cellophane, with copperplate cards bearing messages for the deceased. Who did they think would read them? Were they expecting Miriam to open the door herself and walk down the garden, pausing to inspect each card politely before stepping into the hearse? Unaccustomed to the bizarre rituals, I felt lost and useless.

I meandered from room to room, picking up various objects and carefully replacing them. The air seemed charged with the faintest tingle of excitement, the cause of which I could not define. But I knew that something was about to happen.

In Miriam's bedroom I sat down at the dressing table. It was littered with bright, shiny things, beads and earrings spilling out of glass trays. There were the ornate combs that she used to fasten up her long hair. I always wore mine loose, an unruly cloud of red curls that I used to veil my face. Picking up a hairbrush, I swept the hair back from my brow, twisting it into a knot behind my head and fastening it with matching silver combs. A new face looked back at me from the mirror, an unexpected face. This woman looked surprised, startled even, and somehow familiar.

I turned to the oval mirror in the wardrobe door to judge the full effect. But oh, how drab I looked. Of course I had dressed in black as Hannah said I should, but is that what Miriam would have done? Her perfume of jasmine oils washed over me as I opened the wardrobe door. The colours of her clothes were soft, rich but natural, the fabrics silks and velvets. She loved Indian styles, long and flowing and heavily embroidered with silken threads. Hippy clothes, Hannah called them. There was a swirling skirt of heavy cotton inset with panels of velvet. It was the colour of crushed fruits, blackberries and dark cherries, worked with silver flowers and tiny spangles of glass. I found a silk shirt in a paler lilac and an ornate leather belt with a silver buckle that sat tight around my waist. A neat-fitting jacket in mulberry velvet toned perfectly with the skirt.

I closed the door and stared at the stranger in the mirror. I had never seen this woman before, and yet I had. There was something so familiar about her, but I just couldn't make the connection. I was both frightened and fascinated. She was like some bright, exotic bird, twirling and sparkling in a way that I would never dare.

The neckline was cut low, exposing the talisman glinting at my throat. No, that wouldn't do! There must be something . . . yes, in a drawer, a long gossamer-fine purple scarf. I wound it around and over the collar to hide the jewel and tossed the ends over my shoulders to trail down my back. Yes, perfect. Then I was skipping down the stairs. I had to show Miriam.

The morning sun illuminated the still unfinished portrait as I posed and danced before her, spreading the skirt wide in my hands. 'I hope you don't mind, but my outfit looked so awful. You would have hated it. It was the only black coat I had, all heavy and shapeless. You always said I used clothes to hide myself in. This feels so . . . so free.' She looked at me with patience, an enigmatic smile lighting her eyes, as if she knew something I didn't and was waiting to surprise me. I was still for a moment, trying to read her thoughts. Then I whispered, 'You will help me through today, won't you? Please be there.'

I left the room quietly, then wondered if I ought to lock the door. There would be people all over the house. This was my studio, my secret place. I didn't want it discovered, not today. I turned the small key, removed it and tucked it deep inside my pocket. As I turned back down the hall I was startled by a rapping at the door.

Hannah and David stood in the porch. I stepped back to let them through, but David remained still, staring at me, while

Hannah reeled back, her eyes widening in fear. Her prepared smile melted as both hands rose to cover her mouth, stifling a pathetic whimper.

'What is it?' I gasped. 'What's wrong?'

David pushed past her, his eyes blazing, roughly grabbing my elbow and dragging me back inside the house. 'What the hell do you think you're playing at, Chloe?'

'What do you mean? I don't understand.'

'You've gone too far this time! Haven't you done enough to hurt your mother without staging this ridiculous pantomime?'

'But I haven't done anything!'

'Don't play innocent with me! Do you think I don't know what you're up to? Final twist of the knife, is it?'

Then, somehow, Paul was there, forcing himself between us, shielding me with his arms as David shouted and pounded at the air with clenched fists. Paul herded me down the length of the hall and pushed me onto the stairs, then went back to face the others at the doorway. I hunched into a tight ball on the bottom step, hands clamped over my ears to shut out the hail of words ricocheting off the stone floor and walls of the hollow passageway: '. . . fancy dress party . . .', '. . . overwrought . . .', '. . . neurotic . . .', '. . . under tremendous strain . . .', '. . . no excuse . . .', '. . . her doctor . . .', '. . . bloody psychiatrist more like . . .'

Gradually the shouting match subsided and Paul returned to me, crouching down to stroke my shoulders and speak softly.

'It's all right now. Hannah's still very shaken, but I think I've convinced them that you didn't mean anything by it.'

'But I didn't, Paul. I don't understand. What have I done wrong?'

'You mean you really don't know? Surely you've looked in a mirror?'

'Yes, but they're Miriam's clothes. Mine looked so awful and she wouldn't have minded . . .'

'Don't you realise you look just like her? No, not even that. You *are* her! When you opened the door, Hannah thought you were Miriam.'

I was shocked into silence as realisation crept up on me. Of course, that's who she was, the woman in the mirror, that's why she looked so familiar.

'Oh, my God! Oh, Paul, I didn't think . . . I would never have . . .' I glanced down the hall at Hannah, who was now inside, sitting on a high-backed chair and clutching a white handkerchief. David stood beside her, the image of our father in his dark suit and shiny shoes. I wasn't the only impostor here.

Paul pulled me to my feet. 'Anyway, it's all over now, Rabbit. Just go upstairs and change. You can't go out looking like that.'

There are moments, brief, seemingly inconsequential moments, when the universe pivots on a pinhead. I had turned. I had actually turned and placed my foot upon the stair. Then I stopped, turned and walked the length of the hall to face my family. By now Hannah had calmed down and wore an expression of tragic resignation. David was at her side, like a hound defending its mistress. I took a deep breath.

'Mum, David. I'm sorry my appearance upset you. I . . . none of us . . . realised how alike Miriam and I are . . . were. However . . .' My voice almost cracked. I stumbled, and then regained control. 'However, this is the reality, I *am* like her. I hope that in time we can all get used to it. And I realise that this must be painful for you both and I'm sorry for that. But it can't be helped. That's the way things are. This is who I am.'

Then I walked back to Paul, still waiting by the stairs. 'Paul, thank you for helping just then. I didn't realise. However, I do need to say this. We're not married yet, you're not my husband. But even if you were it would make no difference. You will never, ever, tell me what clothes I can or cannot wear. Is that understood?'

For a moment neither of us moved or spoke. Then I turned away and walked into the living room, closing the door.

My stomach churned. I forced air into my body despite the

steel ball that had somehow lodged in my throat. My hands were clenched together to stop them from shaking. After a few moments I became aware of muffled voices beyond the door but couldn't make out the words. The caterers scuttled to and fro, clattering objects onto the table, and I wondered how much of the family scene they had witnessed. To avoid looking at them, I gazed steadily out of the window. The sun still sparkled on the trees and occasionally a golden leaf would pirouette down onto the overgrown lawn.

There was a sudden movement, a dark shadow among the trees. A branch bowed and swayed as if something heavy had weighed down upon it, then sprang up in a scattering of bright leaves. Then stillness — nothing.

The hall door opened. Someone was standing behind me. I pretended to be busy rearranging the leaves I had gathered earlier, but my hands were still trembling and grass seeds quivered down onto the windowsill.

'You OK?' It was Paul, his voice barely a whisper.

I nodded in reply.

'Is there anything I can do to help?'

'No, nothing.'

'Anything I can get you?'

'No, I'm fine really.' I heard the sharpness in my voice, the unfairness of it. I looked down the garden to the trees but there was no one there. 'Is Hannah all right?'

'Yes, she'll survive.'

'I suppose I ought to go and make my peace with her. We can't go to the funeral like this. Where is she?'

'She's out the front. I think she went to look at the flowers.'

Hannah was bending down to read each card in turn, perhaps trying to decipher the signature, then replacing them among the blossoms.

'So many flowers. She had a lot of friends.' I said it quietly, but she heard me approach and looked up.

'Yes, people seemed to take to her. She was very lucky.'

I didn't think luck had anything to do with it, but I held my tongue and went through the motions of looking at the cards with her. After a few minutes, I plucked up the courage to ask. 'Did you ever come across a friend of hers, a man called Iolair?'

'Who? Iolair?'

'Yes. I met him recently. But he claims to have known her a long time.'

'Well, then you'd probably know more about him than I would.'

The cutting edge of her voice hurt, as it was meant to, but I wouldn't be deterred.

'I got the impression that he was an old family friend. He seemed to know me.'

As I started to describe him, a change came over Hannah's face. It was as if a cloud had blotted out the sun, throwing her eyes into shadow, the blood draining from her cheeks. She suddenly looked older as she stared into the distance.

'There may have been someone, I'm not sure. There was a gardener, at least I saw him in the garden, I think.' Her voice was frail and unsteady.

'In this garden?'

'Yes. When we first came here. No, no it couldn't have been. It must have been in Ireland. No, that's not right. So long ago. I can't remember. Perhaps there never was anyone. There couldn't have been. Miriam never had a gardener. That's nonsense, Cliohna.' Her voice rose. 'If there was someone in my mother's house, I would have known about him, wouldn't I? I would have seen him!'

'Yes. Why are you getting so angry? I only asked—'

'Well, don't ask. This isn't the time to start bringing up all this nonsense.'

'What nonsense? What have I said?'

'All this about gardeners and birds. You know how I hate birds!'

'But I never said—'

'I won't have it. Not now. Richard, make her stop it!'

'Mother, Richard's not here. Richard's . . . surely you mean . . .'

I began to be afraid. My mother was always so firm and precise, always in control. Just then, thank God, the hearse drew up outside the gate followed by a chauffeur-driven car. It was as if a switch had been thrown. Her face suddenly cleared, her eyes were sharp and focused, her back straight. She smiled at me.

'Ah, good. They're on time. We'd better go indoors while they arrange the flowers on the casket.'

Bewildered, I allowed her to shepherd me through the front door, then left her to put on her coat while I went looking for Paul.

I found him in the living room with David. They were shoulder to shoulder by the window, so alike they could have been brothers. David was holding one of Miriam's paintings towards the light.

'As I say, I'm hardly an expert — it could just as easily be a fake. There's the signature but that means nothing. If it were genuine . . . I daren't think what it might be worth. Even a copy could hold some value.'

I knew the painting well: a madonna and child. It was small, barely eight inches square. Miriam and I had looked at it together many times, marvelling at the glowing transparency of the skin tones and the way the child's hand stretched out from the canvas as if he were trying to reach us. She had always talked of the painting as if it were an original. I said nothing.

'What about this one next to it?' Paul took down another small picture, holding it up for David's scrutiny. 'Looks like a print to me, and a poor one at that.'

'Not even a print, I'm afraid. More like a cutting from a magazine. But the frame is exquisite, probably worth a few thousand itself.'

'It's crazy,' Paul shook his head. 'I don't believe all this. Absolutely crazy.'

'Yes, she was crazy all right. And I'm beginning to think it runs in the family.'

'What runs in the family, David?' Hannah was behind me, pulling on her tight black gloves, pressing each finger firmly into place.

'We were just looking at some of these pieces of art. It's like an Aladdin's cave in here.'

'More like a junk shop, in my opinion.'

'Whoa, hold on there, Mum. Some of this old junk could be priceless.' David turned to Paul again. 'You'll have to get someone in, get it all properly catalogued. I doubt any of it's insured. Look at these bronzes. Obviously Celtic, could be thousands of years old.'

I couldn't bear this. Miriam loved these things; their financial value meant nothing to her. They were picking over her belongings like crows pecking at her corpse. I wanted to protest, but said nothing. Hannah looked around the room, unimpressed.

'Yes, well, you didn't have to live in this mess, did you? She never could keep the place clean.'

I had forgotten. That must have been the first time Hannah had been there for many years, but the cottage had been her home when she was growing up.

'Chloe, you could have made an effort to get rid of some of this rubbish before the reception, or at least tidy it up. What will people think? There must be an inch of dust on these books. The whole place needs a good clear-out.'

There was a polite cough and a frock-coated gentleman appeared in the doorway, indicating they were ready to leave. Hannah bestowed one last look of disgust on the room as she ordered us out of the house and into the waiting vehicle.

We sat in a tight little circle, the four of us. I chose to sit with my back to the engine; I couldn't bear to watch the car in front carrying the casket laden with greenery and flowers. Paul was beside me, holding my hand, so I was forced to look at Hannah and David. David was still angry and Hannah gave me looks of pained disappointment. I wished that I had changed back into my own clothes. I wished that I had never visited Miriam. I wished that I had always tidied my room, helped with the housework, been a paragon of obedience. I clung to Paul, certain that I was drowning and praying that the end would be swift. But Paul was there, solid and warm. Perhaps I would survive.

My memory of the service is a patchwork of images. The Great Hall at King's College, chairs set out in rows. Lyrical, powerful music, both sad and joyous. Conspiratorial glances exchanged, nods of recognition and approval, as the clear notes of the harp reached to the vaulted ceiling. Only days before those same notes had filled the cottage and we two, Miriam and I, had hummed the familiar tunes as we worked.

Many people stepped up to the lectern to speak about the woman they had known. They told of fine qualities and great achievements, a glorious life and a painful loss. Sometimes they spoke of the Miriam I knew, and sometimes of a stranger. And there were passages and poems in Gaelic. I recognised the tones and the poetry of it even though I could not understand the words. But others could. I watched their lips move in unison with the readings. These were her friends, her comrades, fellow writers, researchers, archaeologists, historians and translators, all gathered to do her homage. The chosen ones. I hovered on the fringes of this shining throng, knowing enough to claim a place, unlike

Hannah, who sighed and fidgeted beside me, clutching her white handkerchief. She and David were the outsiders, the uninvited. At times she would turn to me, eyebrows raised, questioning this unchristian ritual.

'It's what she wanted,' I mouthed.

Hannah sighed and shook her head. I began to feel annoyed, resentful. Then I remembered the pain in her eyes as she'd told me of her days in Ireland, of the children's taunts.

'I would like my coffin to be covered with willow branches,' Miriam had told me once. 'Weeping willow, weeping for the dead. In ancient Greece there was a grove sacred to Persephone, queen of the underworld, where willows and poplars grew. Mourners would weave the branches into garlands to wear around their heads. It was a protection, a safeguard. A funeral is a dangerous crossing point on the borders between this world and the next. The Chinese knew about the willow too. They would cover their coffins with willow branches to ward against enchantment. Yes,' she had said, 'I would like that.'

I looked at the sad wooden box. It lay in front of us laden with willow fronds and white roses and I tried to convince myself that Miriam was there, inside it. But it seemed to have little to do with her or with what was being said. All the while Paul held my hand and the ancient carved figures above us gazed down. I looked around. A sea of faces, as they say, and I recognised only a few. Was there someone I was hoping to see? If so, he was not there.

Then we were outside again, walking through the grounds of the medieval college, with a human tide surging around us. I almost panicked, gasping for air. People were clasping my hands, hugging me, telling me how sorry they were for my loss, as if it were somehow their fault and they needed to apologise. I didn't know how to respond and mumbled incoherently. Hannah fended them off with all the grace and smoothness of a society hostess at a cocktail party. She knew all the right words, the correct intonation. Many remarked how like my grandmother I was — they had not realised there was such a strong family resemblance. There were strange, startled looks.

Then Paul led me away and into the car and the whole carnival procession started off on its final journey.

By then it was early afternoon. The air was still and sunshine edged the white marble crosses with molten gold. We picked our way between the graves. The grass was slippery with moss and freshly fallen leaves stuck to the soles of my boots. I spent some time debating whether it would be all right to bend down and remove them or if I should leave them there and risk slipping over. Either course of action could turn into another social blunder and I had been the cause of enough family embarrassment already. I held tightly on to Paul's arm.

More words were spoken. The coffin was lowered and yet more words tossed down upon it, with handfuls of flowers and small tokens. I couldn't bear to watch and looked about me for some gentler sight to dwell upon. In the distance, an elderly woman was bending over to arrange flowers. Her dress rode up at the back to display stocking tops and the edge of a pink petticoat. A fallen stone angel with a broken nose read and reread the unturned pages of a book. Death was everywhere.

Then, suddenly, there he was.

Not part of the group crowding around the burial plot, but way over on the other side of the graveyard. Yet, even at that distance, I knew him. I knew the long black coat brushing the tops of the grasses, the slim hands held loosely at his sides. He was motionless. I couldn't see his eyes, but I knew he was looking at me. I would have called out to him had the moment not forbidden it. But he was too far away to hear or be heard. So we both watched and waited.

'Chloe?' It was a whisper.

At first I thought it was his voice. Then I realised Paul was nudging my side. Someone was holding a trowel towards me and it was my turn to scatter the earth. I looked up again and he was gone.

It was when we were walking away from the grave that it happened. Just a slight ripple in the air, the gentlest of breezes. Not enough to stir the trees or set the roses nodding upon their stems. But enough to lift one end of a scarf and toss it over my shoulder. Enough to let it slip from my neck and allow the sunlight to glance off the twisted knot of silver. It was at that precise moment that Hannah turned and I saw the fractured beam of light dazzle her eye.

'Oh, no.' It was barely a whisper, and her clutching fingers twisted the sleeve of David's coat.

For the second time that day her face distorted in fear. Only this time it was more than fear — it was despair. It was useless to pretend I didn't know what was wrong. My hand rose to cover the talisman.

'No, not you, Chloe. Not you, too.' Her voice cracked in her throat. 'Why? Why did you take it?'

'She gave it to me,' I whispered. It was the only defence I had to offer.

'Take it off.' She stumbled towards me, her hand still wrenching at David's sleeve. 'Take that thing off your neck!'

Her voice rose to a scream as she lunged toward me, grabbing at my throat. David threw his arms around her and they both stumbled to the ground. At the same time I felt Paul spin me around, coming between us. I lost my balance and crashed against a headstone, scraping skin from my hand and smearing the grave with blood. Hannah was still on the ground, trying to scramble towards me. Her tights were ripped at the knees and there was mud on her skirt.

'Make her take it off. Please, David, Paul. Make her take it off!'

Paul and David exchanged looks. No, this could not be Hannah, sobbing and hysterical. The mourners making their way ahead of us had reached the line of waiting cars and were turning to witness the cause of the disturbance. A few came running back to help David drag Hannah to her feet.

And then David was guiding Hannah into a car; someone else followed behind carrying her bag and one of the black gloves.

Paul's arms were around me, trying to stop me from shaking. 'What the hell was all that about?'

'I don't know. I've no idea.' I knew I was lying.

'Let me see that hand. That's a nasty graze. I think we'd better put something on it. Let's get you back to the cottage. Poor little Rabbit, you're trembling. Think you can walk to the car?'

'Yes, of course.'

Paul fended off further offers of assistance, and as we reached the pathway he half-lifted me into the back seat of the car, closed the door and climbed in the other side. As we swung through the cemetery gates, I looked back at the freshly covered grave.

In the shadowed foliage of a nearby tree, a heavy branch dipped and swayed.

Seven

'OUCH!' MY hand pulled itself away.

'Look, it wouldn't hurt so much if you'd stop bobbing about.'

I was perched on the edge of the bath while Paul attempted to clean up my bruised and battered skin. We had found a curled-up tube of antiseptic cream and a few wrinkled plasters at the back of a cupboard. Naturally, Miriam's home wouldn't contain anything so useful as a first-aid box.

'Well, as family funerals go, that one was certainly unique.' It was the first comment Paul had made.

'Didn't you think the service was beautiful?'

'Hmm, can't say I understood much of it. The music was nice, I suppose.'

'There was an air of celebration about it. I was dreading it beforehand. I thought it would be morbid and depressing, but I didn't even feel sad. In fact I came away feeling a sort of completeness, as if everything had come full circle.'

Yes, I know that sounds like a load of psycho-twaddle — I can see that now — but I did talk like that sometimes in the old days . . . well, a few weeks ago.

'They say a funeral should be satisfying, that you should feel a sense of accomplishment. After all it's a ritual. That's what rituals are for, you know, to help the social group adjust to change. It's designed to bring about a psychological readjustment.'

'You know you're sounding just like Miriam.'

'No, seriously, a funeral is a process. It's a way of saying goodbye, of letting go.'

'And have you?' Paul stopped dabbing at my hand and looked directly into my eyes.

'Have I what?'

'Let go of Miriam. Oh, look, I'm sorry. I know it's been a bad time for you, and I'm trying to be as patient as I can. But don't forget that I need you too. I almost ashamed to say this, but I keep thinking that maybe now I can have you all to myself instead of having to share you with your grandmother.'

It was then that I realised how forlorn Paul seemed. Perhaps he always looked like that and I'd got so used to it that I hadn't noticed. I saw the ash-golden hair falling in a mop over his forehead, the pale, clear blue of his eyes reflecting my face. I knew the smile that twitched along the edge of his mouth, his lips full and pouting, like a lost little boy. I realised that it had been a long time since we had kissed, not since before the evening Miriam was taken to the hospital. I was suddenly aware of how much I needed physical closeness.

'Of course, Paul, you can have me all to yourself, any time you like.'

I slid my free hand inside his jacket, pulling myself up close towards him. I could feel the warmth of his body, the muscles of his back taut against his shirt.

'Hey, Chloe, what do you think you're doing?'

'I'm giving you all my attention. That's what you wanted, isn't it?'

'Well, yes, but not right now.' His voice was soft, teasing, but his arm tensed as he held me away from him, stumbling against the hand basin. 'And certainly not here.'

I could sense that energy again, as if the air were charged. I felt high on it, my head light and buzzing.

'The bedroom's there, just across the landing.' I was pulling him toward the open doorway.

'Chloe, stop this.' He was laughing, but it was a nervous, confused laugh, as if I were something unknown, something he didn't know how to deal with.

'Oh, come on, it could be fun.'

But he caught my wrist, holding me in check. 'Have you taken leave of your senses?' There was a sudden edge of irritation to his voice. 'Look, Chloe, this isn't funny. We're at a funeral. There are guests downstairs.'

A door banged somewhere. There was a clinking of china and voices drifted up from the floor below. He was right, of course. I suddenly felt very foolish and blood rushed hot in my face. I stammered words of apology. For a moment he seemed even more confused. Then everything was all right again. This time it was Paul who was hugging me.

'It's OK, Rabbit. I appreciate the thought, but your timing's way out. Save it all up for later, hey? There's my girl.' Paul was in charge again, holding me, stroking my back. 'Look, it's nearly all over now. We'll just survive the rest of today, then we can get back to some sort of normality. Don't worry now, everything's going to be just like it was before.'

There it was again, that sensation of drowning. The tap dripped steadily. My face was pressing against his shirt and I noticed that a button was hanging by a thread. Paul needed a wife and I was being dragged down into the undertow and I didn't know how to save myself. Then he was speaking again.

'That business with Hannah? What was it all about?'

'Me looking like Miriam you mean?'

'Well, yes, but I was thinking more about that outburst of hysterics at the cemetery.'

'I think losing her mother has hit her harder than I expected.

When we were outside looking at the flowers, she got really upset and angry. And I hadn't even mentioned any birds.'

'Birds?'

'Yes, she's got a thing about them. Sort of a phobia, I suppose. Only times I've ever seen her afraid are when a bird was in the house. Sometimes a sparrow would fly in through the kitchen window, and she'd sort of freeze in a corner and cover her face while David and I chased it out. She can't stand touching feathers, either.'

'That's not uncommon. Ornithophobia I think it's called. But that scene at the cemetery, that wasn't about birds. What upset her that time?'

'I don't know.'

'Oh, I think you do. It was something to do with that necklace you're wearing, wasn't it? That's what she was getting upset about. Some dark family secret, hey? Skeletons rattling in the ancestral closet? Look, you don't have to tell me if you don't want to, but I think you should take it off. If it's going to upset people like that it would be better if you stopped wearing it.'

I pushed myself away from him, putting space between us. He had to see my face so that he would understand.

I said only one word.

'No.'

It hovered in mid-air, suspended between us, like some fragile crystal globe, and we both were silent, knowing it would shatter if either of us dared to touch it.

After a while he said, 'Look, I think we should ring David and make sure Hannah's calmed down. Would you like me to do it? Might make it easier.'

'Oh, would you? You're an angel, Paul. I don't know what I'd do without you.' Yes, what would I do without him? 'I know I'm being a real pain at the moment.'

'Yes, well . . . But right now there's a room full of people down there, and, without Hannah around, you're going to have to play hostess.'

'Oh, God, yes. I'd almost forgotten. I suppose I'd better go down and face them.'

'Do you feel up to it?'

I thought for a moment and was startled by the realisation. Yes, I did feel up to it. And, what's more, I was actually eager to get on with it. For the first time it dawned on me that this was my house and those people were my guests, not Hannah's, or David's. As I untangled myself from Paul, I pulled the loose button away from his shirt. Then I turned to the mirror, smoothing my hair into place.

'Yes, of course. I'll be fine. You go and make that phone call and I'll see you downstairs.'

'You look very different, you know, with your hair like that.'

'Do you like it?'

'I'm not sure. It doesn't look like you somehow.'

'Oh, but it does. It looks exactly like me.' And then I left the room. Halfway down the stairs I realised I still had Paul's shirt button in my hand. After a moment's hesitation, I tossed it out of the landing window.

I felt very brave until I tried to enter the room and found it blocked with faces. People had gathered in small, disconnected groups, not knowing quite what to do or how they should behave. Others were still arriving from the cemetery. There were discreet salutations. Occasionally a normal conversation would break out above the muted discourse, only to be swallowed up in an embarrassed hush.

I was highly skilled at avoiding social gatherings: it was one of the reasons Paul called me Rabbit. My usual tactic on such occasions was to take refuge in the kitchen and pretend to be helping with the dishes. The atmosphere in the cottage was uncomfortable and so was I, but it was down to me to change it.

The wine might help to relax people, I thought. I took a deep breath and snatched a bottle from a disconcerted waitress.

'There you are, Miriam,' I whispered, 'a good, full-bodied red as instructed. A libation fit to honour a noble warrior.'

I approached a small group of men who were talking earnestly, their grey heads bent close together. 'Let me refill your glasses, gentlemen. This was one of Miriam's favourites. She would want us to enjoy it.' I smiled, which gave them permission to smile in return. I left them discussing the vineyards of Bordeaux and holding their glasses towards the light. Yes, that's how she would have done it, I thought and moved on to another group.

Before long I became aware of the hum of conversation rising, a ripple of laughter, then another. I tipped the bottle, draining it into a glass and the last drops trickled down the side, dripping onto the floor. I touched the hand that held the glass, reassuring the woman, and we laughed together, both apologising. I fetched another bottle and moved on to interlace with the next conversational knot.

I found myself laughing a lot, mostly with astonishment. I was actually enjoying myself, in the most literal sense: I was enjoying my *self*, discovering the pleasure of moving, acting, speaking, causing others to react to my presence. Nothing like the little Rabbit who crouched in a corner, hoping the rest of the party wouldn't notice her. Somehow I had become . . . what was it? Capable? Confident? Liberated? Yes, that was how I felt. Liberated.

Yet, all the while, there was a strange sensation of detachment, as if I were an observer witnessing my own participation. I felt distanced from the crowd, and from myself also, as if none of this were real, as if we were mere images projected onto a three-dimensional screen.

At one point I turned, laughing, from one small gathering to acknowledge the greetings of another. There, in the doorway, stood Paul. I think he had been watching me for some time. He wore an amused smile, his eyebrows raised in mock surprise as he lifted his glass to salute me. In this, at least, I had won his approval. And, apparently, the approval of others. I overheard snatches of conversation.

'How like her grandmother she looks . . .'

'Yes, I can see Miriam in her. She has her mannerisms, you know . . .'

'Yes, that's just how she smiled . . .'

'And her voice, she has her voice, but without the accent of course . . .'

'I never realised, it's quite remarkable . . .'

I smiled and moved on, graciously receiving condolences and refilling glasses. I drank nothing myself, wishing to remain clear-headed and in command.

It was an illusion, of course, I realise that now. I was certainly not clear-headed. And as for being the one in command, well, I'd like to think some of it was me — yes, some of it *was* me. I'm not sure exactly when I began to change, but that day was when I first became aware of it.

I realised that I was hungry, so I encouraged people to sample the trays of delicacies on the lavishly laden table and soon I was helping myself. Paul came up beside me and took my hand, twisting the engagement ring he had given me around and around on my finger. It was something he often did, as if to remind me it was there.

'How am I doing?' I asked.

'You're doing just great. I'm very proud of you.' He selected a curl of smoked salmon and popped it into my mouth.

'How's Hannah?' I mumbled through the unsolicited gift. 'Did you manage to get through?'

'Yes, I spoke to David. She's fine now, resting. I said everything was OK here and not to worry about coming back if they weren't up to it.'

I was relieved. I did not want to face them again today. Besides, this was my show now: I was centre stage and I wanted to keep it that way. I gave Paul a discreet hug as a reward and whispered, 'Thanks. You're my hero. Just to prove how grateful I am, when everyone's gone we'll finish that conversation we started in the bathroom.'

'Well, that would be great except I'm on duty at six, or had you forgotten?' ·

'Oh, damn.'

'Still, there's always tomorrow. It's about time we spent an evening alone together.' He smiled at me and winked as he slipped back into the crowd.

Would some background music be appropriate? Would this be Miriam's next move or was I adding my own touch of whimsy to the proceedings? I moved over to the stereo and took a CD from the top of the pile. A selection of Celtic music, most appropriate. A folk band began to play a set of reels at an unbelievably fast pace. A few eyebrows were raised, to be followed by smiles. Yes, I had made the right move.

I looked around at the gathering and was satisfied. This is how Miriam would have wanted it. She wouldn't have tolerated any morbid repression. Those she had invited to be there, those whom she had loved, soon learned from my example and honoured her spirit by shedding their funeral masks. As ties were loosened, so were tongues, and anecdotes flowed with the wine — tales of her brilliance, of her friendship, of her endearing eccentricities. It was truly a party in her honour, a celebration of her life, and I moved among them all, producer, director and stage manager. Or so I thought.

'Ah, there she is, there she is. Chloe my dear, oh, I'm so glad I managed to catch you.'

'Doctor Sangster, I'm sorry. I tried to speak to you earlier. Thank you so much for being here today.'

'It's Marcus, my dear. Do call me Marcus. Yes, yes, dear Miriam. I don't know what we'll do without her.' The dear man, as Miriam would have called him, shook his head. His eyes were brimming with tears. 'And such a beautiful service. Yes, well now, where is she? I do so want to introduce you to my wife. Miriam told her so much about you and she's looking forward to meeting you. Ah, there you are, Janet. Come along here, my dear, and meet Cliohna.'

A little bird of a woman was making her way towards us. I would have picked Janet Sangster from the crowd unaided. They were a complementary pair. Her grey-white hair, cut into a blunt bob, sat upon her head like a nightcap. She balanced two plates of assorted titbits in her fragile hands.

'Here, Marcus, I've found you some nice lean chicken and a little salad. Now promise me you won't go sneaking up on those awful prawns. He will eat prawns, you know. He knows how they upset his digestion. He thinks I don't notice these things.'

I think she was addressing me at this point, but it was difficult to tell. Her violet eyes crinkled and squinted into a short-sighted smile while her spectacles bobbed on her breast, all forgotten, on a thin gold chain. At this point Marcus tried to introduce us, but his wife simply ignored this formality and continued to talk to me as if we had known each other for years.

'It's not as if he won't suffer for it later. Your grandmother was always telling him, but would he listen?'

'There, there, my dear,' he patted her arm gently. 'Chloe doesn't want to hear about my petty troubles. I'm sure she has greater concerns of her own at present.' But the warmth in his voice belied the admonishment, and her eyes sparkled in response. They had been married forever and obviously adored each other.

'Chloe, my love,' he patted my hand this time, 'if there's anything Janet and I can do to help . . . well . . . such a terrible shock to us all, such a sad, sad loss . . .'

'Actually there is something. A favour I need to ask you.'

'Of course, my dear, I'll help in any way I can.'

'Well, I have to sort out all her personal belongings, you know, clothes and stuff. And then there's all her research material, reference books, documents, notes, that sort of thing. I had a brief look but there's so much that I don't really understand. I would appreciate some expert guidance.'

'My dear, it would be an honour, a privilege, to be allowed . . .'

'Not at all. I wouldn't know where to start. Besides, I'm sure you're the only person she would trust with her work. Perhaps I could talk to you about it sometime soon?'

'Now, Marcus, we should be inviting Chloe round for dinner, then you two can sort things out and I can make sure she gets a decent meal. I shouldn't think you've been looking after yourself over this last week have you, my dear? Don't you think she looks a little pale?'

'Sounds wonderful. Yes, I'd love to.'

'Well, you just call us as soon as you're ready and we'll fix something up.'

'And your poor mother, my dear,' Marcus said. 'So distressed. Is she recovering now? I do hope someone is looking after her.'

'Yes, thank you. She's fine now. David took her home to rest.'

'Yes, best thing to do. Fine woman, Hannah,' said Marcus. 'Strong, capable, always was. Knew her when she was your age, you know. Last person I imagined would break down like that. Very strange.'

I found we were standing next to the bookcase, an easy distraction. I ran my hand along the row of green bindings.

'You must know Miriam's work better than anyone,' I said. 'You've read all her books, of course?'

'Oh, yes. Invaluable, invaluable.'

'But it isn't history, is it? I don't understand why the collecting of folk tales should be so important to historians.'

'Ah, but it *is* history. It's the history of the development of a group consciousness, of the evolution of cultural and race memory.' We had caught the attention of some people nearby who turned towards our conversation. 'These stories tell us what moved those people, what they feared, the inner strengths that helped them survive — what made them tick, if you like. Without that understanding all their actions become meaningless.'

'And that's what made Miriam's work so important?'

A small circle was gathering to hear the professor speak. Marcus needed little prompting.

'Why, yes, indeed. You see, very little was written by the Celts themselves about their religion and customs, even at the height of their power. It wasn't until much later that things were recorded, not until the thirteenth century in fact, and then mostly by Christians. Not the best people to give an objective account. The Celts themselves relied upon their oral tradition, woven into folk tales and legends. The storytellers have always been held in the highest esteem throughout Celtic history, even now.'

'Just like Miriam?'

'That's right. Through her stories Miriam was able to unravel history for the historians so that . . .'

I didn't hear the rest of his words. I had become aware of a transformation, a shift in the atmosphere, subtle at first, then growing, swelling, pressing down on me. No one else seemed to notice. They were all talking and listening, involved with each other, but I could no longer hear them. All sights and sensations in the room had fallen away, leaving one pure sound, that of a lone flute. I remembered now, that particular album, that particular track. 'Lagan Love' it was called. She would play it over and over again. A slow air she said it was, a lament. The instrument sang and sobbed. Each note filled the air, piercing my head with liquid, vibrating sorrow as it rose, wavered, then died away. A tune to break your heart, she had called it, and she would close her eyes, tensed and listening with every sinew of her body, as if no other sound ever existed. That was how I heard it then, and that was all I heard.

And I knew he was listening with me. But where? Yes, it would have to be the garden. I was at the window now, looking out. And he was there, as I knew he would be. Closer this time, almost to the house. I could have reached out and touched him if not for the glass. This time his eyes were not focused on mine, but I knew he was listening with me. Tears trembled on the sweep of black lashes, and the eyes I had seen as yellow now flashed golden in the slanting sunlight. On his pale, translucent face was an expression of such utter grief and despair that I thought I could not endure it. Both of us were motionless, for a second, for an eternity.

Then I was running through the room, pushing past guests with unseen faces, through the kitchen, scattering trays and glasses, before tumbling out through the garden door. He was gone of course, vanished, but where to? There had not been time and yet I looked to the orchard. Shadows slid across the lawn, pursued by the late afternoon. But not a branch stirred, not a leaf quivered.

'Chloe? Chloe, where are you?'

I became aware of the voice, but could neither comprehend the words nor identify the speaker, only that it wasn't him.

'Cliohna, is anything wrong?' I turned to stare at Uncle Greg's shoulders filling the kitchen doorway.

'What? What did you say?'

'I said, is anything wrong? You went rushing out of the house . . .'

'No, I'm fine. It's nothing. I thought I saw someone I knew. I must have been mistaken.'

'Must have been someone pretty important.'

'No, not really.' I hurried back towards him, directing him towards the house, away from the garden even though there was no one there to see, nothing to hide.

'You said earlier you wanted to speak to me,' I said.

'Yes. I just needed to have a word about— Hey, what's wrong, lass? You're as white as a sheet. And you're shivering.'

'Am I? I expect it's been a long day. Really, I'm OK. What was it you wanted?'

He folded his arm around me. 'Nothing that can't wait. Perhaps you need a rest.'

'No, please go on. Tell me.'

I wanted him to talk, to go on filling the spaces around us with questions and answers.

'It's just that I need you to come into the office quite soon, perhaps before the end of next week, but only if you feel up to it. There are quite a few papers for you to sign. And there's a list of gifts for various friends. If you could help me identify them then I'll see that they are handed over.'

I nodded, his words washing over me, barely audible above the music still swirling in my head.

'She left a letter for Harold Shaw with me, of course, but I won't send it off until I've managed to make contact and break the news. I've rung several times but so far there's been no reply.'

'Harold Shaw? You said Harold Shaw?'

'Yes, Harold. Miriam's husband. Your grandfather.'

'Grandfather?'

'Yes. Surely you knew that she was married? That Hannah had a father?'

'Hannah's father's dead. He died in America. That was years ago.'

'Oh, Christ, is that what they told you?'

'Yes, I mean, no. That's what Hannah said.'

Greg took hold of my shoulders, turning me towards him.

'Your grandfather, Miriam's husband, Harold Shaw, is still living. Whatever you were told about his death wasn't true.'

'But why? I don't understand. Why would they lie about it?'

'What can I say? It's a big thing, losing a father at such an early age. Perhaps Miriam thought it was best that Hannah made a clean break. He did go back to America, to Boston. It's been a long time, but I have every reason to believe he still lives near there.'

'Miriam never spoke of him. It's like he never existed for her.'

'That's not quite true. They did keep in touch. Oh, only cards at Christmas, the occasional note with news of the family. But I do have an address and phone number. And she did write him a long letter to be sent in case of her death. I don't know about the state of his health. He would be well over seventy now. That's why I thought I'd better ring first, but so far I haven't been able to get through.'

We were standing by the kitchen door, silent while I took this in. I scraped at the woodwork with my thumbnail, detaching a loose flake of green paint. Of course I had a grandfather. Everybody had a grandfather: it was a genetic necessity. The flakes of paint crumbled between my fingers. So much needed doing. I would have to find a decorator. If Miriam's husband had been there he would have painted the doors. But he had melted into the past, a thing of anecdote and history, an unmentioned name at family gatherings. I had a grandfather. There was an address and a phone number. Press the buttons and up he would pop like magic, brought into existence like a rabbit out of a top hat.

'I'm sorry. This must be a shock for you, on top of everything else. I would never have sprung it on you like this, only I'd no idea . . .'

'Yes, well, it is a bit of a surprise. There's been rather a lot of those lately.'

I buried my face against Uncle Greg's shoulder, breathing in the smell of stale cigars. I wondered if Harold Shaw smoked cigars.

'I can't take it in just at the moment, what with everything else.' But that wasn't entirely true. Somewhere at the back of my mind I was already making plans.

Another hour passed. Guests waited in turn to give their final condolences and I thanked them graciously. A taxi was summoned and Paul went off to don his white coat and play doctors and nurses. The caterers polished the glasses, packed away the tricks of their trade and departed in their mini-van. The cottage was mine again.

I wandered through the rooms, savouring the solitude, yet sharply aware that the air crackled with activity. The spaces between objects felt grainy, as if emptiness held more texture than solid matter. I was aware of Miriam's perfume even though my senses couldn't detect it.

She was everywhere.

The sun was rushing headlong towards the purple horizon. The last, lingering rays of light patched the floors and walls with squares of bronze. As I looked along the hallway I sensed something was not quite right, an irregularity which, at first, I could not define. Then I noticed a wedge of light, a beam of the dying sun, lying across the flagstones in a place where no light should be. Unless . . .

Unless it was coming through the door of my studio. My fingers curled around the door key hidden safely in the deep folds of my pocket. I didn't feel afraid as I walked towards the light though I knew, even before I reached it, that the door would be standing wide open.

Eight

HE FACED THE CANVAS, standing between Miriam and me. At the nape of his neck the sleek, jet hair was bound into a long tail, an inverted question mark. Through the dark, enveloping coat his shoulders stood at sharp angles, held high and taut. Here was tensile strength coupled with fragility, as if the muscles and sinews were made of spun glass: a body through which sunlight slipped and slid.

He continued to gaze at her portrait while I remained silent at the doorway of the sanctuary, a trespasser witnessing an act of adoration. The waves of energy between them were palpable. Seconds passed, minutes; still I hesitated, fearing that the thunderous rushing of my own breath would violate this holy communion. And yet I sensed that some part of him was alert to my presence. Eventually he shuddered, his back and shoulders quivering, and the breath escaped from him in a long sigh that finally came to rest in a choking sob.

'It's too soon, far too soon. There is no sense to it. What purpose does it serve? So fragile an existence, so brief! How can you bear it, knowing that's all there is?' He turned to me, eyes brimming, his face tear-streaked and accusing. 'Tell me, how can you bear it?

How am *I* supposed to bear it? And why must I? Answer me that, Cliohna!'

His hands were clenched, knuckles white as bleached stones. I struggled to contrive an answer.

'Because that's all we have,' I whispered.

'Yes, that is all you have, your three score years and ten. It is a mockery, some divine joke played on a drunken reveller. And I wanted — I needed — so much more.'

'There is no more.'

'Oh, but there is!' His fist slammed down onto my workbench, scattering paints and pencils. 'There is always more. It goes on and on.' He pounded the table, driving home each word. 'Why? Answer me that, will you!'

A jar toppled, sending a stream of water to soak my sketchpad, staining its white pages a muddy green.

'I'm sorry. I don't understand. I don't know what you want me to say.'

There was a rush and tumble of realisation. I was alone in the house — only me and this strange man with his beating fist and his yellow, flashing eyes. He gasped, all his senses now focused on me, as they had been upon Miriam's image.

'Oh, no, Cliohna, it's all right.'

I stepped back as he reached out towards me. He looked at my face, then at his empty fingers. His hands withdrew, curling away inside his coat pocket. 'No, it's all right. I'm sorry. I didn't mean to frighten you. I wouldn't harm you. You must understand that I can never hurt you. It's only . . . I loved her too. It is important you know that.'

'Yes, I can see. But why did you love her? That's what I don't understand. What was she to you? Who *are* you?'

A smile lit up his face. Then, for a fleeting moment, his expression changed to one of confusion. He retreated, hugging his body, folding in upon himself. Then the smile returned. I was learning that moods moved over him like the swiftly changing colours of a chameleon, all equally genuine and transient. He wiped the tears from his cheeks with the cuff of his sleeve and his eyes pleaded with me like those of a small boy who had been caught stealing apples. I held the advantage.

'How did you get into this room?'

'Through the door.' He pointed over my shoulder, eyebrows arching, all innocence. We both knew he was laughing at me, and I nearly let a smile escape but caught it just in time.

'I saw you at the cemetery. But you know that, don't you? You were watching me from a distance. Why didn't you come closer? You could have joined us. If you were her friend, why weren't you with the others?'

He continued to look at me, his gaze running over my hair, my face and neck, following the lines of my throat to rest where my hand had sought to touch the talisman. His lids half closing, his mouth slightly open, he breathed softly.

'I knew her in a way that was . . . different. As you did. You are the only being with whom I could share this, who would understand anything of who she was. I can see from your painting that you have touched her essence. I can trust you with my grief.'

'But what was she to you? And why would you love her for it?'

'It is a rare and special gift, you know, to be able to capture the spirit of a thing, to record it and keep it. But you have done it here.'

'Strange, that's what Miriam used to tell me. She said that I could paint and draw, that I could make pictures, which in itself was worthy of my time and study. But to be an artist I would have to learn to touch the spirit of a thing. She believed I had it in me, but it wasn't something that could be taught.'

'Ah, but it can! I will show you even more. You will let me.'

'Is that how you knew her? Was she your teacher?'

'Oh yes, I learned a great deal from her.'

He smiled slyly, and turned to catch my eye, as if expecting me to share the joke. The insinuation was too unthinkable to pursue.

She was easily three times his age and more. I quickly sidestepped and tried another path.

'What I mean is, are you a student? Was she helping you with research?'

He was suddenly very earnest. 'I apologise. I did not mean to offend you. You really do have a talent, you know. You have captured her spirit here.'

'Perhaps I sensed somehow, or perhaps she did, that this would be our last chance. As I worked on the portrait I felt conscious of something — something more than awareness of light and shadow and form. It was as if she were with me, as if I'd become a part of her and it was my own self I was expressing.'

'There, you see. You have to know a thing in order to be able to paint it. To enter into it, to be in its consciousness so that it can explain itself through you. This is indeed the Miriam I knew. And there is something of yourself there also.'

'People keep saying I look like her.'

'Yes, but it is more than that. What was it Eliel Saarinen said? "No work of art, in any form, can be considered a work of art unless it reveals the basic nature of the artist himself." ' The little boy beamed at me, proud of his homework and expecting full marks.

'I'm impressed. How come you know so much about art?'

'I've learned a little about many things. I wish to know a lot more.' He turned again to the canvas, and we stood shoulder to shoulder, Miriam smiling at us. He reached out with his long, delicate fingers to touch her cheek. Again unashamed tears coursed down his face. He seemed so vulnerable that I, too, reached out and, in turn, brushed his cheek, gathering salt tears on my fingers.

'Who are you?' I whispered.

He merely sighed, then breathed deeply and said, 'What I need is a glass of wine.'

Abruptly he stepped back, turned and left the room. As he brushed past me I smelt the faint odour of freshly bruised grasses and damp moss.

I was sure he had vanished again, but no, I found him in the kitchen rummaging among the surplus wine bottles. Somewhere between the two rooms he had shed the long coat, though I saw no sign of it. He opened a top cupboard, reaching for a tumbler, then took the corkscrew from a drawer. He was at home in this kitchen, perhaps more so than I was.

'What do you think you're doing?' I demanded. 'This is my grandmother's home. You can't go rifling through it as if it were yours!'

'No, strictly speaking this is your house now.' His smile was gentle. 'Who knows, perhaps it will be your home too.'

'Then what are you doing here?'

'I told you. I need some wine. Ah, I think this one will do. Now, this is one of the things I learned from Miriam, how to appreciate a good wine. I never knew there were so many different kinds. Did you know that the soil the grapes are grown in will affect the entire character of the finished product? It's amazing. Some people can actually tell where a wine was grown just by the taste.'

'Really?'

'Oh, yes. It's a fact.'

'Look, are you sending me up. Because if you are . . .'

'No, I wouldn't do that.' He had filled the tumbler almost to the brim and was now savouring the bouquet, admiring the stained light as it played through the wine.

'Look,' I said, 'I realise you were a close friend of Miriam's so I'm trying not to get angry, but—'

'On the contrary, Cliohna, you are trying very hard to *be* angry and not succeeding very well.' He smiled at me and it was like being bathed in warm sunshine.

'Cheers.' He winked and downed half the tumbler in one gulp. 'Yes, I do enjoy a good wine.'

'So do I.' I managed to inject a sting of sarcasm into my voice.

He turned, dismayed. 'What? Oh, I'm so sorry. Did you want some?'

'Yes, please, if you don't mind.'

'No, of course. Here you are.' He handed me the bottle.

I stood there holding it by the neck, waiting for something else to happen and feeling stupid. He carried on drinking. Clearly, so far as he was concerned that was the end of the matter, and if I wanted a drink I would have to pour it myself. By then I not only wanted one, I needed one. The emotions of the day that I had held so firmly in check were flooding in on me. I could feel my legs and shoulders trembling. As I fumbled with the glass my hands shook uncontrollably and the bottle jumped against the rim, spilling wine over the tabletop.

'It's all right, my Little Wren.' His voice was suddenly tender. 'I know how much you are hurting. All the others have gone now. You need no longer hide it.'

I fought against the stinging in my eyes. Standing with my back to him I was aware how vulnerable this made me, but I was determined not to show how weak I felt. The burning sharpness of the wine cut through me. I took another gulp and felt my body steadying, though my head was now beginning to swim.

I turned to face him, but somehow he had travelled to my side of the room and was now perched on the worktop, squatting on his haunches, his long bony legs bent on either side of his body. He took another sip of wine, savouring the flavour, rolling the liquid around his mouth before swallowing. He wore some sort of high-necked, black sweater, the sleeves pushed up to reveal arms that were smooth and white with the same bluish cast as his face. There were no hairs on the backs of his hands, no lines or scars — no imperfections. My eyes traced the path of a vein along the length of his forearm.

'You don't wear a watch,' I said, for something to say. 'I thought everyone wore a watch. For someone so obsessed with the passing of time, it seems strange not to keep track of it.'

'Time used to be my friend. Now we have become close enemies. I would not carry its portrait on my person.'

He tipped his head back, draining the tumbler, then held it out to me. I refilled it for him while he looked down at me from his perch, his head cocked to one side. I backed away from his bright, unblinking eyes and leaned against the safety of a cupboard.

'You have never been to Paris,' he said. 'You should go.'

'No, you're right. I've always wanted to. The Louvre, of course. Have you been there?'

'Yes. The Picasso exhibition to celebrate his ninetieth birthday. First time they ever staged a major exhibition by a living artist. Magnificent!'

'Was he there? Did you see him? What was he like?'

Iolair shrugged his shoulders. 'Yes, I saw him briefly. He looked like any other old man, I suppose. No, now I come to think of it, he seemed rather uncomfortable, out of place.'

'But surely, wasn't that in the early seventies? You would have been too young to remember.'

'Yes, you should see the Picassos. And the early impressionists. The Renoirs, of course. *The Woman with a Fan* reminds me a little of you. I'll come with you if you like.'

I swallowed hard, coughing as the wine caught in my throat. 'You'll what? Come with me? What makes you think—'

'Oh, it's no problem. I would love to see Paris again. And it's not too far. They have a tunnel now, you know. Goes right under the Channel. You don't have to cross the water at all. Quite painless.' He stared hard at his glass before taking another sip. 'Yes, it is important for you to study the works of other artists.'

'I tried to persuade my mother to let me go on a school trip to Paris when I was fourteen. She said that there were plenty of paintings I could look at in Cambridge. She sent me skiing in Switzerland instead.'

'Hannah has always been very . . . very like Hannah.'

I nodded and we both smiled.

'I painted a picture for her once,' I said. 'Cornfields in the rain. It was a birthday present.'

'She didn't like it?'

'Oh no, on the contrary — she thought it was marvellous. She'd just had the lounge redecorated. The corn exactly matched the colour of the new curtains.'

Iolair laughed softly. 'What did you say?'

'What could I say? How do you explain art to Hannah?'

This time he threw back his head and laughed aloud. I started to giggle. I'd been nurturing that particular pain for so long, so avidly wallowing in my own rejection, that I had failed to see how ridiculous it all was. Then, somehow, all that had happened throughout that long day welled up inside me, the dam broke and I was engulfed in a tidal wave of laughter. Suddenly everything seemed hilariously funny — me, Paul, David, Hannah, especially Hannah, with her ladies' Rotary meetings and her Austrian blinds. I could see the corn-yellow curtains whisking aside to expose her in all her absurdity. I doubled over, helplessly clutching my convulsing body, as tears streamed down my face. It was as if some tight binding cord had started to snap, thread by thread, and was about to unravel. The wine hummed in my head, tilting the floor and walls so that I was forced to hold on to stop myself collapsing. Iolair laughed with my laughter. He rocked to and fro with delight, his shoulders heaving, until I fought to control the flood of hysteria, and was left gasping. He too, caught his breath, sniffed and wiped his eyes.

'It's about time you saw the joke!'

'I know, I know. And the punch line . . .', I started to giggle again, 'the punch line is my mother!'

This set us both off on another round of convulsions. Eventually, exhausted and dizzy, I reached for the bottle, refilled my glass and offered the bottle to him. He held out his tumbler, but I stood my ground and he was forced to come to me. He stepped down in one unbelievably easy movement and crossed the room. We entered a calm silence, sharing the peace that follows a storm. As I filled his glass, he gently lifted the stray twists of hair that had tumbled over my forehead and smoothed them back into place. My head filled with the scent of crushed grasses. His hand stroked my face and neck, his fingers following the chain down to where the talisman lay.

'Give it to me,' he whispered.

'No.' My lips formed the soundless word.

'I am begging you. Give it to me now, while I can still ask it of you. Give it to me. Before it is too late.'

I saw Miriam, her face pale against the glazed, hospital sheet, her hand painfully gripping my wrist. *If you give it back you will lose him!*

I looked up but was afraid to meet his eyes. 'I can't. I promised.'

His jaw tightened and his face seemed to grow darker. 'Then damn you. Damn you all to hell!' He twisted away from me.

I cowered as his arm came up and hurled the tumbler across the room and I watched it spinning through the air, as if in slow motion, spewing red wine in an arc above us. The glass exploded against the sink and the wide sweep of red hit the wall, running down in a tracery of fine rivulets like the blooded wing of some gigantic bird.

And then he was gone. And this time I knew there would be no point in looking for him.

For a long time I stared at the floor and the scattered shards of glass, unable to move. Eventually, I dared to cross the room, but as soon as my trembling hands tried to pick at the fragments a sharp pain stabbed my finger. I watched a bright bead of red appear. Instinct took it to my mouth and I tasted the coppery tang of my own blood. And there was something else, something that tasted of salt and musk.

Then I remembered the portrait and the shimmering tears I had gathered on my fingers.

Nine

IT WAS STILL EARLY EVENING, but already the rain ushered in an early darkness in which I felt safely unobserved. I parked the car outside our little terrace and sat for a while listening to Fifi's engine ticking as it cooled. I was reluctant to leave the warmth of her interior and face the household. I had been alone there again all day, at the cottage, and was loath to break the spell. Rays from the street lamps sparkled through a mist of fine drizzle that had started during the drive back into town and now promised to set in for the night.

As I closed the front door behind me, I heard an unexpected clattering coming from the kitchen, then loud, girlish giggles. The hall was filled with the smells of serious cooking. Was there something happening, something I'd forgotten about? Then the kitchen door opened with a gush of steam and Paul came through, smiling, arms open wide to engulf me.

'Ah, here she is: the guest of honour.'

'What are you doing here? I thought you were on duty?'

'Hi there, Chloe.' That was Ruth calling from the kitchen.

Then Paul was speaking again. 'Yes, I was. Did a swap, managed to get the night off.'

'Why? What's going on?'

'Welcome back celebration. Well, just a dinner party really.'

Then Angie's head appeared around the kitchen door. 'And nothing very ambitious, I'm afraid. All a bit short notice. Just vege lasagne — Malcolm's vegetarian. Ruth's making a Greek salad, lots of black olives.' She vanished again.

'What dinner party? I don't understand.'

Paul took hold of my shoulders, a little too tightly. His face became serious. 'Look, Rabbit, you've been away from us too long. All this involvement with Miriam and the funeral. It's like you've been in another world. We've missed you. *I've* missed you. I want you back.'

'But what's that got to do with a dinner party?'

'Don't worry. It's just us. Ruth's invited Eddie — you know, he helped her with her stuff when she moved in — and Angie wants to show off Malcolm.'

'And who the hell's Malcolm?'

'Well, that just proves how much you've been out of it. Malcolm's the latest boyfriend. I think she's counting on you for a second opinion. You know what she's like with men.'

'Great, but not now. I'm tired. I need an early night.'

'No you don't. It's all arranged. The others will be here any minute. They're your guests.'

'Oh no they're not. You invited them. They're your guests.' I banged my bag down on the hall table and headed up the stairs. 'I hope you all enjoy dinner. I'm going to bed.'

I slumped down onto the mattress, my head pounding. I didn't know what to do with my anger. To make it worse, I felt guilty about being angry, and then angry about being made to feel guilty. I get — I used to get — like that quite often, and it usually meant that I would back down, though I was determined not to this time. But why did he always have to look so hurt?

Rain spattered the windowpane. In the darkness I watched the droplets race each other down the glass and run together, leaving trails like silver serpents against the night sky. It was a few minutes before I heard the stair boards creak. The door inched open and a shaft of light hit my aching eyes. I turned away as Paul entered.

'Look, I've brought you some wine. I bought a few bottles of that nice red we found. Thought you might enjoy it. Peace offering.'

I took the glass from him and stared at the contents. If I drank it, would that be giving way? Then I jumped as the doorbell reverberated through the house. Angie's exaggerated laughter lifted over deeper, muffled tones. The kitchen door opened then banged shut. Of course Paul knew I would have to give in. The wine tasted as good as I remembered.

'Oh, I'm sorry. I know you meant well,' I said, 'but you should have asked.'

'If I had asked, you would have said no.'

'Paul, it's only been two days since the funeral. I need time.'

'Time for what? You've spent the last two days shut up in that cottage doing God knows what. You won't let anyone near the place. When you do come home all you do is sleep. We've hardly spoken to each other. I'm seriously worried about you. You've been so . . . so closed up in yourself, so absent. And you look dreadful.'

'Oh, thanks a lot.'

He sat down beside me, head leaning against mine. 'Now listen, Chloe. Miriam was an old woman and she died and that's sad. But it happens. We deal with it and then we move on. I know it's going to take time, but meanwhile you can't shut yourself off from everyone like this. Now, it's only Angie, Ruth and me and a couple of passing boyfriends. You can manage that, can't you?'

I took a few sips of the wine, twirling the glass stem between my fingers.

'You're probably right. Give me a few minutes to tidy myself up.' I switched on the light and sat in front of the mirror, struggling with a lipstick.

'I see you're still wearing your hair pinned up. I guess I'll get used to it.'

I said nothing and he left the room.

The talisman glinted against midnight-blue satin. I was wearing another of Miriam's dresses. It would have to do; I couldn't be bothered to change. For the first time I noticed the bruised shadows around my eyes. A smut of brown mascara flicked onto my cheek. When I tried to wipe it off, it smeared into a dark stain. I was looking more haggard by the minute.

We found Ruth and Eddie in the sitting room. Ruth turned and smiled as I came in and we gave each other a little hug. Our Victorian dolls' house was never designed for social gatherings. With the dining table moved into the centre of the room and fully extended, there was barely space to squeeze around it.

'Chloe, you remember Eddie, don't you?'

'Yes, of course. Hello again.'

Ruth was a Dresden shepherdess. The sweeping line of her cheekbone and her light delicacy shone through, despite the nose ring and torn denims. Eddie was her masculine counterpart, as pale and fragile as she. Ruth had moved in with us quite recently, and I remembered how confused Angie and I were when she brought her stuff around. She seemed to be everywhere at once until we realised Eddie had come along to help. It was difficult to decide who was imitating who: same closely shaved hair, same ear studs. They should be sharing the same flat, and it was obvious that Angie and I would soon be advertising for another third girl to share.

I sidled around to where Eddie was crouched over a coffee table looking through some of my drawings.

'I've been showing him your art,' Ruth said. 'Hope you don't mind.'

'No, of course not.' I felt a tingle of flattery.

The wine was doing its work and I thought I might as well

accept the inevitable and enjoy the evening. Paul was opening another bottle, so I held out my now-empty glass. He looked surprised but gave me a refill.

'These are good.' Eddie was sifting through a pile of rough sketches.

'Yes, she's a clever girl, my Chloe.'

Eddie gave Paul a withering glance. 'No, I mean these are really good. Who are you studying with?'

'No one, though I was thinking of taking some classes. It's just a hobby.' I turned to Paul. 'Ruth and Eddie are doing a commercial art course.'

'I'm right about those, aren't I?' Ruth said, leaning heavily on Eddie's shoulder. 'She won't believe how talented she is.'

'Well, someone should convince her. Is that yours, too?' He nodded at the portrait over the fireplace.

'Yes, it's supposed to be Angie.'

'I'm not too sure that it looks like her,' said Paul.

'It's not supposed to look like me, Paul, it's not a photo.' Angie had entered the room carrying a bowl of something hot. 'I sense myself in it. I look at it when I feel unsure of things. Like a touchstone.'

'I think it looks like Angie.' This was a new voice. 'You've managed to show that unselfconscious strength she has, that lack of physical awareness.'

'I'll take that as a compliment.' Angie smiled, her eyes shining. I turned to find the source of her pleasure and came face to face with an expanse of sweatshirt. Somewhere high above me was a hairy face and a pair of brown eyes.

'You must be Chloe. I'm Malcolm.'

Angie edged up beside me and dug me in the ribs. It was her way of asking what I thought of him. All her boyfriends look like dogs; I think she picks them up at the surgery. The last one was a forlorn-looking whippet. Malcolm looked more like an Airedale, elegant yet sturdy. I smiled an OK. Then Angie suggested we all sit down and we shuffled around the table. I contrived to move between her and Malcolm, sitting opposite Paul, wilfully sustaining the line of tension between us.

Candles were lit, more dishes fetched and passed from hand to hand. Paul, custodian of the wine, topped up the half-empty glasses. I drained mine in readiness.

'Hey, steady on there.' He held the bottle back.

'You said I should relax and enjoy myself. That's what I'm doing.'

'You've already had two, you know.'

'This will make three then, won't it?'

I thrust my glass forward and held his eyes until he relented. Malcolm, on my left, coughed gently before he spoke.

'Angie didn't tell me what you did for a living.' His voice had a soft, lyrical quality; Welsh perhaps.

'Computers,' I responded. 'Data research. Finding new ways to bend statistics to fit the company image.'

Ruth waved her fork in my direction. 'Don't you find playing with numbers boring? I can never reconcile number-crunching with your creative ability. The two things seem diametrically opposed.'

'If you're talking about fifth form maths, yes, you're right. But it's more than that. Numbers are abstractions. There comes a point where you leave figures behind and enter the realm of principles. Numbers show us the patterns which shape the universe.'

'Yes, I'll grant you that.' Eddie was talking now. 'Even so, Chloe, I really am surprised you haven't taken your artwork more seriously.'

'Become an art student,' Paul laughed, 'like you and Ruth, you mean.'

If Eddie heard the derisive edge in Paul's tone, he chose to ignore it.

'No, of course not. We're both studying commercial art. Fine art is a different matter altogether. Chloe needs a chance to develop, she needs expert nurturing.'

'Yes, well there'll be time enough for that after we're married. She won't have to work, of course. A doctor's hours are long and she'll need something to occupy her time at home, won't you, Chloe?'

'That's not what I meant.' Eddie bristled, glowering at Paul. 'I don't think you appreciate—' Ruth gave him a silencing glare; I think she may have kicked him under the table.

I turned to Angie. 'You see, he's got it all planned out. He'll play the leading role in some hospital drama while I tend the nest and turn out insipid landscapes. I know, I could do them in assorted colours to match the decor. Very stylish. No nudes of course, too controversial. Might shock the consultants' wives.'

Angie and I continued to look at each other. She stifled a smirk while I started to giggle.

'Oh, come on, Chloe. That's not what I meant and you know it. Stop making out I'm some sort of Neanderthal. It's just that now isn't the right time for you to be thinking of changing careers.'

'Why? Are you frightened I might upstage yours?' I snatched the wine bottle before Paul had a chance to refuse and refilled my own glass.

Angie thrust the salad bowl at me.

Ruth's voice was unnecessarily loud. 'Talking of careers, Angie, when are we going to see you on TV? There's been all those programmes recently about animal surgeries.'

I continued to drink steadily, sipping and swallowing with theatrical precision, while the conversation lurched painfully through the RSPCA and abandoned puppies. Malcolm tried asking everyone about their plans for the millennium celebrations but that went down like a concrete balloon. Candles spluttered and our shadows leapt on the narrow walls like encircling giants closing in on us. Paul watched me, ignoring the conversation. Neither of us ate. I pushed food around on my plate while Paul turned a chunk of bread in his hands, tearing at it, gradually reducing it to a pile of crumbs. Meanwhile, Angie urged food onto plates, removed discarded dishes and replaced them with sweeter things. I thought about the wine I had shared with him. Was it only two days ago? The stain still ran down the wall. The ridge of a small scar marked my finger.

'How are things going at the cottage?' Angie touched my arm as she spoke, shepherding my wandering mind.

'Oh, OK, there's such a lot to do.'

'It must be awful,' said Ruth, 'having to search through someone's things, personal stuff. Having to decide which of their belongings to keep and what to give away.'

'Yes, it's . . .' My voice faltered.

Is that what I was supposed to be doing? Is that what they thought? I'd spent two days there. Waiting and watching, working hard at becoming part of that house of treasures. I'd searched through things, opened drawers and cupboards, touching, smelling, absorbing, knowing the things that she had known, learning to own them, allowing them to own me. I could claim a feeble attempt at tidying the garden, sweeping up the fallen leaves. It was an excuse to linger in the orchard. But I remained alone. I tried on all her clothes, deciding which suited me best. I had taken to wearing her perfume. The afternoons turned chilly so I lit a fire of logs and curled up in her armchair. I started to read a book of folk tales but fell asleep instead. Mostly I just listened to the silence.

I watched and I waited.

'It's a bit of a daunting task,' Paul cut in. 'The place is a shambles. I've offered to help, but Chloe insists on doing it all herself, don't you?' He looked directly at me as if it were an accusation. 'Still, you may have to get some professional help in. Time's running short.'

'What do you mean?' said Angie.

'Well, the housing market slumps towards Christmas. If it's not up for sale before the end of September, it probably won't move until the spring.'

'What makes you think it's for sale? Why does everyone assume that I want to sell it, that I want to dispose of everything that was my grandmother, bundle her life up in a black bin liner and leave it out for the dustman?'

'No one's asking you to do that. But we've got to be realistic. You can't hang onto that place. What would you do with it?

'I might want to live in it.'

'Oh, now you're being ridiculous. We can't possibly live in that crumbling old heap.'

'Actually it's not, and I certainly can. Where you choose to live is entirely up to you.'

There was a momentary silence during which Paul lowered his head into his hands. Then Ruth initiated diversionary tactics by clearing dishes from the battleground, Angie joining forces with her.

Eddie said, 'Some of these old places are worth a fortune. Depends on a bit on its history. Is much known about it?'

'I've been there a few times,' Angie offered. 'Looks very ancient. Surrounded by trees and buried in ivy. Loads of atmosphere.'

Ruth was suddenly animated. 'Does it have a ghost?'

'Now that's something Malcolm would know about,' Eddie said. 'Angie told me you're into all that sort of thing.'

Malcolm had been very quiet up till then.

'Not ghosts, nothing like that. Just psychic research. Telepathy experiments, statistical odds of coincidence. That sort of thing.'

'That's not true,' Angie protested. 'He's too modest. It's much more than that. Malcolm is a psychic, a psychometrist — is that the right word?' He shrugged his shoulders in self-effacing agreement. 'He reads vibrations from objects, he can tell things about their owners.'

'Oh, come on now . . .' Paul's exasperation widened, eliciting support from the rest of the company.

'No, really. It works. That's how we met, isn't it? Malcolm was helping an owner to trace their missing cat.'

'But how does it work?' Eddie asked. I'm not sure if he was

genuinely interested or if it was his way of annoying Paul.

'No one knows really. I just hold an object — it has to be something personal, something worn close to the subject. Pictures come into my head. Like thoughts but clearer, more insistent.'

'And does it work with people too?'

'Yes, it does sometimes. Can't guarantee results, though.'

Ruth leaned forward, excitement flushing her face. 'Let's try it. Would you, Malcolm?'

'I know,' said Angie, 'I know what you could use.' My hand darted to my neck. 'Oh, come on, Chloe, it can't do any harm. He may be able to pick up traces of Miriam.'

Then everyone was talking at once with Paul protesting and no one listening to him.

'I can't take it off,' I said.

'That's no problem,' Ruth argued. 'He can still hold it if you're wearing it, can't you, Malcolm?'

'Yes, I suppose so. But only if it's what Chloe wants.'

I was still hesitating, afraid yet excited. 'Can you reach from here? The chain's not very long, I'm afraid.'

'Angie, can't you stop this! Don't you think she's been under enough strain without involving her in these psycho games? You can see what a state she's in.'

'I'm not in a state, Paul, and I'm not a child. I'll decide what I want to do.'

'Chloe,' Paul's voice rose above the others, 'I absolutely forbid you to get involved with this!'

I looked at him through the silence that had caved in upon the room. Slowly and deliberately I drained my glass, placing it carefully on the table. Then I turned in my chair to face Malcolm.

'What do I have to do?'

He glanced sideways at Paul, then looked directly at me.

'Are you sure about this? I don't want to do anything that might upset you.'

'Yes, of course I'm sure. After all it's only Miriam.'

Malcolm leaned towards me, taking the talisman gently between his fingers. The others gathered around us, looking over his shoulder, except for Paul who remained seated.

'A strange metal,' said Ruth. 'It looks like silver, but I'm not so sure. Look, at certain angles you can see other colours running through it, like a seashell. I can't make out the design. What's it supposed to be?'

Then Malcolm said, 'Just keep still and allow me to talk. I'll say whatever comes into my head. It doesn't always make sense but it's important not to interrupt the flow.'

He moved closer to me: I could feel the warmth of his body. His eyes closed and he allowed his fingers to trace the intricate lines of the patterned surface. He sighed deeply, then his breathing became loud and irregular. I hardly dared to breathe at all. A chair moved, scuffing the floor. The candles burned steadily and giant shadows hunched around us, waiting.

Malcolm shivered. The words came slowly at first.

'I feel cold . . . a damp coldness, that goes through to my bones . . . whiteness all around . . . a thick fog . . . the grass is wet with it . . . silence . . . a heavy silence . . . like creeping fingers touching the hairs on my neck. Why am I so afraid? A cry — just a fox, surely, but my heart's beating in my throat. There it is again — no, that was no fox. I want to run. The hill is steep and my legs feel rooted to the earth. Now hooves, pounding upon the turf, pounding through my head. The mud sucks at my feet — something is clinging to my legs: a skirt, wet from the long grass. Have to warn them . . . ow, my ankle! I dare not allow myself to cry out loud. Move . . . faster . . . I bite on my lip to silence the pain. Oh Dana, why does he not come?'

Malcolm's breath had become laboured, his face distorted. We pressed close around him, less sure of ourselves now. He started to speak again.

'More sounds, above me this time: shouts, the clatter of swords on shields. The stockade gates are opening even as I run towards

them. They swarm out, leaders on horseback, others following on foot with axes and knives. They flow around me, like breaking waves. There's Elwyn. He's wielding our father's great sword. Wild, he looks, upon the black stallion. It crashes past me — I can feel heat from its flanks. And there's Fahran. Oh, that I could ride with them. Elwyn is turning in the saddle. "Look to the young ones," he calls, "get them to safety." His words give purpose to my feet and I am running again, though I can scarce breathe. Never was I so afraid. The gods damn this accursed skirt!'

Malcolm was becoming more distressed. Beads of sweat appeared on his forehead. One hand gripped the talisman while the other clutched at his mouth. We huddled around him, silent. Paul's face had lost its anger and he was looking concerned. Then Malcolm was coughing and gasping, tears streaming from his eyes.

'Smoke, black smoke, and the smell of blood. Pray, Dana, my brothers live. My hands are pressed against my ears, but nothing shuts out the cries of the injured. Heedless, I stumble over their bodies. Oh Dana, forgive me. Over there I see red hair, a deerskin jerkin — yes, it has to be Fahran. Please, let it be him, let him be alive. I must kneel in the blood to reach him. The cold wetness oozes through to my skin, my stomach heaves with the stench. Would that I had the courage to flee from this place, but I cannot leave until I find him. Though I have not the strength left in my body I must turn him over — I must know if this be my brother. My hands, red and sticky, slip on the wet leather. Oh, why is he not come to help me? Ah, there, I have done it. Oh, look at you, all smeared with mud. Let me wipe your face. Your eyes are forever open. I know you — you are my clansman, yes, but you are not my brother, not Fahran. Oh Dana, where are they?'

'I think we should put a stop to this,' Paul whispered.

'Shush. He said we were not to interrupt.'

'A shout, the ring of hooves on rock . . . Through the smoke, a black stallion — Elwyn? Praise the gods. No, the enemy! The horseman bears down upon me. The wing of a bird in flight? 'Tis the sharp edge

of an axe. No! I hear a scream and the ground is rushing towards me. The scream dies in my throat.'

Malcolm slumped forward onto the table, still clinging to the silver around my neck, pulling me with him. Paul was up from his chair and clambering around to where we struggled to support Malcolm's body. He was still muttering.

'Lightning . . . in my head . . . black lightning. Perhaps it is pain. The earth is soft and warm . . . I press my face into its wetness. And that smell, the blood smell. The blood of my clansman was cold — this is warm and flowing. It must be mine. Will he come in time? Something is moving nearby . . . something small, snuffling and scratching. Oh, sweet Dana, don't let me die where there are rats . . .'

Then Malcolm fell silent. I think he lost consciousness.

'Open a window, get some air in here.' Suddenly Paul was there, lifting him.

I was pushed aside. The spell was shattered as electric light flooded the room. Malcolm was still slumped in his dining chair and Paul was forcing his eyelids apart, feeling his pulse.

'He's in shock. Fetch something warm — blankets.'

Ruth ran from the room. Angie and Eddie cleared a space and helped manoeuvre Malcolm into an armchair. I backed towards the door.

'I'm sorry,' I whispered, but no one was listening. What if he dies? I thought. It will be my fault. After what seemed an eternity he groaned and tried to pull himself upright.

'Malcolm, can you hear me?' Paul was using his professional voice.

'Yes. Yes, I hear you.' He gripped Paul's shoulder with trembling fingers. 'Please don't leave me. Please.' He sounded terrified.

'No, we're all here. We won't leave you.' Angie's face was pale and her hands were shaking.

Ruth had come back into the room carrying a quilt. 'Here, let's put this round you. Would a hot drink help? Shall I put some coffee on?'

'Yes,' said Paul, 'good idea.'

Ruth left the room again. Paul was still kneeling beside Malcolm, holding his wrist.

Angie put a hand on Malcolm's shoulder. 'What happened? What went wrong?' she asked. 'Can you remember any of it?'

'Not now!' Paul snapped.

But Malcolm was trying to answer. He clutched at Paul's sweater, kneading at it and twisting it out of shape.

'I don't know. There was a battlefield. My head, a dreadful pain. And then . . . oh, God, how long have I been away?'

'Only a few moments. You're not hurt but you need to rest. Just take it easy.'

'A few moments? Can't be. It seemed . . . forever, and yet no time. There was a woman. I remember that. I think she died.'

'Yes,' said Angie, 'there was some sort of battle. Swords and horses, bodies everywhere. She was looking for her brothers. Then someone whacked her with an axe.'

'That's right.' Malcolm lifted his hand to his head. 'God, I can still feel it. Then everything closed in on me, like a black cloud. That's when she must have died. That was bad enough. But what happened next, that was worse, far, far worse.'

'There was more?'

'I became someone else. Someone, or something. I was a man, but not a man. And I existed and yet I didn't exist. Didn't I say anything?'

'No. We didn't know about anyone else, did we?' Ruth looked around for corroboration. 'The woman said something about rats and then it was like you fainted.'

'That's right,' said Eddie, 'but you weren't out long — couldn't have been more than a minute. What happened? Can you remember where you were?'

'Nowhere. That's where I was, nowhere. An endless tunnel of . . . nothing. I was alone. Like a bird, flying, but there was no land to fly over and no sky to fall through. I flew on for ever and ever, yet

I knew I could never move. And I would always be alone. I never want to be in that place again.' Then he lowered his head onto Paul's shoulder and muffled sobs shook his body.

Coffee arrived and Paul had to prise Malcolm's fingers loose and coax him to take a drink. Gradually he came back to us, but he remained pale and shaken.

'I'm sorry, folks. It's not usually like this. I've never experienced anything so powerful.'

'It's me who should be sorry.' Angie knelt beside him, holding his hand. 'I feel awful about this. We should never have pushed you into it.'

'It's OK, love, occupational hazard. Though not one I'd ever want to experience again in a hurry.'

'Who do you think those people were?'

'Some sort of ancient tribe, hill fort dwellers it seemed like. Iceni, maybe, or Celts. Obviously that thing is very old, so God only knows what it's been through. But that doesn't explain what happened afterwards, that emptiness. It's that pendant. There's something . . . I don't know, something wrong with it.'

'I wonder who he was, the one she was waiting for?' Eddie was pouring coffee and handing it around.

'That name: Dana.' I found my voice at last. 'I've heard it before.'

'Isn't she some kind of Pagan goddess?' said Eddie.

'Yes, that's right. I remember Miriam talking about her.'

'I might have known we'd get back to Miriam sooner or later.' Paul spat the words at me.

'Oh, Paul, that's not fair, I just said . . . I didn't know this was going to happen.'

'I told you not to wear that thing. Now you see what damage it's done.'

'Oh Paul, for pity's sake, you don't even believe in this sort of thing. You're just using it as an excuse to get at me.'

'I'm sorry, Chloe, but I have to agree with Paul.' Malcolm's voice was steady now and his eyes full of concern. 'I don't think you should be wearing it. I tell you, nothing would induce me to touch that thing again.'

'No, you're right, I don't believe in all this psychic nonsense.' Paul was standing now. 'But ever since Miriam died, ever since you've been wearing that necklace, you've changed. You've become moody, irrational. Nothing I say or do is right. Hannah thinks your attachment to Miriam is becoming an obsession. She thinks you're living out some kind of fantasy, that you think you're Miriam. You're even starting to look like her. And it all comes back to that damned thing round your neck.'

'Hannah thinks. So you've been talking with Hannah, have you? Discussing me?'

'Well, of course I've talked to Hannah. I had to talk to someone. I've been worried sick about you. We both have.'

'Hannah has always hated Miriam, you know that. And so have you. You're plotting together. Trying to take her away from me.'

'Now you're being paranoid.'

'You just can't bear to think of me having anything of my own, anything that might take my attention away from you. It's not a wife you want, it's a bloody audience.'

Paul looked down, his eyes suddenly tired and defeated. 'Chloe, I don't think I know you any more.'

'No, you don't. In fact, I don't think you ever did.'

I had to get away from him, from them all. I threw myself at the door, struggling with the handle that refused to turn. Then suddenly it flew open and I stumbled through. It slammed behind me and I was alone in the dimness of the hallway.

I stood at the bottom of the stairs, clinging to the banister. The staircase swayed above me. How much wine had I drunk? I couldn't remember. I could hear their voices through the closed door and knew they were talking about me. Paul would be telling them things, private things, justifying his accusations while I was unable to defend myself. Tears of anger scalded my face. There was my bag on the hall table. And then my hand was searching for the car key. They were making too much noise to hear the sound of the front door latch opening and closing. The rain was heavier now. I'd parked the car a few yards from the house, far enough away that they wouldn't hear the engine turning. Rubbing tears and rain from my eyes, I switched on the wipers.

The road swam into focus as I pulled away from the kerb.

Ten

GOD ONLY KNOWS what I thought I was doing.

I was heading for the cottage, but *why* I had no idea. I knew I'd had too much to drink and I was driving too fast. In fact I shouldn't have been driving at all, but that only seemed to make it even more urgent. The windscreen wipers beat water from side to side. I wiped my streaming eyes with the back of my hand.

All I remember of the journey was the lights. At first it was the lights in the city streets. They spangled through the lashing downpour and dazzled me. Coloured neon signs reflected luminous, coiling snakes on the wet tarmac, while the beams of oncoming cars wavered and warped like spectres against the blackness. Then I was away from the main roads with only Fifi's headlights to guide me through the chicane of sudden walls and looming trees. An occasional street lamp confirmed the way, a token of civilisation in a lost world.

I thought I knew this road so well, but suddenly all I could see was that tree, its giant arms waving frantically, warning me to stop. My head was thrown back against the seat and there were bright lights all around me — little fairy lights — and the sound of tinkling music. Everything was happening slowly and it took me a while to realise that I was being showered by fragments of shattered windscreen. A moment later all was darkness and silence; there was only me and the rain.

I don't know how long I sat there. No cars passed and no one came. I wasn't sure if I was injured or not, but nothing seemed to hurt. Eventually I realised that I must do something. I can remember the sharp coldness as I opened the car door. Fragments of glass scattered like confetti as I fell to my knees in the mud. I managed to pull myself up. No, I wasn't injured, but Fifi was badly damaged. I ran my hand over the front wing where the metal was crumpled, and flakes of paint stuck to my wet fingers.

I had to reach the cottage; there was nowhere else for me to go in this unreal world. But the rain was real enough. As I stumbled through the darkness, it stung my face and hands like a thousand wicked needles. I tried to follow the grass verge, slipping on mud and twisting my feet in puddled holes. The thin satin dress quickly became a sodden burden that dragged cold against my skin. My eyes were fixed on the next street lamp, then the next. Surely it couldn't be far now, just around the next curve in the lane, just a hundred yards more.

Then, there it was ahead, a square of gold, a lighted window. But how could that be? I'd left the rooms dark and empty. Miriam of course. Miriam was there. She would make everything all right. But she couldn't be there, could she? And yet there was that warm glow to welcome me and I knew I would be safe. Branches snatched and tore at my hair as I tugged at the gate and tumbled onto the front path. My frozen hands scrabbled through my bag in search of the door key. But as I reached the door it opened wide and the warmth of candlelight flowed out to envelop me and take me in.

'Fifi's all broken,' I blurted out. 'It's all my fault. I was such a bitch!'

'Shush! It's all right. You're safe now.' His arms went around me and the coolness of his jaw rubbed against my temple. I clung to his neck, shivering.

'They were only trying to be kind and I spoiled it for everyone. It was like I was someone else. Like, there was someone inside me, making me drink all that wine so they could get out and . . . and he'll never speak to me again! Oh, God, he hasn't rung, has he? If he comes here I don't want to see him!'

'Nobody has rung and no one will come looking for you. I promise. They won't even know you went out.'

'How do you know that? I never said . . .'

'Well you're obviously running away, aren't you?'

'Yes, but——'

'And, I would judge by your appearance, not very successfully.' He held me at arm's length and pulled the ragged tails of wet hair from my face. 'You look like a cat that's been for a swim.'

'But what about the car? I'll have to call a garage or something.'

'Nothing that can't keep until the morning.'

'But——'

'The car will be fine. You are not to worry. I promise you, all will be well. You do believe me, don't you? Say you believe me.' He looked straight at me with those yellow eyes and I couldn't look away.

'Yes, I suppose so.' I was exhausted and it was too easy to give in.

He rubbed my icy hands between his. 'You're shivering. Come on, this way.'

We went through to where a log fire cracked and spat. Candles were set anywhere there was a space and the room was a magical cave of shimmering light. A blanket was draped over Miriam's chair and cushions heaped on the floor.

'Here, use this.' He handed me a towel from a pile warming by the hearth. 'That dress is wet through. You'd best take it off.'

I looked down, realising that I had dripped a trail all through the house.

'Oh, I'm sorry. I must have . . .' About to apologise for making him wet, I reached out and laid my hand on his shoulder. His clothes felt bone-dry. Yet, I knew I had leant my body against his. Before I could say any more he was behind me, unfastening the buttons. Then I felt a tugging. The dress had become caught up with the chain and Iolair worked to disentangle it.

I expected, perhaps I even hoped, that he would ask for the talisman again. I think if he had, at that moment I would have given it to him, despite my promise to Miriam. It had only caused trouble — Hannah and now Malcolm; at least Paul was right about that. But Iolair didn't ask. It was as if he had forgotten all about it.

'Malcolm. He was there tonight, he did some sort of psychic reading on it. He said there was something wrong with it. That it was bad somehow.' No response. 'He said I shouldn't be wearing it. I'm beginning to think he's right.' Still nothing. 'You seem to know about it. What do you think?'

'I think this Malcolm shouldn't meddle with things that are beyond his understanding.' His voice was sharp and brittle.

At last he managed to free the chain. His mouth pressed against the nape of my neck. The fine hairs on my skin rose with his breath. Then the dress was undone and he slipped the soaked material down onto the floor, stepping back to look at me, his eyes unblinking. I could neither move nor speak, a small, helpless creature held fast in the gaze of a hunter.

'There are plenty of towels. I can fetch more if you need them.'

'Thank you, they'll be fine.' I made some meaningless gesture with my hands. His eyes were unwavering, but he said, 'Would you like a drink?'

'I think I've had quite enough alcohol for one night, don't you?'

We both laughed and the tension between us was broken.

'I know, I'll make us some tea. I know how to do it.'

'Yes, that would be nice.'

He darted away into the kitchen, a small boy on a vital mission.

Eventually I stopped shivering, curled up in Miriam's chair, the blanket tucked around me. The heat of the fire seeped through my skin and I stretched my toes out to meet the flames. The logs shifted with a loud crack, sending out a gasp of spark and ash. I had no desire to leave. The world outside the cottage had ceased to exist. It was part of some fantasy. The people I had left only a short while ago had faded into some other world. Here I was real. I would be safe with Iolair, despite his strangeness. It occurred to me that he might be mentally unstable. But what did that mean, anyway? Paul thought I was coming apart at the seams. He'd virtually said as much.

'Here, I've done it. Fresh tea!' He came bearing a tray to the rattle of spoons and the chinking of china. Descending gracefully onto the pile of cushions, his legs folding beneath him, he held it perfectly balanced. I recognised Miriam's favourite blue Delft teacups and there was a teapot with a knitted cosy.

'I made sure the water was properly boiling and I warmed the pot like you're supposed to.'

'Well done. Looks wonderful.'

'Now, you take milk, don't you, but no sugar.'

I watched him pour. His pale hands moved with the deceptive grace of ballet dancers performing a *pas de deux*. For his own tea he took up the silver tongs and delicately pincered eight cubes. His fingers curved elegantly to stir the lumpy concoction. Then he spooned out two half-dissolved cubes and popped them into his mouth, crunching with mischievous relish. A minute trickle of syrupy tea ran between his lips. He flicked it back with the tip of his tongue. I laughed until my cup rattled in its saucer and I had to steady it with both hands. He smiled, delighted with himself.

'I've amused you. I like to hear you laugh.'

'This reminds me of when I was a child. On rainy days Miriam and I would have dolls' tea parties in front of this fire.'

'You were a pretty child.'

'How would you know? David said I was odd. I suppose I must have been difficult — argumentative and defiant, or so I've been told. I drove Hannah to despair at times.'

'Sounds rather like the way you behaved tonight.'

'Oh, don't remind me. I was awful.'

'If you were to tell the truth, you would say you thoroughly enjoyed it. Now don't deny it, you know I'm right. You should be yourself more often.'

'That wasn't me. It wasn't, was it? And even if it were, I won't allow myself to behave like that again.'

'Why not? I wouldn't mind.'

'Yes, but you're not . . .'

'I'm not Paul?'

'People expect things of you.' I traced my finger around the china rim. 'Love is such a temporary gift. So easily taken back. My father left. Now I've lost Paul. He'll send me away, I know he will. Just like Hannah sent Miriam away. That was all my fault too.'

I watched the flames dance across the logs and remembered another fire. I could still smell the charred paper and see the burning fragments tossed in the wind.

'Strawberry jam on toast. With bananas.' It's my birthday and I can have anything I want for breakfast. 'And lemonade. Please.'

Today all the usual rules get ignored and I can do whatever I like. Well, almost. And it's Saturday so I don't have to go to school. The breakfast table is littered with torn wrapping paper, and a half-circle of cards surrounds my plate, a wall marking off my special space. Lots of them had badges and I've pinned them all over my T-shirt: '9 today' and 'I am 9'. Next year it will be double figures and that's almost a teenager.

David pretends to be unimpressed. 'You're still my little sister. And you're still a pain in the butt.'

'That's not true. Anyway, at least I don't play stupid football and I haven't got spots.'

'Give it a rest, you two. Can't we have just one breakfast that doesn't turn into a battleground?'

Mum never eats breakfast. I think that's unfair because we have to. She just has coffee and cigarettes. I hate that smell. It gets all in her hair. My teacher, Miss Barnes, says smoking is very dangerous and you can die from it. Why does she have to puff it all over the table? If it goes in my food I might die.

I wonder what it would be like to die young. It would be a great tragedy, of course. I would be draped all in white satin and carried in a glass coach pulled by six white horses. People would throw rose buds under the horses' hooves. Everyone would cry for weeks, especially David. He would realise how cruel he had been, but it would be too late by then. He would be so sorry that he would join a monastery and pray eighteen hours a day for the souls of lost children. She'd be sorry too. She'd have to devote her life to running an anti-smoking campaign as an act of penance. Or is that just if you're a Catholic?

'Chloe. Wake up and eat your toast. David, I think your father's bringing the car around if you still want that lift.'

'Oh, right. Is my sports shirt dry? Right, thanks Mum. See you later.'

'Enjoy your game, love.'

David heads for the door. He takes a sharp yank at my hair as he passes.

'See you later. Have a nice birthday, monkey.'

'Ow! Stupid football.'

We're alone now. She sighs and lights another cigarette as if his teasing were all my fault. Actually the jam and banana mixture doesn't taste quite as good as I thought it would. But I'm going to eat it anyway.

'Well, Chloe, what would you like to do now? Miriam won't be here for another hour or so.'

My grandmother has promised to take us out to lunch. A real grown-up restaurant with wine and everything. I don't suppose Hannah will let me have wine, though Miriam might be able to persuade her. But I'll be able to choose anything off the menu. I wonder if it will be in French. Young ladies learn to read French menus at finishing school and which knife to use for what and all that sort of stuff. If I came from a very aristocratic family, I'd have to know all that so I could capture the heart of a wealthy European Count. He'd beg me to marry him and I'd save my family from the disgrace of genteel poverty and my aged grandfather could retain his family seat. I wonder where they keep the family seat? I suppose it would be in the drawing room. Unless we lived in a castle, then it would in the top room of the highest tower . . .

'Chloe, I realise it's difficult for you, but do you think you could stay tuned to this world for a few minutes. I said, What shall we do now?'

As birthday girl I have certain privileges, like not having to wash up, so the rest of the morning is mine to do whatever I please.

'I think I'll paint something for Miriam.'

'Fine, well you'd better do that in your room.'

She is suddenly busy at the sink. The plates seem to be making a lot of noise. They do that when she's annoyed.

David did give me a present, so I suppose he must like me a bit really. A big box of paints and a pad of white paper. That's the best so far, but I know Miriam's will be even better. Not like the Barbie doll Mum gave me. Oh, it's all right I suppose. She's dressed in a pink ballgown so she could be a princess. I'll call her Amaryllis and make up a play about her. She can be under a spell. That awful plastic garden gnome can be the wizard. Silly-looking thing. Real gnomes don't look a bit like that. Amaryllis is being held in the tower of an ancient castle. Miriam will help me act it out. I know, I'll paint a picture of the castle for her. Better not tell Mummy about Amaryllis, *though. She likes things to be what they're supposed to be. She gets angry when I change them.*

There, it's finished. Just let the paint dry. There's a dragon curling its tail round the bottom of the tower. I'm not sure about the wings, how they are supposed to fold. I'll ask Miriam, she knows all about dragons. I must clean the paintbrush before I put it back in the box. I run it under the tap until the water runs clear, then wipe it carefully on a tissue, smoothing the hairs into a fine point. The little squares of colour shine like bright gemstones. A treasure chest.

Was that a car? Yes, it's Miriam. I'm running down stairs so fast I almost trip over my feet. Then I'm out through the front door and I'm swept up in a cloud of pale blue muslin and the lovely jasmine smell of her perfume.

'Happy birthday, my Little Wren! Are you taller? Yes, I'm sure you've grown an inch overnight.'

She's so beautiful, her long red hair tumbling down her back and her skirt almost sweeping the ground. There are rows of shiny beads around her neck and that silver charm she always wears. Her earrings jingle when she laughs. That's how I want to look when I grow up. But I don't think I'll ever be so elegant. Anyway I'll be too short, just like my mother. She says Miriam dresses like a leftover hippie and that it's about time she learned to act her age.

I think she's jealous.

Miriam is reaching into the back seat of the car and bringing out a parcel, then an envelope, which she balances on top. I have to pretend I don't know they're for me. It's polite. We walk her up the driveway, Mummy on one side and me on the other, crunching through the pebbles. A sharp stone has found its way inside my sandal and is digging into my foot with every step. I can't stop to take it out now.

Miriam tosses her hair back and places the parcel in the centre of the kitchen table. It's something special, I know it, and she knows

I'm going to love it. I can tell by the way her eyes are crinkled. The envelope is a sort of mottled yellow. It's always good manners to open the card first, even though you're dying to get at the wrapping paper. I wriggle my finger into the gap and tear. No, not a birthday card. It's more like a sort of postcard. It's the picture of Oberon and Titania by Joseph Paton. I've seen it in one of Miriam's big glossy art books. She's written a special message on the back. I'll keep it on my dressing table. Perhaps I can copy some of the figures with my new paints.

Now the parcel. I've never had a present wrapped like this before. It looks too special to spoil but Miriam is impatient for me to open it. It's quite heavy. Not paper, but gold foil wrapping with diagonal stripes of emerald green. A huge butterfly bow made from gold satin ribbon sits on top. I take one end and pull gently. It's so smooth that it slips through my fingers. This time I give it a definite tug and like magic it unravels and the wrapping wafts down onto the table. Oh, that smell. The dry spicy smell of new leather. Inside is a dark green box. Is it a box? More like a small, leather bookcase. It matches the row of books; there are seven of them. They look just like her own books, the ones she wrote. The lettering is golden, all curly tails and pointed lines. I think it's what they call gothic. I run my fingers over the deep embossing. I can almost read it by touch: The Chronicles of Narnia.

'All of the stories. Oh, Miriam, that's fantastic. Oh, thank you, thank you, thank you.'

Inside they're creamy white and as smooth as the satin ribbon. And the smell, the wonderful new-book smell, like nothing else. I bury my nose between the pages and sniff it in.

'I haven't read The Last Battle or Prince Caspian.'

'Well, you can now. We can start at the beginning and follow the history right through.'

'Haven't you read them all, Miriam?'

'Yes, but that was a long time ago. I'd love to hear the stories again.'

Why is Mummy looking at us like that? Strange, sort of angry and sad all at the same time. Now the two grown-ups are looking at each other, as if they know what the other one is thinking. There's a nasty, tight feeling in my stomach. Mum's turning her back on us and leaving the kitchen. Miriam has followed her and the door is pushed to. They're shutting me out. She must be angry. I must have done something wrong. Even with the door closed I can hear her.

'Of course I don't approve. You knew that when you bought them.'

'I can't see what is wrong with a few harmless children's stories.'

'Harmless? How can you say they're harmless? Fantasy worlds and talking animals. You've stuffed her head with so much nonsense she hardly knows what's real and what isn't. Telling lies all the time, saying she's seen things. And this constant daydreaming. When I try to reason with her all I get is tears and tantrums. I just don't know how to cope with it any more.'

'What's so wrong with make-believe? She's a child, Hannah. Of course Cliohna has imagination, but, more than other children, she has the talent to express it. We should be nurturing her creativity, not stifling it. She desperately needs you to understand her.'

'Don't tell me what my daughter needs. Yes, of course she's a bright, intelligent girl. Don't you think I know that? What she needs is to concentrate on her schoolwork, to spend time with children of her own age. She needs books about real people that tell her what real life is about.'

'Why can't you try to see the world through her eyes?'

'Your world, you mean. Through your eyes. It's this world she has to live in. This is where she has to earn a living, make a home, bring up a family. How is she going to survive with her head in fairyland?'

'Those are your values, Hannah. We can't all live your way.'

'Chloe is my daughter, I'll decide how she lives.'

Why is she being so horrible to Miriam? Miriam loves me better than anyone in the whole world. That's the best present I've ever had. She can't take them from me. She can't. I won't let her.

I have the box tight in my arms and I'm running up the stairs. Not *the bookshelf. Where, where? The wardrobe, she won't look there. That's it, right at the back. I'll cover them with my old sweaters and pile shoes on top. My birthday's all spoiled now. I can feel myself getting angrier and angrier. It's like a big red dragon, growing inside me. My face feels hot and my eyes hurt. Why do I always cry when I'm angry? It's not fair.*

All my best books are the ones Miriam gave me. Why should Hannah tell me what to read? She doesn't understand anything about stories. Look at the silly books she gives me. I pull one book from the shelf and hurl it onto the floor. Stupid Girls' Adventure Stories. *I hate it! Then another and another:* Patricia and the Bloody Pony Club! *Stupid bloody* Ballet School. *As if anyone would want to read this rubbish. Another book hits the carpet and bounces open. Silly, stupid children with their silly, stupid games. Wouldn't know an adventure if you rammed it up their noses. None of them can even draw a sword. Couldn't tell a basilisk from next door's cat. I won't be made to read this rubbish, I won't!*

My arms seem to be working all by themselves, picking up the scattered books. I'm heading down the stairs as fast as I can. I stop when I get to the kitchen. Can they hear me? No, she's too busy shouting at Miriam. Shouting about me. I start to cross the kitchen on my way to the dustbin. But there's something on the kitchen table, next to her cigarette packet. Well, I'll show her! I snatch up the lighter and run out into the garden.

There, I've thrown them all down in a heap. I grab one and wrench at the pages, all the silly, smarmy pages about soppy, useless children. One after another they rip and tear and are hurled onto the pyre. How do you work this lighter? I flick with my thumb and a little blue spark jumps and fades and jumps again.

I've got it — a flame. It's running up the edge of a page and leaping across to another. Salamanders, that are what they are, fire spirits. They're scampering all over the dry paper, blue and yellow salamanders eating up words and paragraphs and whole chapters.

Only the fire's getting big. This doesn't feel right any more. I'm scared. I'm trying to stamp out the flames but they are running too fast for me to catch them. A gust of wind flips the curling edges and lifts burning fragments high into the air like a swarm of winged insects, scorched and shimmering. They look nasty. One lands on my shoulder. Its wings are glowing as red as hot coal. It's eating at my T-shirt, gnawing through the cloth, its fiery teeth biting into my skin, and biting and biting...

'Mummy! Mummy!'

Hands are on me. Miriam's hands, beating at my shoulder, beating until the insect falls dead. But the pain is still eating at me. Oh, it hurts so much.

'Mummy, I'm sorry, I didn't mean it.'

She has me now, wrenching me away from Miriam. I bury my face in my mother's arms. She's shouting again. 'This is all your doing!'

'Oh, no, no. Hannah, I didn't mean for this to happen.'

'You're to stay away from her, do you understand? I won't let you have her.'

'Hannah, no, you can't mean that.'

My shoulder feels like one big hurt and Mum's so furious that I can't understand what she's saying. Things about Ireland and Miriam not loving her own child. If I hold onto Mum, she won't be so angry. The pain is biting deeper and deeper into me and I don't care how much I cry. I look around at Miriam and she's crying too. She is trying to reach out to me but she's not allowed.

'I'll make it up to you, Cliohna. Somehow. I promise.'

And she turns and walks away.

'Where have you been?' It was Iolair's voice. He reached up and pulled my hand from my shoulder. I had been rubbing the mark, the little patch of white, puckered skin, a traitor's brand.

'I was remembering my birthday. That dreadful row. I watched her leave. Part of me went with her and part of me clung to my mother. I was terrified I would be banished too. It was like being ripped in half, like those pages, torn and jagged and not one line of me left whole. I never meant to cause so much pain.'

'Yes, Miriam was hurt, and Hannah, too. But it was *their* quarrel. They were each responsible for what happened to them.' He ran his fingers over my scarred shoulder. His hands had lost their pallor in the glow of the fire and his face now shone with a soft, golden light.

'And what of you?' he whispered. 'What of *your* pain?'

'I suppose that's when I started to change. Up to then I'd been awful. I could sense my mother's vulnerability, the soft, fearful places in her tough shell. I would poke and prod at them, to make sure she wouldn't crack I suppose, like most children do. All I had to do was to mention fairies or elves. She wouldn't say anything, but her nails would dig into the palms of her hands until they left a row of little half-moons. A few times I told her I'd actually seen things. Or perhaps I *had* seen something, I'm not sure now. Anyway, she'd get practically hysterical. That was the only time I was smacked, but even that didn't deter me. And of course I knew how I could hurt her with my worship of Miriam. I had no idea of the consequences until it was too late.

'After that I worked hard at being Hannah's daughter. I figured out that there were parts of me that belonged to her, things that she would approve of. And there were parts of me that belonged to my grandmother and it would be as well to keep those to myself. Hannah and I got on better after that. No, you can't go around just saying and doing whatever you feel. People get hurt. If you need people to love you, then you must be what they want to love.'

He ran his hand along my arm, rubbing gently on my skin. 'Even if it means sacrificing your own being? Do you think being loved is worth that much?'

'I suppose it's better than not being loved at all, better than losing it.'

'No, you are wrong.' Suddenly his fingers were digging into my arm. 'There are some kinds of love which cannot be withdrawn.' He grabbed the poker and jabbed violently at the burning logs. They cracked and broke. A spark leapt towards me and I pulled back, dragging the blanket away from the hearth. 'We do not all have a choice.' There was bitterness in his voice. 'There is a love that is beyond the will of the loved or the lover. It is as inescapable as death.'

There was a long silence. I thought I'd lost him again and I didn't know what to say to win him back. Although he stared into the fire, his eyes were darkened as if they no longer gathered the light in the room. Then, just as abruptly, the little boy returned to tease me.

'What about this Paul, then? You're not seriously intending to marry him, are you?'

'No, of course not.' That wasn't the answer I expected, but the words were said and I couldn't retrieve them.

'Another attempt to please Hannah, was it?'

'Oh, no, though I didn't doubt for a moment Hannah would be pleased with him. At first I was more concerned about Miriam's approval. I took him to meet her, secretly. They didn't get on. She said he was a pleasant enough boy but I was being betrayed by my own feelings. She said that I craved emotional fulfilment and I was ready to fall in love with love itself and would project this onto the first likely candidate that came along. It all got quite heated — in fact it was the only argument we ever had. I set about proving to her how mature my feelings were by getting engaged to Paul.'

'And how did Miriam respond to that?'

'I expected her to be exasperated. Instead she thought it was hysterically funny. She said, "That's more like the little girl who set fire to Enid Blyton." Then she became very serious. She made me promise not to marry just yet, to wait just a little while longer. It was as if she were plotting something.'

The light was shining on Iolair's face, his eyes gold and amber. He moved nearer, perching himself on the arm of my chair. His arm went around me once more and I leaned back against his shoulder.

'She was right, of course. I'm not the person Paul thinks I am, and I'm beginning to resent this other Chloe he has in his head. It's as if he doesn't see me at all. He gives me no idea of myself and I don't know who I am any more. It's like looking in a mirror with no reflection. I'm afraid that if I go on with him I might completely disappear.'

'And do you see yourself when you look at me, Little Wren?'

I looked up into his eyes and saw the fire crackling red and black. For a moment I thought there was something else there, something fluttering.

'Why do you call me that? That's what Miriam used to call me. In fact, I think it was her idea to name me Cliohna.'

'It certainly was not your mother's.'

'Yes, I've often wondered why she would choose an Irish name, knowing how she felt about the place.'

'Well, there are ways of persuading people to favour a certain course, often without them realising it.'

'What do you mean?'

But he merely smiled and said, 'She knew you would be irresistible, like that other Cliohna. You must know the story. She's said to be a strange, unearthly spirit who dwells in the hearts of rocks and at the sea's edge and lures young men to their doom with her haunting cry. She would sometimes appear as a wren, did you know that? The Druid's bird, the people called it. At one time young men would hunt them down as a sacrifice to her. They'd decorate branches with the corpses then go rampaging through the countryside with them, terrifying the peasants.'

'No, you're making that up!'

'No, I'm not! It's the honest truth.'

'I'm not sure I'd want to be a sacrifice.' I suddenly felt lost and desperate. I buried my head in the coolness of his neck. 'It's all such a mess. What am I going to do?'

He kissed the top of my head. I moved my face up to his but he held me away.

'No, it's too soon. There are things you need to know first.'

Hot blood flushed my cheeks. Had I misunderstood, misread the signs? I drew away from him and pulled the blanket tight around my shoulders. There was an awkward silence. Then it was almost as if I felt his mood shift.

'I have a gift for you.' He smiled as he spoke and everything was easy between us again.

'What sort of gift? Where is it?'

'You have to close your eyes to see it.'

I thought it was some sort of game, but I did as I was told. He held me close to him, softly humming that slow tune, the one that Miriam loved so much. It laid the gentle coverlet of sleep over me. I do not think he spoke and yet I heard his voice.

'There are things only I can show you. You must come with me. I will guide you.' His gentle music filled my head. Then there was darkness and I must have dreamed, though I'm not sure. Even now I can recall every sensation. I kept changing, becoming one thing and then another, transformed into their very essence, as if I had entered into the soul of nature itself.

At first all I was aware of was rhythm and motion, blood pumping, limbs straining and wrenching, one wing-beat, another, and another, flying, soaring. I was not alone. Someone — a bird — moved beside me. His wings were broad and they swept long and hard. His feathers were brown and his eyes golden. His rhythm was stronger than mine and he drove the air beneath my wings, lifting me, holding me to the sky as the morning sunlight poured down upon us. What I felt was pure joy, as if this was why I existed, to leave the earth turning far beneath and lay my wings upon the wind.

And then it was as if I became the wind, no shape or form, just an endless dance. I knew that I could play, could tease dandelion clocks and ruffle the feathers of roosters. But I was also the roaring, raging blast that curdles foam on the rocks and I laughed as I ripped branches from trees, pulling their fibres until they screamed.

Then I became a tree, born in darkness, season upon season, reaching, straining for light, until the yearly night drew me, weeping, back into the ground. I went down into the earth itself, churning and slowly turning the rich, rotting life to feed the roots that twisted through me, feeding on the black juice of my body. As the earth I was greedy, devouring all I was given, then returned it, reformed and renewed.

Lying on the ground beneath fronds of bracken, I was small and trembling. I was some little creature and I found I could snuffle the soil and read signs on the wind. But I also felt fear, a driving fear that made me hide in burrows, flee from the terror of — I don't know what. I only knew that it pursued and that I had to run — run from the cracking of bones, the slashing of flesh and the splashing of blood...

And suddenly I was the hunter with the salt taste of gore upon my tongue, fresh and warm as it dripped from my mouth. Then somehow I was the blood, the blood that flows and carries life, that pours onto the earth, blood flowing like rivers, sweeping to the ocean.

I was the sea, in it and part of it, on a journey that knew no arrival, only the endless movement of current and tide. And I was strong, so strong that I could grind the rocks and tear the mountains from their high places.

Stillness. Solitude. I was stone, a rock cracked by the sun and punished by the tide, but I could change nothing. I was a mountain and I witnessed the ages pass and I knew it all.

Then I was far above the mountain again with the warmth of the sun on my wings, and the other one, he was beside me, with the light turning his body to gold. The earth was spread out below me and I was a tiny splinter of life. The joy of flight and the sun's orb of gold were all that existed.

In the end I was the sun, a golden blindness that sees everything. Like the light, I was in all things and all things were in me. I was *the length and the breadth and the depth, the single point where all things meet. I was everything that had ever been or will be, and I said it over and over like a mantra: I am, I am, I am . . .*

I awoke suddenly. I was alone. He had gone.

The tattered fragments of the dream still hung around me, momentarily transforming familiar surroundings into an alien landscape. A grey morning light suffused the room. Gradually, my consciousness latched on to mundane things: discarded teacups, looming bookcases, cold ash powdering the hearth. I tried to move and pain shot through my protesting muscles. The blanket had slipped down and my shoulders were icy cold. I pulled it about me, and as it moved something fluttered from my lap. A feather, a small brown feather, flecked with gold.

The room gradually lightened. I remained in the armchair, running my finger along the edge of the tiny plume. There was a difference within me, a shifting of perception. I gazed at the burnt-out wood and knew the tracks where the fire had eaten its life away, and sensed the emptiness. The pale dawn filtered through the window as on any other morning. Yet I could discern, in the subtle texture of this light, the hesitancy that distinguished it from that of the bright noon.

I was aware of being part of these things; myself and yet no longer separated. I remembered Miriam telling me how I would have to learn to touch the spirit of a thing in order to know it. Perhaps this was what she meant.

Eventually I stirred, wrapped the blanket around me and went into the kitchen intending to make coffee. Instead, I stood gazing out over the orchard. It had been the longest night; yesterday was now a thousand years beyond my reach. I turned the little feather between my fingers.

There was no going back.

Eleven

BY MIDDAY I WAS BACK at the house in town. Thank God both Angie and Ruth were out and I could leave a note. Far easier than verbal explanations. Coward's way out, I told myself, but what could I say to them anyway? How could I explain to them what I couldn't explain to myself?

It was just a few hours since I had woken from that strange dream, but twice already the world had jolted on its axis. Twice, within a few hours, all the little pieces in the kaleidoscope had shifted again and still the picture made no sense. No, better just to make a run for it.

But I'm going too fast, getting ahead of myself.

For a long time I stood in the kitchen at the cottage, gazing out at the orchard, desperate to capture each precious sensation, locking it safely inside me before it melted into the day. Then, somehow, the decision was made; there was no choice really. But there were things I would have to do.

The first was to make that coffee.

Then there was Fifi. I couldn't just abandon her, besides it was only a matter of time before the police came looking for me. Still wrapped in the blanket I carried my mug through to the sitting room. The first few gulps gave me a kick-start before I forced myself to reach for the telephone and the unreality of the mundane world. A search through my bag had proven fruitless, so I assumed the keys were still in the ignition. My friendly neighbourhood garage man said he would sort it all out right away, I was to leave it all to him.

Then I noticed that the answering machine was flashing. By now they must have realised I was missing and where I had run to. I was surprised Paul hadn't come after me. I made myself press the playback, resisting the irrational urge to hide behind the door.

'Chloe, Greg Uson here. Just thought I'd give you a reminder. If you possibly could drop by soon we can sort out that paperwork. Sorry to push you, but it is important. I'll try to make it as painless as possible.'

That was the only message.

I wasn't sure if I was relieved or disappointed. Iolair had said they wouldn't notice I was gone. He had promised. But that was last night and it was now nine in the morning. Surely someone had missed me? Never mind, I had other things to think about. I ordered a taxi for ten o'clock, then bathed and dressed in one of Miriam's soft, flowing shirts and some old denim jeans. I pinned up my hair and found a string of jade beads, tucking the talisman inside my shirt. The taxi arrived on time.

The lane, still wet from the previous night's rain, sparkled in the morning sun as the cab wheels sprayed muddy puddles over the grass verges. My stomach tightened as we neared the curve in the road. There it was: that bend and that tree. And there were the skid marks, two deep gouges cutting parallel arcs across the grass. There was no sign of Fifi.

'It's Susan, isn't it? I don't know if you remember me, Cliohna Blackthorn. Greg asked me to call in. I'm afraid I haven't a proper appointment.'

'Yes, I do remember.' But she sounded unsure and paused a moment before she spoke again. 'Well, if you don't mind waiting ten minutes. There's a client with him now, but I know he's anxious to see you.'

It had been just over a week since I was last there, but it could have been a hundred years ago. I tried to sit on the leather sofa as I had done then. There was a pile of magazines nearby, but the words had no meaning and the pictures were just blobs of colour. Instead I paced about the room, touching things, pulling books from the shelves and replacing them. Susan attempted to look as if she were concentrating on her work, but I knew she was watching me. It seemed a long time before the inner door opened and a mousy woman in a headscarf shuffled out. Greg's square shoulders loomed behind her and he smiled and ushered me in.

'You got my message? Good! I've done most of the work, just need signatures really. But rather a lot of them. Coffee?'

'Yes, Greg, I'd love some. And, before you ask, I'll say yes to the brandy too.'

'Greg, is it? What happened to Uncle?'

'Some things you grow out of.'

He paused, eyebrows raised as he looked at me. 'You've changed, you know. There's something different.'

'Don't tell me: I look like Miriam?'

'Yes, you do, but it's not just that. You seem . . . older. It suits you. You also look tired. Here, you're going to need this. And this.' He handed me a brandy glass and a fountain pen. He was about to light up a cigar when I said I would rather he didn't smoke. He hesitated, gave me a long look, then closed the lid on the table lighter.

The procession of papers seemed endless, most of it beyond my understanding. There was the transference of deeds for the cottage. I was expecting that and felt a shiver of satisfaction as I flourished the signature that made it my own. Then there were the various holdings, shares and bonds that left me thoroughly bewildered, to say nothing of royalties. She seemed to have a number of accounts, all for different purposes, none of which I understood. Greg tried to explain it all. He was very patient. I was very bored. I had been only half-listening, remembering the coldness of the rain and the dancing firelight, the little feather in my pocket. I was impatient to get back to the cottage. It wouldn't take long to collect my stuff. The sooner I left Greg, the sooner I could go around to the town house and start packing.

'You don't need to worry too much,' he was saying. 'We arranged it so that it more or less runs itself. But it will take a few days to move the bulk of the money and the interest payments into your own account.'

'That should please my bank manager. I'm usually overdrawn.'

'Not much danger of that now. I'll deal with the bank directly if you like. In the meantime you'll need some pocket money. Would ten thousand do?'

'Sorry? Did you say ten thousand? What, *pounds*?'

'Just to tide you over. No doubt there are things you want to do straight away.'

I suddenly wished I'd paid more attention. 'Look, exactly how much money are we talking about?'

He took a small piece of paper, scratched his pen over it, then slid it across the desk to me. I looked at it for some time, waiting for it to do something. My mind formed the black lines and loops into pictures. A black swan on a white lake, leading a string of cygnets bobbing along behind her. Or was it a sea serpent arching its long neck from the deep, endless coils of body breaking the surface in its wake? Greg's hand was on mine.

'I know it's a lot to take in all at once. I've been trying to break it to you gently.' He reached into his desk for the brandy bottle.

My stomach twisted with fear. 'I don't understand. Where did it all come from?'

Greg shook his head. 'I often asked myself the same question. But it's all quite legitimate. She just seemed to have a knack for making money.'

'I can't take this! What about Hannah?'

'Wouldn't take a penny from Miriam. And God knows Miriam tried often enough. Now, this is just between you and me. You know I handle all your mother's finances, the divorce settlement and maintenance payments. Well, Miriam and I have been leaking money into her account for years. Just small, regular amounts, so she wouldn't notice. If she ever found out . . . well, you know Hannah. Perhaps, in time, she might accept something from you, but I wouldn't broach the subject just yet. Meanwhile I take it you'd like me to continue the arrangement?'

I nodded, then said, 'But what am I supposed to do with the rest of it?'

'Well, you could try spending it. Being wealthy isn't all bad, Cliohna. Who knows, you might learn to enjoy it.'

Greg was laughing at me, but I was close to tears. I was lost. My hand groped at my neck, clutching the talisman. Where was he when I needed him? Some place beyond my reach, somewhere only he and Miriam knew about. I doubted Hannah would know anything, and even if she did she would only deny it. Ireland, that was part of it, along with all the money. 'Chloe? You all right? You know I'll help in any way I can . . .'

'My grandfather, Harold Shaw? You were trying to reach him.' I was grasping for something concrete.

'And we're still trying. As I said, Miriam left me his address and a phone number. But no answer yet. Here, I'll write it down for you.'

'You said there was something for him from Miriam. A letter?'

'That's right. To be sent after her death.'

'And you still have it?'

'Yes, I wasn't going to send it until I had made contact personally.'

'Let me take it to him.'

'What? To America you mean?'

'Yes. Is there any reason why I shouldn't?'

Greg shrugged his shoulders. 'No, no reason at all.'

And that's how it was left. He would inform me as soon as he managed to make contact, then I would go in search of Harold Shaw.

Greg insisted on walking me down the stairs. I think I was still shaking. I refused the offer of another taxi: the house wasn't far away, a sunlit walk through the morning city streets. I needed some time and space to think about the money, but I can only remember wondering if there would be many blackberries in the orchard this year. I had noticed the tight little knots of fruit appearing a few weeks ago, green and glassy red. I had bitten into one. The dry flesh soured my mouth.

I turned into our side street. There were no front gardens here and the crowded houses shouldered onto a narrow pavement. A line of cars hunched into the kerb. I edged along the path, dusty brickwork on one side, glaring metallic paintwork on the other. There was a splash of bright red near Fifi's usual parking spot. I wondered how she was, just how bad the damage had been. As I neared I could see that it was exactly the same colour red. In fact . . . no, it couldn't be. Same make, same colour, but it had to be a different car, just an odd coincidence. Then I read the registration number. There was my old jacket on the back seat and the pile of mint wrappers spilling off the dashboard. I ran my hand over the front wing. It was smooth and polished. Last night the metal had buckled like crumpled paper. I had brushed flakes of paint from my fingers. Shards of windscreen had flown all around me. I backed away, groping for the front door. Stumbling through, I trod on a bunch of car keys. There was a folded sheet of paper.

Dear Miss Blackthorn,
We collected your car as requested. It was parked at the side

of the road. No apparent damage to the bodywork. We gave
it a quick check over and it seems OK mechanically. Sorry,
but we'll have to charge you for a call out and delivery. If
you have any problems with it give me a ring.

I read the note several times, hoping there was something I'd missed. But there was no explanation. *He* had promised, that was all. I couldn't think about it now, not on top of everything else. I was just thankful the house was empty and I didn't have to explain any of this, or where I'd been all night.

God, I'd been awful to Paul. I waited for the usual pang of conscience, but nothing came. I tried prodding about among the confused numbness of emotion, hoping to feel something, like the reassuring pain from an aching tooth. Nothing. Then a small part of me suddenly wanted to laugh. I went upstairs to pack.

People who say 'I won't let it change my life' are fooling themselves. Money changes everything — everything you own, everything you do. Already choices were opening up before me like cracks in the earth, yawning chasms of empty space where once there had been the firmness of necessity and obligation. I was supposed to return to work in a few days, but was that really what I wanted to do? I could no longer justify my compliance with Hannah's career plans by the collection of a salary slip. I was certain Miriam had known all this would happen. The money was just a means: it opened up the way.

I brushed the dust from my old suitcase and folded some clothes into it. Then I took most of them out again and stood, bewildered, amid my worldly goods. Concentrate on the suitcase. It was small and the plastic covering had split. I had bought it when Angie and I had gone on a bargain package holiday to Spain. It was all I could afford at the time. Now the value of everything had changed. Everything I owned, or nearly everything, had become instantly replaceable. I refilled the case with other things, presents mostly, books and CDs, a few ornaments and some jewellery. It was soon full. I would have to resort to black bin liners to carry out the rest of my possessions. How did the song go? 'Carrying her home in two carrier bags.' I was turning into a bag lady. I thought about all those noughts Greg Uson had dashed off and started to giggle.

There was my artwork, of course, folios and the paintings from the walls. They left squares of lightness when I took them down, proof that I had once been here. No doubt she would soon cover up my spaces with someone else. The colour would soon fade and blend in. I left the portrait of Angie for her as a gift. It took several trips to fill Fifi's back seat and boot. Yes, and that was something else. Fifi. No, I couldn't think about that.

I used a silk blouse to wrap up my little green poodle. Made of cheap plaster and flaking into white patches, it's the ugliest thing I've ever owned. I won it at a fairground when I was seven. The few things of Miriam's I had collected went into the car. I dumped most of my own clothes on the bed. They might fit Ruth. Oh, hell no: Lady Bountiful's cast-offs. She would be so insulted. God, how could I be so clumsy? I stowed another bag in Fifi and ran back up to sort through my dressing-table drawer.

There was a sound from downstairs, a key in the front door, then other doors opening and closing. Paul's footsteps echoed on the stairs and I stood by my bed waiting for him to find me. If I closed my eyes I might become invisible. I tried it but the sound of his steps came nearer and the door burst open.

'What's going on? What's all that stuff in the car?'

'I'm moving into the cottage.'

His shoulders drooped. He looked at the ceiling, and then at me again. His voice was deliberately slow and steady. 'I thought we went over all that last night.'

'No, *you* went over it—' I stopped myself, determined to remain serene. I was resolute on this so there would be no need for a confrontation. 'About last night. I had too much to drink. I should have waited. Explained things properly. I'm sorry.'

'No. It was just as much my fault. You've been through a rough time. I didn't realise that you were— how badly it had affected you. I shouldn't have sprung that dinner party on you. It was far too soon. I see that now. I'm sorry.'

'You didn't come upstairs then, before you went.'

'You'd had quite a skinful. We thought it best to leave you to sleep it off. I rang this morning but Angie said you were still in bed. She didn't want to wake you.'

'Oh, I see.'

'Look, about the cottage—'

'I told you, I'm moving in there.' I was trying hard to keep the defiance out of my voice. I turned back to the drawer, grabbing at the small personal scraps that accumulate in such places, throwing them into a carrier bag.

Paul walked around to where I stood, hands spread out in front of him as if to pacify an unpredictable animal. 'It's all right. I've thought about it. I realise this cottage means a lot to you. It would be unfair to expect you to give it up. Well, not straight away. Why don't you keep it on for a while? No need to move in completely. We could go there at weekends. Perhaps spend Christmas there. That could be fun, you know, real tree, log fire, have some friends round for New Year. Then in the spring . . . well, who knows?'

It all sounded so reasonable, so rational.

Beware reasonable arguments, Miriam's voice whispered at the back of my head, *they're a honey-baited trap.*

'That's not what I plan to do.' I continued sorting out the drawer. I could feel something harsh and jagged welling up inside me.

'You'll be back at work next week. It will be further to travel from there.'

No it won't, I thought, but I said nothing.

'And it's further from the hospital you know, I'll find it more difficult to get there.' That was true.

'Actually, I'm not going back to work. I've quit my job.' The words surprised us both.

'What do you mean? You can't just throw up a job like that.'

'I can and I have.' Yes, I know I should have explained everything, I owed him that. Instead I was taunting him with feigned irrationality, wielding it like a sword.

'What do you think you are going to do?' His voice rose ever so slightly, piercing the thin veneer of calm and reason.

'I'm going to America. It's all arranged. I'm going to find my grandfather, Harold Shaw.' I would not wait on Greg.

'What? Miriam's husband? But you told me he died years ago.'

'Well, it seems he's made a remarkable recovery.' I looked up from my packing and smiled sweetly. He was starting to fray round the edges like the cuffs of his jacket. I should buy him a new one. Least I could do.

'All right, all right. Look, I'll tell you what we'll do. You go back to work. It won't be a problem. Just tell them you've been under a lot of stress and you weren't thinking straight. You can keep the cottage on, for weekends like we agreed.'

'No, I never agree—'

'No, listen to me, Chloe. Go back to work and in a few weeks we can both take some time off and I'll go with you to America. Yes, that's the way forward. We'll both go. We can see your grandfather, if he's still around, and we'll have some time together. There hasn't been much chance of that lately. Yes, that's what you need. A holiday.' He was more confident now, getting into his stride. 'Besides, you're not used to travelling. You can't go all that way by yourself, can you?'

He did have a point there. I'd hardly been out of the country before, and never on my own. America suddenly seemed a long way away. For a moment I wavered. He must have sensed the weakness in my shield and moved forward, wrapping his arms around me. If he had just left it there I might have given a little. But not Paul. He had to win all the way.

'There, you see. We've worked it all out. All you needed was a break. I'll arrange it all. Meanwhile, perhaps you could go to your mother's for a few days.'

Like hell I would!

'Come on, Rabbit, I'll help you to unpack.'

And that was it. He had said the magic word — the spell was broken. Every muscle in my body tightened. A wave of energy surged along my spine, lava boiling up through a volcano.

'I am not a rabbit!' I spat the words out as venom.

'What was that? What did you say?'

'I said I am not a fucking rabbit. I will not spend my life digging a hole to cower in. Not for you, or Hannah, or anyone else.' My voice rose. Fury possessed me and I watched myself in wonder, realising that I was actually enjoying it. More than that, I was rejoicing in it. 'What's more, *I'll* decide where I live and what I do and what I want!' I pushed Paul away, so hard that he stumbled backwards against the bed. I was a child again and I was free.

'Just what do you want then?'

'I want to fly, that's what I want to do. I want to fly with the eagles!'

'For God's sake, Chloe, calm down.' He staggered to his feet, clutching the bed cover. His hair was sticking up and there was spittle on his chin.

'I'm perfectly calm, thank you—'

'You're out of control. You know that, don't you?'

'— and rational. In fact, I think I've finally come to my senses. And guess what, Paul? You're no longer part of the deal.'

'You're acting like you're crazy!'

'Am I? Really? Then I suggest you leave here now, while you still can!'

I looked around for something to throw. Damn, I'd packed nearly everything. There was that hideous vase, a present from my mother — I'd always hated it. With cool calculation I hurled it at the doorpost just to the right of Paul's head. He ducked and it landed with a bang, failing to shatter. Disappointing. I was hoping for the full dramatic effect. However, the outcome was the same. Paul's feet thudded down the stairs and the front door slammed behind him.

Silence.

I could feel blood pulsing in my ears, the zing of adrenalin rushing through my veins. I threw myself backwards onto the bed, breathless and exhilarated. The weight of gravity had fallen from my body. There were no wings, but I was flying.

After a while I finished packing, dashed off a letter and pinned it to Angie's door, then said goodbye to the little house. On the way out I paused by the telephone table and picked up the *Yellow Pages*. Flipping through, I scanned the ads for travel agents.

Twelve

IT WAS ALL ARRANGED.

Only five days, then I would board a flight for the United States. The tickets arrived as promised and I resented the brief visit to the bank for dollars. One hasty trip to the local shop for food, then I surrendered totally to the cottage, huddling down into it, waiting.

There was a long phone call from Angie. I refused to budge and forbade her to come to me, so we talked in circles for ages until, eventually, I persuaded her that I was OK. I convinced her I needed some time out, that was all. And she was to take no notice of anything Paul said; he'd had his ego badly dented. Apart from that one call, no one intruded upon my isolation. Perhaps I was forgotten, and if so I didn't mind.

This is how it will be, I thought, this is the shape and pattern of my future. For those few days I moved in solitude, adrift upon a slow, winding river while time relinquished its hold over me. Whenever September burnishes the trees and the ripe, rotting smell of harvested fields taints the evening air, I shall think of those silent days.

Asleep and sleepwalking, I spent the hours filling my senses with the essence of my new home: birds pecking and squabbling among the fruit canes, the mustiness that rises from sun-drenched plaster, ancient timbers creaking and sighing throughout the night. Although isolated, I cannot remember being afraid there. Nor was I idle, exploring cluttered cupboards and hidden spaces, coming to know what was mine. I told myself this was contentment. For the most part I believed it. Yet every rational thread in my mind should have been screaming out to me.

I found something.

I was in her bedroom, rooting around among some old clothes in the bottom drawer of a chest, when I felt the corner of something hard. It was a shoebox, a large one, white cardboard and tied round with a limp yellow ribbon. Of course I opened it. Envelopes — the box was full of them, all shapes and sizes, white and cream and blue. Love letters, I thought at first, wondering if I ought to not intrude further. Then I noticed they were still sealed. I quickly sifted through the box. No, not one of them had been opened. The stamps were all American, the postmarks mostly from Boston. And the dates, they went back years, but all December and April, December and April, Christmas and—

Of course. They were addressed to *Miss H. Shaw*. Not Miriam, but Hannah. Every Christmas and birthday, year after year after year. Every one remembered and not one of them reached her. For a long time I sat on the floor, turning them over in my hands, counting the years and wondering what to do. They were rightfully Hannah's. I would have to talk to her, find the right moment. But not yet.

So I replaced the lid, retied the ribbon and put the letters back where I had found them.

I finished Miriam's portrait. I tried to read her thoughts as I worked on her likeness, expecting there to be some understanding between us. I was convinced she was listening, but she gazed down and said nothing. I told her of my plan to find Harold and waited for her approval. I asked her about the letters, but she gave nothing away. I begged her to tell me what it was she was doing for me. Or *to* me. At times I tried to feign indifference. In the end I would despair of her.

'Why are you doing this?' I would shout at her. 'Who is he? Why me?'

Several times I turned my back on her and slammed the door behind me. But those outbursts were short-lived. It was easier to relinquish all volition and drift with the tide.

I had a string puppet once, a clown dressed in chequered trousers and a tailcoat. He had a mop of bright red curly hair, rather like mine. His mouth, outlined in white clown paint, was wide and distorted, a parody of a smile. I used to play with him, jerking him around on his strings, forcing him to move this way and that. No matter what I did to him, he smiled. Eventually, of course, the strings became incurably tangled and he hung there, pinned to the wall, helpless, his limbs contorted like the victim of some horrific accident. And still he went on smiling his fixed, idiot grin as I, too, went on passively smiling.

Did I say I was alone? No, not really alone. Iolair was there. Any moment I might have turned around and come face to face with him. A sudden stirring of branches in the windless orchard and my heart would leap into my throat. The faint trace of damp moss and crushed grass as I entered a room set every nerve in my body alive.

And there were gifts. Feathers and flowers would fall into my lap, a bowl of fresh strawberries would appear at breakfast time. One morning I awoke to warm September sunshine sliding across my pillow and found handfuls of snowdrops, their petals heavy with crystals of snow melting into the warm linen. Most of the time it was enough that I knew he was with me, close, very close. But there were moments when I wanted him so much, when I thought of him so hard that I was sure the air itself would crack in two and he would step through. Yes, he was there and he knew. But he never came.

No, that's not quite true. I did talk with him once, although it wasn't at the cottage. It was early in the morning of the third day. I had woken, aware of a heavy silence outside, to find Grantchester cocooned in a layer of mist that muffled all the usual morning sounds. I couldn't resist creeping out into a world where I could move unseen. Pulling on warm clothes I slipped out of the door, across the lane and into the field. The mist lay low, saturating the grass and draping the hedges, yet betraying an oyster-shell sky streaked with pink and violet.

The pathway, no more than a track, took me across the field, over a stile and up to the river. Yes, I did say *up* to the river. The fens make a strange landscape, much of it below sea level. Those early Dutchmen who once lived there dug ditches and dykes, draining the earth with a network of waterways feeding into natural rivers. The soil is black and rich, but repeated harvests and the north winds of winter have robbed the fields, leaving them to sink even lower, so that in places they lie below the roads and canals. Despite the work of modern drainage engineers and conservationists the fenlands exist on the brink of disaster; the fen people are stubborn and relentless.

In the days before there were roads and railways, canals carried the traffic of commerce. A pathway runs alongside the river, a narrow strip where heavy horses once pulled barges all the way to villages and market towns. Now the towpaths serve leisure boatmen, anglers and families out for a Sunday stroll. That's where I walked, watching white vapour roll over the surface of the water, the strong current teasing it into curling tendrils.

The path led me towards the rising sun, still low and red on the horizon, and my vision was blurred by diffused sunlight transmuting the air into a haze of dusty gold. But I could see something ahead on the path, a dark shape like a bundle abandoned by the river. It could have been anything. I walked on and was much nearer before I realised it was a figure crouching on the bank. It was not a good place to meet a stranger, and common sense would have turned me around, but then I recognised the long black coat draping the ground around him and a quiver of warmth ran through my body. He gave no sign but I knew that he was aware of me. He was bending over the edge, sleeve pushed up to his elbow as he trailed his hand in the water.

'What are you doing?'

'Shush. You must speak softly or you will frighten him. They are very sensitive to sound, you know.'

'Frighten who?'

'Come down here and see.'

I crouched beside him and looked to where his arm entered the water. There was a fish, brown and silver scaled with a red flush on its underside. About the size of a small cat it was, and like a cat it caressed itself on Iolair's hand; yes, that's it, a cat, the way it rubs your legs with its body, then turns to stroke the other side. Back and forth it went, slipping itself over his hand as if entranced by the movement and the touch.

'That's wonderful,' I whispered. 'How do you do that?'

'Actually, it's this fellow here who's doing all the work.'

'What sort of fish is it?'

'Oh, a very splendid fish in my opinion, and quite old as fishes go, a wise old man of the river.'

'No, I meant what is it called?'

'I don't think fish have names. They are at a much earlier stage of evolution, without our self-awareness, so they would have no need of personal titles. Not like cats. They usually have several names — depending on who's speaking to them.'

As usual I was never quite sure if he was sending me up or if his answers were genuine. Perhaps a bit of both.

'Would he let me do that?'

'He might if I ask him. I think your arms are shorter than mine, so you'll have to lie down. But move carefully, don't startle him.'

So I did. I slid down onto my knees then stretched out full length with my nose in the grass. Pushing my sweater sleeve up as far as it would go, I dipped my hand slowly and gently into the water next to Iolair's. The coldness of the river gripped my arm like a manacle of ice. Almost immediately my fingers started to turn blue.

'Now keep very still, let him get used to you. He will come to you as he wishes.'

The fish continued its stately dance with Iolair's hand, unperturbed by my appearance over the water or my limb's unexpected entry into his world. I tried to be patient.

'I'm going away, you know,' I whispered.

'Yes, I know.'

'It's only for a little while. I'm going to find my grandfather, Miriam's husband.'

He said nothing.

'I've never been that far on my own before.'

'I can't come with you.'

'Oh, I didn't mean—'

'I would if I could, you know that. But the flight from Ireland was more than I could bear.'

'You mean you're afraid of flying? Lots of people are. Can't say I'm that confident about it either.'

'Oh, no,' he turned to look at me at last, 'I have no problem with flying. It's the water.'

'What about the water?'

'Too much salt.'

I felt we were heading up a blind alleyway, so I tried a different route.

'Is that where you came from? Ireland?' I asked.

'Not exactly. But I did have to cross the Channel to get here. And I managed to get to Europe, although, of course, there's less water to pass over, but salt water all the same. To go all the way to the New World, the Atlantic Ocean… No, it's not possible.'

'Oh, I see.' Though I didn't.

I watched the fish again, still turning its figure of eight. My whole arm was purple by then, but I had ceased to worry about the cold. Suddenly the creature changed direction, looped around and swam through my palm. I felt it. It was neither warm nor cold, but a sort of pressure, like the water itself. I held my breath, afraid to move or speak. The fish turned again and brushed over my arm, pausing to nibble at my fingers. Satisfied that I was not edible, it made another turn through my hand then went back to its double loop around Iolair.

'That was amazing. I felt it. I mean I *really* felt it. Not just the touch of its body, it was as if, for a moment, I felt that I was *with* the fish. It was like the dream. But you knew that, didn't you? That's why you did this.'

Iolair smiled his 'am I not clever?' smile.

'Was it a dream?' I asked. 'Or was it real? It felt real.'

'Are dreams not real, also? What did you learn from it?'

'It was like . . . everything has a soul, the rocks, the trees, and yet it's all part of the same thing. And because everything is connected it's possible to feel as if you're part of something else. Does that make sense? Is that what it was supposed to do?'

'That's good.'

'I think it changed me. Everything looks different now, including myself.'

The fish altered course and glided around my arm again, only this time it stayed with me and continued its dance around my hand, pushing its body against me. Its skin was like velvet. I could sense the joy it derived from that simple movement, losing itself in the pleasure of the water, the sensation of touch and the motion of its own body.

I don't know how long we stayed like that, only the three of us in the whole world and nothing beyond the mist but silence.

Eventually Iolair said, 'I think we had better stop before this old fellow wears himself out. Besides I have another gift for you. Something different. You will have it tomorrow.'

As I slipped my arm out of the river a volley of sharp sounds fractured the air. A dog barking. I jumped as if I had forgotten that anything else existed, and twisted around to look along the towpath. Yes, there was an elderly man with an even older collie that padded stiff-legged towards me, barking loudly.

Behind me Iolair laid a hand on my shoulder. 'Remember tomorrow. Be alert for the fish. It is a sign and may have more than one meaning.'

I turned to him, but he was gone. And so was the fish, darting away into the reeds.

They had left me to scrabble to my feet and face the dog and its owner, my clothes soaking wet and covered in mud, while Iolair vanished like the mist from the river.

The next morning, with one day to go, I was feeling nervous about the whole trip — the flight and Harold and everything.

As an enforced distraction I made some attempt to clean up. The rooms were untidy although not really dirty. I wiped away thin films of dust and wondered at the absence of cobwebs. Then I realised that there were no spiders. At least, I'd never seen one here, or any other living thing for that matter. The garden was full of life, yet the house was deserted. No mice to scrabble behind skirting boards, no moths to tap themselves against the windowpanes; not a beetle, or a late, lingering bee. For one fleeting moment I felt utterly alone and desolate. But that feeling soon passed.

Miriam's worktable had to be tackled, that huge circle of inlaid wood piled high with papers; decades of research, millennia of history. Oh, why hadn't I paid more attention? I'd listened to her stories, of course, fed upon them, licked up each morsel and crumb. And I'd watched her labour for hours on end over her notes, seen her strain until she clawed her cramped fingers and her eyes were red raw. Yet I never consciously made any connection. This was her life's work and I understood nothing of it.

The afternoon wore away as I grew more despondent, heaping more blame on my own neglect. So much was in Gaelic, which at least I recognised, and there were other languages that I did not. I scraped away layer after layer, exposing centuries, learning nothing. Eventually I declared defeat. Gathering cardboard boxes, carrier bags, even the laundry basket, I scooped up the lot and rang Marcus Sangster.

The promised invitation to dinner jarred me from my isolation. Feeling like a hermit crab being forced out of a comfortable shell, I was reluctant to go out. But I had agreed on impulse and was now committed. Besides, it would be simpler to just hand over all her work and be done with it.

It was as I was about to leave that I noticed it. Was this the next gift that Iolair had promised? He had said tomorrow, and it was; and yes, this was something different.

Exposed for the first time in years after my clear-out, the table's dark surface had robbed the room of light. However, it showed promise. I had set to work, attacking the grime with soap and water, then drying and polishing with beeswax until the beauty of the wood shone through. I had set a little white jug in the centre, arranged the snowdrops and stood back to admire my work. This was the first time I had imposed something of myself upon this place. Yes, I was pleased.

Heading for the door, I gave the table a final, satisfied glance. And there it was, next to the jug of flowers, a small book, no bigger than a pocket diary. The cover was of soft leather, deeply embossed with swirls and knots. I hesitated before picking it up. Page after page, all yellow-edged and brittle, were filled with Miriam's handwriting. Some of it I recognised as Gaelic, but there were also pages full of strange lines and crosses which signified nothing to me.

I slipped the book into my pocket as I went out.

Thirteen

THE SANGSTERS' HOUSE is tall and narrow, one of those Victorian villas that line the city avenues near King's College. It was intended for wealthy owners in wealthier times. There are two floors of high-ceilinged family rooms, all moulded plaster and creaking floorboards. The kitchen was originally below-stairs in the basement, with the servants quartered in the cramped and draughty attic. Now the attic is filled with domestic clutter, except for the one room Janet has made cosy for her sewing machine. A modern kitchen fills half the ground floor, with Marcus's study taking up most of the basement. The rest of the house ought to be filled with the echoes of family laughter, dressers proudly laden with framed memories of children and grandchildren. But there are no memories. Janet spends her days running between the top and the bottom of the house, tending to Marcus's needs and neglecting her own. The rooms between the basement and the attic remain silent.

It was to the basement study that Marcus and I struggled with the boxes of papers, dumping them in the centre of the room. I had explained that I wanted none of it, that it was all his to do with as he saw fit. I knew Miriam would have trusted him. He protested and flustered and stuttered and lost his glasses several times. Eventually I rallied Janet to my side by refusing to sit down to dinner until the car was unloaded. Between us we bullied the poor man into submission.

While we made trips back and forth, heavy clouds shadowed the houses, darkening the evening before it was time. A cold wind whipped around us and dry leaves scuttled across the pavement to nip at our ankles. I was thankful when we finally closed the door.

'So, when do you leave?' asked Janet as she hovered round the table, piling vegetables onto our plates. I'd had to explain about the resurrection of Harold and the trip to America. They knew nothing of his existence. 'Marcus, have some more carrots. He never takes enough vitamin C, then wonders why he gets cold after cold. And you, Chloe.'

'No more, thank you. I'll never eat all this. Tomorrow. I leave tomorrow, Friday, late afternoon. I managed to get a cancellation.'

Marcus shook his head, murmuring into his plate. 'I can still hardly believe it. All these years and never a word about a husband. I'd no idea. Strange that Hannah never said anything either. Surely, she must have known . . .'

'So what will you do with it all? The papers, I mean.'

'He'll bury himself in that basement, that's what he'll do. At least it'll keep him out from under my feet.' Janet gave him a mischievous smile.

He reached across and brushed the back of her hand with his fingers. 'Well, from just a brief glance I can see it means a lot of work. It's really exciting. So many unpublished articles. Invaluable. Some have been only partly translated. Of course it will be in the Goedelic form — that's the Gaelic developed in Ireland.'

'I thought the Celts were all over Europe. Why is Ireland so significant?' I froze, stunned by my own words. Of course, why Ireland? So that was why I had come here. Or had I been sent? Ireland was Marcus's love, his obsession. Once started on the subject he would talk and talk. He could tell me things. But I would have to tread so very carefully, give nothing away. I looked up. Marcus was still speaking, but now I was alert to his every word.

'—originated in South Germany and Bohemia in about 500BC. They reached Ireland two hundred years later. But, you see, most of Europe was either conquered by the Roman Empire or in some way influenced by their culture and religion. Only the Irish managed to develop in isolation, along with their storytellers.' He strained to look over his glasses, then pushed them higher onto his nose. 'That is, until the coming of Saint Patrick in the fifth century.'

'Didn't he banish the snakes from Ireland?'

'So they say, though I think he was more concerned with banishing the Pagans. He had less success there.'

The wind sang through the chimneybreast. I wished they would draw the curtains, shut out the encroaching night. I struggled to keep my voice light. 'But the Irish did convert to Christianity, didn't they?'

'Well, yes and no. They certainly changed one set of gods for another. The Celts worshipped the forces of nature. There were literally hundreds of gods, greater and lesser ones, mostly local deities, woodland spirits, that sort of thing. They worshipped in the places where the spirits dwelt, a sacred grove of trees, a rocky hill . . . It's difficult to overthrow a religion when there are no temples to destroy, no statues to deface. Celtic Paganism was enshrined in the minds of a highly imaginative and creative race. As far as I'm concerned it still is. It's only the names that have changed.'

'That's what he would have us believe, my dear,' Janet cut in. 'Nearly all the Irish people I've known have been staunch Catholics.'

I forced myself to smile and to go on eating, at least enough to satisfy Janet, despite the knot tightening in my stomach. I tried rearranging the food on my plate to make it look smaller.

'Indeed, they are,' Marcus went on. 'And are the psychological forces of Catholicism so very different from those of Paganism? Perhaps that's why they were so easily converted. All those saints they talk to as if they were personal friends. The candles and the little bribes laid out before the altar. A good Catholic will go to Mass on Sunday morning and leave milk sops out for the little people that same night. They see nothing incongruous in this. Whatever they choose to call themselves, as far as I'm concerned the Irish are still a Pagan race.'

'Well, if that's your definition of a Pagan, then I think there's quite a few of them in my Ladies' Christian Circle.' Janet winked at me. She would have made the perfect grandmother, I thought, straight out of a storybook. She started to clear away the dishes. 'Chloe, we're going to have to work on your appetite. I've got something special for dessert that might tempt you.'

For a few moments, Marcus and I sat in silence. I was moving closer to something, step by step, as if walking toward a cliff edge, drawn by the very fear of falling. Outside bare branches scratched at the windows, urging me forward. I fingered the talisman, aware of its weight around my neck, remembering that awful dinner party, Malcolm sitting beside me and the woman on the hillside, the woman who had died by the fall of an axe.

'What about Dana? She was a goddess, wasn't she?'

'Dana? Yes, a major deity, possibly the same as Bridget. She was the goddess of one of the mythical tribes. The Tuatha de Danaan, the Children of Dana.'

'Mythical tribes?'

'Yes. You see the Celts seem not to have had any creation myths like most religious cultures — no Adam and Eve, that sort of thing. Apparently, according to them, Ireland has always existed. In one of the earliest texts called the *Book of Invasions*, they explain their own arrival by claiming descent from the pre-human races of gods who invaded Ireland in successive waves. The Tuatha de Danaan were the fourth arrivals.'

'What happened to the other three?'

'Defeated by the newcomers, mostly. The first wave was nearly all destroyed in the great flood, another commonly occurring legend. Except Fintan, of course.'

'Yes, Miriam spoke of Fintan. Wasn't he the patron of traditional lore and storytelling?'

'That's right. He escaped the deluge by changing into the form of a salmon, or in some versions it was an eagle or a hawk. Shape-shifting is quite rife in Celtic mythology. It was he who witnessed all the subsequent invasions and was able to pass on the history.'

'And he changed into an eagle?'

The wind threw itself against the house, shaking the windows in their ancient frames. Invisible claws tapped and scraped at the panes. My head was throbbing. I pressed the coldness of the wine glass against my temple. Marcus, undeterred, talked on.

'Now, the Tuatha de Danaan are interesting. They were said to have come out of the west, out of the misty seas. They were known as the beautiful people, tall and graceful, well versed in music and the arts. However, they were also powerful warriors and they brought with them their own magicians. That's how they managed to conquer the land so efficiently, by the use of magical weapons. There was a bottomless cauldron that fed everyone, a magic sword and spear, and a stone that sang truths and fate to the world. Even so they were eventually defeated and went to live in the fairy kingdom.'

'The golden apples of the sun!'

I jumped, startled at Janet's voice as she entered the room holding aloft a steaming hot plate.

'Ah, one of your famous apple pies, my love,' said Marcus. 'You'll never taste better, Chloe.'

'No, no. I mean yes, it *is* apple pie, but that's not what I meant.'

She placed it in the centre of the table and reached for a knife. A little cloud of steam arose at the first cut and with it the aroma of cinnamon and cloves. 'These apples came from Miriam's orchard. She sent a tray over just a few days before . . . Well . . .' She cut a huge wedge, placing it in front of me. 'I should have made two, Chloe, then you could have taken one home with you. Oh no, you're going away tomorrow, aren't you? When you come back, then. Though I suppose they must be your apples now. Are you really going to live in the cottage?'

'Yes, I think I am. I think that's what she wanted.' I looked down at my plate. Yes, my apples, my orchard. 'What did you mean about golden apples?'

'Yeats.'

'Sorry?'

'Yeats, William Butler. You were talking about shape-changing when I was in the kitchen.'

Marcus peered at her over his glasses. 'I don't quite follow you, my dear.'

'Yes, you do. Now, how does it go?

And pluck till time and times are done,
The silver apples of the moon,
The golden apples of the sun.

'That's it, you see. Only that was a salmon . . . or was it a trout?' She continued to dissect the pie as Marcus and I looked at her in blank silence.

'Of *course* you know what I mean.' In feigned exasperation she snapped the knife down on the side of the plate. 'Just a moment, I'll go and find it.'

She bustled out of the room and I turned to Marcus, who was smiling and shaking his head.

'You were telling me about these Tuatha de Danaan people. Were they really only a myth?'

'Well, I dare say there was originally a powerful tribe of conquerors upon whom the legend was based. Rather like the Ancient British leader who united tribes under one banner and became known as King Arthur. Naturally, all that stuff about round tables and Merlin and swords coming out of lakes is pure fantasy. It was the same with the Tuatha de Danaan. They probably did exist. A tribe of refugee invaders, a bit more cultured than most, who just got lucky for a while.' Marcus smiled, pleased with himself, expecting me to share his little joke. He was unaware of the wind pounding at the doors, the scratching at the windows. He didn't know I was being driven toward the edge, that I could fall and go on falling.

'What would they have been like? How would they have lived?'

'By our standards very poorly, even for kings. They were herdsmen and warriors, constantly involved in minor skirmishes with neighbouring tribes. They would have built simple huts and lodges surrounded by a wooden stockade for protection, probably on a hill. The wealthy and powerful among them would have had horses and metal jewellery and weapons, but little else. Life was short and hard for everyone. Death always at their shoulders.'

'And the rats,' I murmured, *'don't let me die where there are rats.'*

'What's that, my dear?'

'Oh, nothing, please go on.'

'Well, they had their kings and spiritual leaders, of course.'

'The Druids?'

'Yes, but the Druids were more like administrators of religion. It was the Filidh who were the experts in spells and divination.'

'Yet, you say they were defeated?'

'Yes, that's right. Eventually their power waned and they were overthrown by the Sons of Mil, the immediate ancestors of the Irish people.'

Janet came back into the room holding a book. 'Here you are, I was right, it was a trout. Listen.

… I dropped the berry in a stream
And caught a little silver trout.

When I had laid it on the floor
I went to blow the fire a-flame,
But something rustled on the floor
And some one called me by my name:
It had become a glimmering girl
With apple blossom in her hair
Who called me by my name and ran
And faded through the brightening air.

'There, you see, shape-changing. I was right.'

'Yes, my dear, you were right, as always. And, of course, Yeats was an Irishman, too. A politician, among other things, and an authority on Celtic legend. A poet and mystic with a vision of a united Irish culture founded in its mythology.'

'Well, you and he would have had a lot to talk about then, Marcus. And, of course, he did take a great interest in Faerie lore. Are you interested in the Faerie legends, Chloe? Perhaps I could lend you something to read.'

What was it he had said? *Be alert for the fish. It is a sign and may have more than one meaning.* Yes, that was it. But what did it mean? We all concentrated on the dessert for a while, and I did manage to eat some of it. Then Janet said she would make coffee. I offered to help but was dismissed: guests weren't allowed to work. Marcus went back down to his basement study, muttering something about the four magical weapons and a link with alchemy. We had come close, so very close. I would not be turned back now. I followed him down.

He entered the room and switched on a table lamp which threw a yellow circle over the desk. Unlike Miriam, who worked amid chaos, Marcus kept his space neat and orderly. Or perhaps it was Janet who filed his papers and tidied away his pens. The corners of the room, outside the circle of light, were full of shadows. The darkness had entered the house now, and the wind heaved and sucked at the curtains. He pulled out several books from the shelf and flipped through them. I perched on the desk, looking over his shoulder and trying not to shiver.

'You said that these people — the Tuatha de Danaan, is it? — went to live in the Faerie kingdom?'

'Well, there's some confusion. In some of the tales, the Danaan tribes seem to be human, living side by side with the Faerie and able to interact with them. In others, the roles become blurred, as if they were actually Faerie themselves, or at least became the Faerie after their final defeat. It's really not at all clear.'

'The Irish still choose to believe in fairies, don't they?'

'Oh, no, I don't think the Irish *choose* to believe in them exactly. Rather, it's something deeply rooted in the Celtic psyche. The Irish have always lived on easy terms with the supernatural, and historically their belief in the natural order of things has always seemed somehow vaster and more flexible than ours.' As he spoke I noticed a picture hanging above the mantelpiece, a large print. It was *A Midsummer Night's Dream* by Joseph Paton, the same as the card Miriam had given me for my birthday all those years ago. Not an incredible coincidence, considering Marcus and she shared a fascination for the subject of the painting. I moved over to look at it more closely.

There were the figures of Titania and Oberon, as I remembered them, amid a magical gathering of ethereal spirits and sprites with beautiful faces and gossamer wings. But now I could see that they were not all beautiful. Some among them were ugly and misshapen. A wild-eyed male, his arms muscled like knotted wood, dripped poison from a flower cup into the mouth of a sleeping human. Gnomes and dwarves with leering grins urged him on, gleeful in the torment of their plaything. Nearby a winged fairy looked down. She had breasts as white as porcelain and the blessed face of a madonna. A dark-bearded satyr clung to her naked thighs. Such a sweet and innocent corruption.

The Faerie King and Queen stood amid their court, their bodies entwined with ropes of flowers. They had no thought beyond the tricks of love and betrayal they devised for each other to while away the long night: mind games, with human lives as the gaming board. And all the while the tiny subjects danced about their feet and plucked their harps and sang their songs while their victims slept on, oblivious to such an exquisite and dainty depravity.

'Chloe? You're miles away. What are you thinking?' Marcus's voice cut through my thoughts.

I went back to his desk, laughing a little to hide my embarrassment. 'I'm sorry. It was the picture. I was thinking that Miriam was always very passionate about the nature of the Faerie. She hated the storybook images of little people flitting among the flowers or sitting on a toadstool. She often got quite angry about it.'

'Well, the new culture of Christianity needed to diminish the power of the old ways by diminishing their gods to harmless picture-book creatures. The Faerie, or the Sidhe as they were also called, were remarkable beings to be provoked at one's peril. Some believe that they're fallen angels, ejected from Heaven but not wicked enough for Hell. Certainly, by human standards, they seem to be amoral, but then they're of a different social order and less, well, solid and bound by physical laws. They were able to change shape at will, to come and go, make themselves invisible. I suppose they would seem more like devils than angels.'

I wanted to run out of the room, to run upstairs to Janet's domestic sanctuary. The gloom beyond the circle of light held me fast. I forced myself to speak, to tell myself what I already knew; what I had known all along.

'Of course there were all kinds of beings, but Miriam said the Elven races were the most powerful and the most feared. They were tall and slender and beautiful. Their very presence could weave a spell over the human mind. To hear their voice was an enchantment, one would be lost to them forever.'

'Oh, yes,' said Marcus. 'There are countless tales of young men

175

and women being enticed away by the fairies. Legend would have us believe they actually interbred with the ancient tribes. Their sons and their descendants are said to be the ancient Kings of the Celts. Mind you, it's not all one-way. The Sidhe have been known to attach themselves to humans. There have even been claims of them following people who have emigrated to America and Canada. But that seems highly unlikely. Apparently they have some aversion to crossing salt water.'

I was at the very edge now, looking down into my own fear. There was something deep and dark here, threatening to rise up and engulf me. But I had to know.

'Marcus, this talisman?'

'Yes, I noticed you were wearing it. Strange, I always meant to ask her about it but never got around to it somehow.'

'You don't know what it is then?'

'Well, no, but let me see it.' He took the pendant in his hands. 'A strange metal. I thought it was silver, but it's much too bright. The colours seem to shine from under the surface. Mithril, I bet.'

'Mithril? What's that?'

'Just my little joke, Chloe, all this talk of Faerie. You must have read Tolkien?'

'Of course.'

'Then you would know all about Elven silver.'

I couldn't answer. Sweat prickled the nape of my neck and my palms were damp. He continued to hold the talisman, tracing the intricate lines with his fingertips.

'Celtic, no doubt, though I have no idea how old it is. Iolair, of course, highly stylised, like most of their creatures.'

'That name!'

'What name, my dear? Why are you taking on so? What's wrong?'

'You said his name. Iolair.'

'Ah, no, no. That's not a name. Just a word from the Gaelic. It means eagle. Look, you can just make out the wings and the beak— What's the matter, child? Come, you'd better sit down. Perhaps too much wine at dinner, eh? Where has Janet got to with that coffee? Janet? Janet!'

It was too late. The room was spinning and I was drifting down into emptiness.

'There, are you feeling a little better?' Janet had her arm around me. 'I told you not to keep her down in that stuffy basement. Young girl like that needs fresh air in her lungs.' She had coaxed me up into the dining room and opened a window, and was now wiping my face with a cold, damp cloth.

'I'm fine now. I'm sorry. I feel so silly. Must be the journey tomorrow. I'm feeling a bit nervous. About flying, I mean.'

'Perhaps an early night then. Marcus, you must drive her home.'

'Oh, no. I'm all right now, really. Perhaps if I could have that cup of coffee.' Janet went off to the kitchen. 'Marcus, there's something else I want you to look at.'

I took the book from my pocket and handed it to him. I had been undecided as to whether I should show it or not. Now things were different. He held it under a lamp for some time, scanning the pages in silence. Then he sighed and shook his head.

'Miriam's writing, obviously. Some of it Gaelic, but a very ancient form. Much of it is Runic. Look, there are the signs for *Peorth* and *Haga*. But, again, it's a form I'm not familiar with. I don't think I know enough to make any sense of it.'

'You couldn't translate it, then?'

'No, but I think I know someone who may be able to help. This is obviously something special. Could you bear to trust me with it for a few days?'

So of course I had to leave the book with him. There was nothing else I could do.

Fourteen

I DIDN'T SLEEP that night, or rather I fell asleep over and over again, only to awaken suddenly with my mind racing. I threw myself from one side of the bed to the other as the wind battered the windows and doors. The cottage felt deserted. Loneliness pressed down on me until I thought I would suffocate. If he was aware of how much I'd learned, he gave no sign.

I'd become afraid, and not before time. I was terrified that this fantasy might be real; even more terrified that it was not real and I was going insane. There were so many things to fear, so many strange and awful things that had been told to me by Miriam. Most of all I was afraid that I would never see him again.

Eventually, morning light crept across the bedroom wall. The wind had dropped, but the overnight gale had stripped much of the orchard and naked branches stretched against an oatmeal sky. I stumbled from room to room, trying to organise myself for the journey, making mental lists of things I needed. It all seemed so complicated and I was beginning to have serious doubts about the wisdom of this wild-goose chase. Thank goodness I wouldn't have to drive in rush hour and the motorway would not be too busy. Even so I would have to leave at lunchtime to be sure of checking in two hours before the five o'clock flight. I was so anxious about the time that I was packed and ready by ten o'clock.

About mid-morning I was startled by a knock. It had to be Paul. What could I say to him? I had a momentary urge to pretend I was not there, to hide behind the sofa. Oh, grow up Cliohna, I thought and forced myself to open the door. It was a shock to find Hannah on the doorstep. Had I actually forgotten she existed? She had melted into the past, relegated to another part of time. We stared at each other for ages, then she broke the silence.

'Am I allowed to come in?'

As usual, I heard this as a criticism. Stepping back to let her pass I realised, with a twist of guilt, that this was the first time we'd encountered each other since the funeral. The last time I had seen her, she was being dragged into a car in a state of hysteria. I hadn't even telephoned to ask if she was all right: that was left to Paul.

As I followed her I became aware of how cold and bleak the sitting room felt. I hadn't bothered to light a fire. She started to remove her coat, then hesitated, looking to me for permission. She was nervous, not sure how to act in my presence, as if she were somehow afraid of me. This was a Hannah I didn't know.

'You look tired, Chloe.'

'I didn't sleep well last night. The wind.'

'Yes, yes of course. Did it do much damage?'

'I'm not sure.'

We looked at each other, reappraising. I thought she looked smaller than I remembered, less imposing. Time does change people. That was silly, it had only been a week. I wondered what she saw in me, apart from Miriam. I was desperate for some sort of diversion.

'Would you like some coffee?'

'Yes, that would be nice.' She sounded relieved also and walked behind me into the kitchen, surveying the rooms as she passed through. 'The place looks tidier. I see you've cleared that mess off the dining table.'

Something caught me full in the stomach — a revelation, and a bitter one. That was the only real difference I'd made here and it was made by some part of me that was Hannah, not Miriam. I fumbled at the taps and splashed water down my skirt. Hannah sat down, snapping open her handbag and reaching inside.

'I'd rather you didn't smoke in here.'

She froze, her hand clutching the small red box. Her mouth slackened as she looked at me. I made myself look directly at her in return, unwavering, unrelenting. Slowly she returned the box to her bag and closed it, threading the strap through her fingers.

'I hear you're going to America.'

'Yes, that's right. Leaving this afternoon as a matter of fact. Who told you? Paul?'

'No. I've spoken with Paul, yes, but it was Greg who told me about the trip.' She crossed one knee over the other, straightening her back against the chair.

'Oh.' I said. No, I hadn't informed her myself and, no, I wouldn't apologise for that, either.

'Paul was very upset.'

'Why did you lie to me?'

'He said that you'd had a row, that you two had broken up.'

'I said: why did you lie to me? My grandfather. You know, Harold Shaw, your father? Surely you must have heard of him?'

She was about to speak, then let the words go, her narrow body folding in on itself. I could see that she was hurting and that wasn't what I'd meant to do. At that moment I wanted to reach out to her. Instead I pushed myself hard against the wall. I was determined to go through with this.

'Miriam never spoke of him at all. It was as if he never existed for her. But you told me he'd died. That's not what you believed, is it? You knew he was alive, didn't you? You must have known.'

There was a silence; it hung between us, sharp as a knife. When she eventually spoke, she looked down at her hands. Her voice was hushed, the words carefully placed.

'It was his choice. I had no idea what had happened to him. I never bothered to find out. He may as well have died. As far as I was concerned he *was* dead.'

'But why?'

She shook her head and looked at the leather twisting through her fingers. Colour had drained from her face, and the frail morning sunlight seeping through the lattice did nothing to warm the room.

I moved to the table, sliding down into the chair nearest to hers.

'I need you to help me. I need to know what happened in Ireland.'

'I don't know what I can tell you. I never really understood it myself.'

I waited, expecting more. Then she said, 'We came from Boston on a three-year grant that my father had been given by the university. That's how long he worked there. Then he went back home and we stayed behind. I never heard from him again. That's all I can tell you.'

'No. There must have been more to it.' I slid her cup towards her. 'Something happened there. I need to know. You owe me that.'

She glanced up at me, just for a moment, then nodded and took a sip of her coffee.

'You told me some of it before the funeral, the day that David came. You said Miriam was happy there.'

'Yes, they both were. I suppose I was too, at first, though I was never really at ease. There were others there when we arrived, of course, some English people, professional colleagues of Harold's. They all worked on the sites as well as at the university, but I don't think Miriam ever got to know them properly.'

'What about the country? Did she love it, hate it, or what?'

'We were all shocked by the little stone cottage they gave us. Then Miriam seemed to take to it, loved the primitive nature of it all. She was like a child herself, playing house in that little hovel, cooking on a peat-fired range, scrubbing clothes in the stone sink. I suppose we all ran a little wild.

'At first she would help out at the dig and I would climb up the hillside with her. My father had taught her how to brush away the fine layers of earth and spot the tiny slivers of bone or fired clay. They always called to me if they found something and I got caught up in their excitement even though I didn't understand it. They wouldn't let me too close to where they were working in case I disturbed the earth. I was supposed to watch from a distance, but I usually got bored and wandered off to play on my own.

'Then Miriam would come after me. She'd take my hand and we'd follow the little stream as it tumbled down the hillside over slippery rocks. She showed me where to look among the reeds for wild flowers — orchids and violets and the tall foxgloves. There were so many. She knew all the proper names, and the common names the local people knew them by. She taught me how to string them together, to split the stem with the nail of my thumb till the milky sap bubbled out. If you're very careful, you can do it without breaking the end. Then we would thread the next stem through the slit, then another and another. Chains of bright buttercups and wild marigolds. Jewels fit for a princess, she would say and laugh and slip them around my neck and twist them into a crown for my head. You're my little princess, she'd say, and far prettier than any flower.'

'But it wasn't always like that, was it?'

Hannah shook her head, then took a deep breath, as if it were hard to push the words forward. 'After a while we spent less time at the dig. She started to visit the village people and I would go with her. I didn't like that so much. They were . . . Well, they would look at us strangely and wipe a seat for her to sit on. They crooned over me, telling her how pretty I was, but I knew it was only words to charm her. Then they would talk for a long time and she would write it all down in her notebook. She was always so excited, and they appeared to be friendly and respectful. The older women all wore black shawls wrapped about their heads. I felt embarrassed by my mother's bright clothes. She often wore shorts, even on Sundays. No one ever said anything, but I saw the way they looked at each other.

'The children were dirty. They always had runny noses — I don't think anyone owned a handkerchief. I tried not to touch anything, and I always refused the bread and scones they offered, no matter how hungry I felt. I scrubbed my hands when I got home. Miriam didn't seem to notice the dirt. She was too excited about the things she'd written down. She tried to explain it all to me on the way home. I didn't really listen. I don't think it ever occurred to her that I mightn't want to go with her.'

'What about your father?'

'In the evening Harold would come home — muddy boots in the hall and a fine trickle of brown dust falling from his clothes. He was a tall man, broad-shouldered, with hands like spades. He stood over me like a huge bear. He must have sensed that. He was always so careful with me, lifting me gently as if I would break. I suppose all fathers do that. He would take me up to the little room he used as a study and I was allowed to watch while he sorted through his trays of precious fragments. He had tiny brushes to clean them with and special knives with miniature blades, like surgical instruments, to scrape away the dirt. They were kept on his worktable in a black leather box, each with its own velvet-lined compartment. I was never allowed to touch. I suppose they must have been very sharp. In the evening they would build up the fire and she would tell him her latest story while I fell asleep on his lap. Yes, I suppose we were all happy at first.'

'Something must have happened to change that.'

Hannah's hands tightened their grip on the leather.

'Please, I have to know.'

She closed her eyes for a moment. 'Your grandmother became more and more absorbed in her writing. That's when they started to argue. After a time it seemed that was all they did. They would fight and then there would be long days of silence. I don't know which was worse.'

'What did they argue about?'

'Anything. Everything. There was one big row. I'm not sure if that was the start of it.'

'What was it about?'

'Harold had spent a lot of time working at the dig. There was something important going on. He had come home late the previous night and went off early again that morning. In the afternoon Miriam went up to join him. I wasn't allowed to go this time. I stayed in the house with one of the village women who sometimes helped out.

'Suddenly Miriam came back. She burst in and ran upstairs, right past me, and slammed the door. She must have locked it, because Harold went running up after her and knocked and banged at it for ages. "You can't do this!" he kept shouting, "You know it's wrong. Have you lost your senses?" But she wouldn't let him in.

'The shouting went on for days. He kept saying she'd done something unethical. I didn't know what that meant then. I still don't know what she'd done. But I knew it was important and I was afraid. Nobody spoke to me or told me what was happening.

'After that they sort of retreated into their own separate worlds. It was like the cinema when they show a split screen, two different scenes with different people doing different things and each unaware of the other. My father would go off to the university or to the site. Often he and the other men went to the pub after and he wouldn't return until late. I think he may have started drinking, I mean seriously drinking, but he wasn't around enough for me to be sure. When he was home, he shut himself away in his study. I kept out of his way.'

'And what about Miriam?'

'She spent more and more of her time visiting the local people, then working over her notes. She'd become so engrossed that she often forgot to cook a meal and we'd have to eat sandwiches. The kitchen table was always covered with piles of paper. Harold would get really annoyed.'

'So you spent your time with her, went with her, not with Harold?'

'Yes, well, my father . . . I think he just assumed that's how it should be, mother and daughter, you know. He always left me behind. She didn't exactly take me with her. I just followed her because I didn't know what else I was supposed to do. Sometimes she would talk out loud about something she was working on, but I'm not sure if she was that aware of me. Most of the time I don't think she even knew I was there.

'I would follow her down into the village, into the tight little houses reeking of burnt peat, or up into the hills to some isolated crofter's hut. The cramped rooms were always dark, even at midday, and the smoke from the open fires was choking. I would stand behind her while the women whispered their tales of leprechauns and banshees. Often Miriam sat in the only armchair. It would have been the man's chair, but she was privileged. Sometimes it was the man she spoke with, and then the women would keep out of the way. But it was always the women she paid when she left. Just a little something for your trouble, she would say and they would smile and shake their heads in modesty. Even so, their hands would snake out from under their shawls and snatch at the few coins.

'No matter how poor their home, there was always a crucifix and picture of the Virgin Mary in a blue dress. Sometimes it would be a statue. Some houses had a little candle burning in a red glass cup. The women would light the candle before they started their whispered tales, and they would drop their voices even lower and cross themselves when they came to the part about the magical people.'

'What about the children? You told me how they used to torment you.'

'Ah, yes, the children. So many children, with thin, sickly

bodies and small for their age. They must have known hunger. We were the rich Americans. They would watch me from the far side of the room, a little crowd of them all hunched together. They hated me. They were always watching me. They hated me because my mother was beautiful and my hair was shiny and I wore pretty cotton dresses that were clean and starched. They dared not move against me there, in their parents' homes, where the stick was always in the corner. So they would stare at me from the shadows and poke their tongues out and claw their fingers at me when the grown-ups weren't looking. I knew they would wait until we were in the school playground, that's where they'd get their revenge. And all the while their mothers and grandmothers would be muttering tales about gnomes and hobgoblins and evil things that lived in the dark.'

'Oh, God, no wonder you hated Miriam's work! No wonder you got upset when I went on about magic and fairies. I'd no idea. I'm so sorry. I must have been awful.'

'That doesn't matter now. It's all in the past.'

'No, but it isn't, is it? You're still afraid, aren't you?'

'I'm afraid for you, what she's doing to you.'

'Didn't you ever tell her how you felt?'

'I tried. She would laugh and tell me not to be foolish, that they were only children playing. It was as if she didn't hear me. I would follow her home afterwards, with her striding out, her notebook in her arms and her mind full of the latest revelation. The sun would have already set. I would run after her, desperate not to be left behind in the gathering darkness. We could barely see the way ahead, but she was unconcerned. I was sure there were evil things lurking behind each bush and bramble, waiting to tear at me and carry me away into the blackness. But she would touch that thing around her neck and laugh and say that nothing could ever hurt us.'

'That thing? You mean this, her talisman?' I reached my hand to my neck and held the chain.

Hannah flinched. 'Yes, her talisman, if that's what you want to call it.'

'When did she start to wear it?'

'I can't remember. Please don't ask me any more about it.'

'But I think you *can* remember.'

Her fingers pulled and wrenched at the strap of her bag. The bones of her knuckles were sharp.

'Please, you must. I know this is painful, but I need you to help me.'

'I really can't remember. It just seemed to be there. She certainly had it before Harold left. That was one of the things they argued about. He tried to take it from her once. She was shouting at him and he lunged across the table and grabbed the chain. She screamed and clawed at his face. I screamed too, but I don't think they heard me. His chair fell over and there was blood on his chin.'

'And what happened when he left?'

'Nothing really. He just went. He took me for a carriage ride. He had borrowed a pony and trap from one of the farmers and we drove along the lakeside, just him and me. We watched the swans land on the water and he showed me where there were wild deer hiding in the trees. He said it was time for him to go back to America and I was to stay with my mother. He said it was for the best. The next day she drove us to the station and I waved goodbye. That was the last time I saw him. She never spoke of him again.

'For weeks afterwards I would go up to his study, hoping to find him there, but it was always empty. The trays of little bits of history had all been taken away and only a fine layer of brown dust remained over the tabletop. It left a clean square where his instrument box had stood. He'd taken that with him, you see. It was too precious to be left behind.'

There was that other box, the white cardboard box, upstairs in the bottom drawer. I could have retrieved it in seconds. I could have shown her the letters, birthday cards, Christmas cards. I could have forced her to open them, made her see. But I didn't. Perhaps her pain was too raw. No, it wouldn't have been right at that point. Salt on an open wound. No, not yet.

'And then what happened?'

'Nothing happened. We just went on as before. Only in some ways it got worse. She worked at her stories, became completely obsessed by them. I think there were whole days on end when she forgot I existed. I managed to survive, kept up appearances. I didn't want people to know, you see. I suppose I felt guilty, as if it were somehow my fault. I tried to keep the cottage clean. I washed my own clothes and made sure my hair was brushed. Often there would be nothing to eat in the house so I took pennies from her purse and bought food on the way to school. If she noticed, she never said anything.

'Then suddenly there seemed to be more money. I think that was when she started to sell her work. She hired a housekeeper to look after me. It didn't help. We were more despised than ever. I kept expecting Harold to come back, or even send for me. But he never did. Then, after a while, she decided we should move to England.'

Hannah bent over the kitchen table. She looked broken, beyond tears. I moved close to her, putting my arm around her shoulder. The weight of that white box lay heavy on my conscience.

'Go on, Mum, have a cigarette.'

'You sure you don't mind?' Her hands shook as she struggled with the packet. I took the lighter from her and held it while she breathed hard on the smoke.

'I'm sorry I have to do this to you. I must ask you one more thing. I know this is hard for you, but I have to know. Was there someone?'

'I don't know what you mean.'

'Yes, you do know.' Her shoulders trembled under my hands. I held my voice calm and steady. 'I mean, was there a man? Did she have a lover?'

She sighed and tapped at her cigarette ash and looked at the rim of her coffee cup, turning it in her hands. 'I'm not sure. Sometimes I think there might have been someone. There was a little wood nearby. She would spend hours there alone. Or that's what she said. I was forbidden to follow her but I didn't need telling. Things moved in there, branches shook . . . Sometimes I thought there was someone in the house. That was after Harold had left. There were sounds in the night. I would wake suddenly and think I could hear laughter. It may have been just a dream.'

'What about when you moved here? Did you ever see anyone in this cottage, or in the orchard?'

'No. Well, yes, there might have been someone, a young man, dark hair. For some reason I thought he was the gardener. No one ever said.'

'Did you notice anything about him, anything strange?'

'No, I only saw him once or twice and that was from a distance. Only . . . I think he kept some sort of bird, like a falcon.'

'Or an eagle? Could it have been an eagle?'

'I don't know. It could have been. I could hear scratching at the windows. Sometimes Miriam would pick up a feather . . .' Her voice had fallen to a whisper. 'I really can't remember.'

'It's OK, Mum, I'll get you some more coffee.'

I stood by the kettle and watched her as she lit another cigarette. It was as if I were seeing her for the first time, not as my mother but as a separate person, a woman on her own — a lonely woman. Whatever happened in Ireland had robbed her of both her parents. Even her husband had abandoned her. David and I were all she had. She was always going on at me, like mothers do, I suppose. Brush your hair, Chloe. Wipe your feet before you come into the house. Don't read this, don't play with that, she'd say, or you'll end up like your grandmother. Stick to numbers, they're nice and safe. Don't mess with paints, Chloe, or the goblins will get you. No, she didn't actually say that, but now I know that's what she was thinking. Perhaps she was right. Perhaps they already had.

'Chloe, about Paul . . .'

'Yes? What about him?'

'That's really why I came. I was hoping I could persuade you to let him run you to Heathrow. Perhaps if you talked to him again . . .'

'No. It was all a big mistake. I can't marry him. It's just not possible.'

She was silent for a moment. Then she shifted, her chair leg scraping the floor. 'Very well. I can see you're determined. But you can't just leave it like that. You're both, well . . . he's so upset. Perhaps he could still do that — take you to the airport, I mean. It's easy enough for him to cyle here and pick you and Fifi up. It might be easier to talk like that, explain things calmly and sensibly. Tidy the ends up.'

There was something in what she said. I hadn't been very fair to him. Besides, I could hardly throw things at him on the motorway.

'You're probably right. OK. We'll tidy the ends up, as you put it, part on civilised terms. But that's all.'

She nodded. 'I suppose I'd be wasting my breath if I asked you to take that thing off your neck?'

I didn't answer. She sighed heavily and slipped her cigarettes back into her bag.

'Is there anything you want me to say to Grandfather?' I asked.

My mother looked at the floor and shook her head.

Fifteen

I'M NOT USED to flying, and it's still a strange experience for me to hang in the sky, hour upon hour, while the earth turns beneath. At first I tried to maintain awareness of where I was, up there suspended in space, looking down at the strings of city lights threaded far below. But it's a long flight and soon the duty-free magazines and attendants jostling in the aisles turned the world outside into an illusion. Before long I surrendered to the comfort of the airtight capsule and a glass of wine, then slept for most of the flight.

The journey to the airport had been tense. Paul came to collect me and insisted on driving Fifi. We discussed the weather, the flight times and the traffic problems on the M25 — anything safe and civilised. We were no more than polite strangers. He actually looked relieved when he left me at the check-in desk. He said he would take the car back to the flat and return in seven days' time. I said he was welcome to use it in the meantime. He said he hoped I would enjoy the holiday, that I certainly needed it. I clenched my fists inside my pockets and thanked him for driving me down.

'My pleasure,' he replied. 'Besides, you'd never have managed the motorway on your own.' And with that parting shot he left.

I tried to think up a stinging retort as I moved through Customs, not noticing the little nicks I was tearing in my boarding card. The flight attendant showed me to my seat and helped to stow my hand luggage. As soon as I was alone, I wrenched off the diamond ring Paul had given me and slipped it into my purse. It left a raw red mark around my finger. Then I determined to be calm and enjoy the luxury of being waited upon.

It wasn't strictly true about my getting a last-minute cancellation. Vacant seats are no problem if you can afford to fly first-class. This was the first time I had seen Miriam's money as anything other than a threat. I lay back and dozed in comfort to the hum of the engines. I had Harold's letter from Miriam tucked away, safe in my bag. A dozen times I stroked the cool, silky surface of the thick envelope. It would be my key, my password to . . . to what? If I ever found him. If he could remember anything. I tried to relax. I told myself there was no point in anticipating difficulties.

That was fine until they woke me an hour before landing and I realised I was nearly across the Atlantic. In an hour's time they were going to make me get off the plane, and all I had was an address on a scrap of paper:

Aquinnah Lodge,
Harrisville,
Lake Wampanoag,
Massachusetts.

The travel agent had told me Harrisville was just over an hour's drive from Boston Airport. I had some vague idea of Boston being a big city, like London or New York. Harrisville must be a suburb. Perhaps the lodge was an old folks' home. Why hadn't I looked at a map? I was on the other side of the world with no idea where I was or where I was going; few people even knew I was there. Right up until the time I left, Greg had kept on trying to contact Harold Shaw. There continued to be no reply, just an answerphone and an abrupt voice saying, 'Aquinnah Lodge. There's no one here. If you want you can leave a message.'

I should have listened to Greg. I should have waited. Even if I found Harold, he wouldn't know who I was. He could be sick, or senile. Perhaps he was already dead. Perhaps they had all died and the nursing home had closed down and I would find it all boarded up. I thought about going straight to the desk and booking a flight home. I could make up some story about an emergency, stay in the airport, sleep on a bench.

Pull yourself together, I told myself. I was booked into a hotel, and it should be easy enough to get a taxi there. I could stay in the room for a few hours, calm down a little, have a bath and a decent meal, a good sleep. And if I still felt like this in the morning, *then* I could turn around and run home.

I managed to recover my baggage and was walking out of Customs and through to the exit hall. I'm not sure what I expected, but I was surprised to find Logan Airport looking very much like the Heathrow I'd left behind. Even though it was late evening, there seemed to be lots of people around and they looked harmless enough. Perhaps it wouldn't be so bad. Security guards were everywhere. I would have asked one of them where to get a cab, only they were carrying guns.

Suddenly I was hit by a wall of tartan and sheepskin, a wall that tossed me into the air, spun me around and set me down again. Was I being mugged? Yes, this was America, of course I was being mugged. Why didn't someone help me? Then I was being crushed. No, I was being held at arm's length and shaken by the shoulders. Then I was looking into watery blue eyes and a stained and straggly beard and a woollen hat pulled down hard over bushy eyebrows.

'God, you're so like her. I didn't think it was possible.'

The voice was gruff and broken. I tried to call for help. Barely a whimper came out.

'Oh, I'm sorry, girl. I'm sorry. I didn't mean to scare you. It's me, Harold. Your grandfather. Hey, listen to that: grandfather!'

He shook me again, then relinquished his grip to snatch up my suitcase and propel me towards the doors.

'Come on, let's get you out of here. Get you somewhere I can take a proper look at you. Only just made it. Needed to catch a few hours' sleep. Woke up just in time.'

I managed to regain my breath and thought I ought to say something. 'We've been trying to contact you for days. I didn't know if I would be able to find you.'

'Been up in the mountains, staying with a friend. Did some fishing. Got back this afternoon and found a message on the machine. That Uson fellow. Said you were on your way.'

A strong arm was locked firmly around my shoulders and I was being marched past the line of cabs, my last means of escape. We were heading for a white truck, some sort of four-wheel-drive. He tossed my suitcase in the back and pushed me up into the passenger seat.

'Where are we going?'

'Home, of course.'

This was all happening too fast. 'I've booked into a hotel, The Meridian.'

'Nonsense, girl. You've not come all this way to stay in a hotel. Besides, the lodge is only an hour away. It would take us that time to fight through the city traffic. Driving through Boston isn't for the faint-hearted.' He wrestled the engine into gear and pulled out on to the road.

Floundering in a whirlpool of trepidation, I attempted to organise some rational thought. If he was who he claimed to be, he was remarkable. Harold would be well into his seventies. The man beside me was as strong as a man twenty years his junior. Tall, though I could see his shoulders were bent. Glaring street lamps illuminated his face. His jaw was square and firm beneath the grizzled beard, skin leathery and deeply lined, and his hands, gripping the steering wheel, were taut and wiry. Yes, I suppose it could be possible. He turned to glance at me, shook his head in disbelief, laughing to himself, his eyes shining. He reached out and slapped my knee, and chuckled. Yes, perhaps this could be Harold.

The truck swung away from the airport and on to the motorway. The man beside me screwed up his eyes and peered forward through the windscreen. He's too old to be driving, I thought. God, we're on the wrong side of the road! Then I realised that everyone else was too. I was still in a daze. It's probably jet lag, I thought, though I wasn't sure exactly what that meant.

A terrible thought struck me. 'You say you found a message on the answerphone? You haven't actually spoken to anyone, then?'

He turned to me for a moment, then looked hard at the road. 'It's OK,' he said, softly, reaching out to pat my hand, 'I phoned him back, that Uson fellow. He told me about Miriam. Strange, I knew it had to happen one day. Either her or me. Always thought it would be me. Couldn't picture her growing old, you see. In my mind she's the same as when I last saw her. It doesn't seem right.'

We drove on in silence. Traffic signs and place names flashed by in the headlights. We seemed to be in the centre of several lanes of traffic sweeping in terrifying formation past the edge of the city. Then he manoeuvred the truck onto another, less threatening, highway, and I saw that we were heading along a coast road.

'Don't know about you,' he said, 'but I could do with some coffee. I know a good place up ahead. It's on the Salem road. A truckers' stop, but clean and the food's excellent.'

'Salem? Isn't that where there were witches?'

'You bet. It's where I met your grandmother.'

This time he rocked with laughter and I joined in. Yes, this had to be Harold Shaw.

The diner was brightly lit, all chrome and melamine, scrubbed and gleaming. I expected waitresses out of fifties Hollywood movies, dressed in gingham aprons and chewing gum. Instead they wore jeans and neat shirts, were well-spoken and polite. Nobody said 'Have a nice day'. They all seemed to know Harold. He explained they were students, working their way through university. I was paraded before everyone.

'My granddaughter, from England.'

American-sized plates appeared and endless hot coffee. I didn't think I was hungry until the smell of food hit me and I found I was ravenous. Harold ate too, but with less enthusiasm. He hardly took his eyes off me.

'Same colour hair. Hers was straighter. Fell down her back like a waterfall. Same eyes, too. First thing I noticed about her. Worked in the library, University of Salem. My first teaching post. Nearly wore out my library pass before I asked her for a date.'

'I thought you used to live in Boston?'

'Yes, that's right. I was born in Boston. Studied at Harvard. Miriam's family were from Salem. Irish stock originally. After we married, I got a lectureship at Cambridge. This Cambridge, that is — it's a sub-department of Harvard. Odd that when she left Ireland she chose to live in an English university city called Cambridge. Anyhow, we settled in Boston. Fourth generation of Shaws to establish there.'

'Hannah still remembers Boston.'

A shadow came over his face. His voice shook. 'How is Hannah?'

We both reached for photographs. I showed him a picture of my mother and David, taken this year. He recognised them both. I was amazed to find he had a picture of two small children on a beach: David and me, building sandcastles. Then David on a motorbike and another of me in Guide uniform. There was one of Hannah as a teenager. I had forgotten how pretty she was, although shorter and darker than her mother. Then he showed me a Miriam I never knew, a young woman in shorts, her hair tied in a ponytail, smiling and waving. She was standing in long grass, dwarfed by giant standing stones. The photo was in black and white, the corners cracked and dog-eared. I turned it over and saw there was writing on the back: *Wicklow Mountains, Ireland, August 1957.*

I showed Harold a Miriam much older than he remembered, a Miriam he had never known. He gazed at the picture for a long time. I told him he must keep them all. He returned his photographs to the wallet in which they had worn a grubby space as if they were taken out often. So much we had to say to each other, but it was far too soon. There would be time.

The truck ambled on through the night. A half-moon rose in a clear sky. I watched it playing on the ocean before we turned off the coast road to wind through fields and gentle forest-clad hills. Occasionally the line of trees broke and I caught the surface of still water, milky in the moonlight. This wasn't the country I'd expected. Nor was this the man I expected.

Harrisville turned out to be a small-town settlement of white-painted wooden houses. *Population 6,420* the sign read, hardly more than a village. Harold slowed the truck and followed the main road through the centre of town. Eventually, on the outskirts at the far side, he turned off on to a dirt track and headed down towards a lake. We came to a halt in front of Aquinnah Lodge. It reminded me of a log cabin, but huge, with walls of glass and wide verandas overlooking the water. I clambered down, stiff and exhausted from hours of travel.

He led the way through the front door and flooded a huge, vaulted room with light. It was like a museum. The wood-lined walls were hung with Indian weapons, shields, leather tunics worked with brightly coloured beads. There were old maps and sepia pictures from the nineteenth century: severe-faced Indians, their arms crossed, sitting in motionless ranks as if posing for a school photograph; white men in fringed leather with rifles, one foot on the mound of a dead buffalo. Books were scattered everywhere. An entire canoe hung suspended from the ceiling. It was another version of Miriam's cottage, more exotic, but equally eccentric and chaotic.

Harold insisted on carrying my suitcase through to the guest room.

'You make yourself at home while I just catch my breath,' he said. 'Then I'll light the stove.'

He dropped down into an armchair. By the time I had taken off my coat he was asleep, his hat pulled down over his ears.

I knew nothing until the next morning, having found the shower and put myself to bed, falling asleep instantly. I was woken by the whizzing of the coffee grinder and the clatter of pots and pans. Harold took the whole issue of food seriously — catching or shooting it, preparing it, eating it, and then sleeping it off. As he was no longer lecturing, food had taken over his life and he considered it only right and natural that I should participate fully. I was certainly hungry for the scrambled eggs and slices of venison, but the syrupy pancakes first thing in the morning defeated me.

I gave him Miriam's letter after breakfast. He took it from me without speaking, and carried it into his study, closing the door behind him. I waited for him in the silence of the vaulted room, turning the pages of a book. I tried to read line by line, but remembered not one word. An eternity passed before he emerged, slapped his hands together and asked me what I fancied for lunch. My disappointment was bitter, but I held back. Perhaps, I told myself, when we had a chance to know each other and he could trust me, then it would be safe to talk. Or maybe I had thought I might find some happiness here and was afraid to break the spell. Whatever the reason for my reluctance, I asked nothing about the letter and kept the talisman well hidden.

Over the next week I grew to know Harold Shaw, both as my grandfather and as my friend. He's an astonishing man, made more so by his age, living in bursts of outrageous energy between sitting down to 'just catch my breath'. Often this took him several hours and, while he snored on the veranda, I would walk the gentle, sloping hills around the lake. We did talk of my grandmother, of course, and sometimes he forgot and talked to me as if I were her. It is as if, through her death, he had found his Miriam again. We both put a lot into those few days, knowing time was against us and so much of it had been lost already. I'll go back there, perhaps in the New Year, but it must be soon, very soon.

Harold showed me the mountains and forests of Massachusetts. I'd heard about New England in the fall, but nothing could have prepared me for what I saw. There were burnished golds and beaten coppers, citrines, topaz and amber, gems scattered on swathes of saffron and cinnamon, and all set against a satin sky: the cargo of a treasure galleon strewn across the landscape.

As evening drew in, the lake would turn to blue-tinged marble, as pale as Iolair's skin. I kicked at the carpet of fallen leaves and picked through them until I found one to match the yellow of his eyes. The damp earth below was the colour of his long, dark hair. I tried to imagine how far away I was from England. As the moon ripened towards full, I wondered if it rose in his sky as it fell in mine.

Word soon got around. On the second day, while Harold was asleep, I wandered into the centre of Harrisville. Several people waved to me or stopped to say hello. They seemed to know who I was and why I was here, and asked me all sorts of questions about England and how long I was intending to stay.

I had come prepared for the elegance of the big city, a five-star hotel and discreet visits to a hushed sanatorium. In the one and only clothing store, I managed to purchase some jeans and sweaters, a pair of walking boots and a lumber jacket like Harold's. Then, passing a toyshop, I spotted pads of drawing paper and something twitched in my fingers. There were no proper art materials, so I compromised with pencils and a box of Mickey Mouse poster paints. While Harold continued to sleep I sat cross-legged on the veranda with my pad and paintbrush.

At first I paused to study the shape and composition of the landscape. Then something else began to happen. I could hear the trees; I could hear them whisper, one to the other. I wanted to reach out, to touch each one; touch their sadness and make it my own. Amid all this beauty, they were dying, sinking into the long sleep, the small death of winter. My limbs weakened with theirs. I was being drained as their life force was drained, spent in that last triumphant blaze of fire. I felt myself drifting and I pulled back, brought myself down to the solidity of paper and brushes. Then my hands began to work, following the line of my eye, but listening, listening all the while to the trees that died and the leaves that fell and the earth that welcomed and enfolded them.

'Where did you learn to do that, girl?'

I was startled. I was so absorbed in what I was doing that I hadn't heard him move behind me. I scrambled to my feet, holding up the pad.

'I was trying to capture the colours of the trees, but the paints aren't really made for it.'

He took the painting, stared at it, then at me. 'Who taught you to paint? And don't tell me this is a schoolgirl hobby. I know what I see.'

'I don't know. I just paint, that's all.'

He looked so serious that I began to feel uncomfortable, as if

I'd done something out of place. Confused, I reached out for the paper to look for myself and the breath caught in my throat. This was my work? The scene was alive! It would capture the observer and draw them in; would force them to see and understand what I had seen and understood; feel what I had felt. I could not trust myself with this and thrust the paper at Harold.

'Here, you keep it. Please.' I fumbled with the paintbox and spilled the water.

He said no more about it that day. Later I found the painting tacked to the wall of his study.

We had talked about Hannah, and there was sadness in his voice whenever he spoke of her. I knew I would have to tell him about those unopened letters. There was never going to be a right time, but there was a moment when it all came out.

We had been working outside. Harold showed me how to use his powered chainsaw and he let me help cut logs for the coming winter. We were laughing a lot and it ended with me kicking up leaves and throwing them at him like a child. I realised, in the middle of all that play, what had been missing from my childhood: I should have had a grandfather. And what about Hannah? How different would she have been if Harold had stayed with her? Why had Miriam kept them apart? For the first time, those formless doubts about Miriam that I had always pushed into some dark corner of my mind started to assert themselves, solidifying into something tangible. And at its centre was a tiny core of resentment.

He was sitting on the veranda, still laughing and picking leaves out of his coat while I brewed tea. I carried the mugs out to him and crouched on the steps at his feet.

'She never got your letters. Hannah, I mean. They never reached her.'

'What do you mean?'

'I found them. Miriam had kept them, hidden them away. They are all unopened. Hannah didn't know. She thinks you didn't . . . That you . . .'

He was silent for a while, nodding slowly. 'That doesn't surprise me. Miriam said we had to make a clean break. I suppose I wrote them more for myself than anything.'

'I've no idea why she kept them. She stored them away carefully. I found them hidden in a drawer.'

'Does Hannah ever speak of me?'

'No, never. The first I knew about you was after the funeral when Greg told me about that envelope I brought. That's why I'm here now.'

He nodded again and sipped his tea.

'But the point is that Hannah didn't know about the letters. She thinks you abandoned her completely.'

'In a way I suppose I did. I can't explain it. I had to leave. It was like there was something pushing me out. But I tried to keep in touch through Miriam. It got easier as time went on and we fell into a pattern. I'd write to them both, every Christmas and birthday, and there was always a card for Hannah. Miriam usually wrote back. There'd be news and photographs. But whenever I suggested a visit she refused. She kept saying it was better that way. Going back gets more and more difficult as the years pass. You get to a point where it's just not possible.'

'No, it's not too late. I'll talk to her, make her understand how it was. I've got the letters. I'll *make* her read them if I have to.'

Harold shook his head and said nothing, drained his mug and set about stacking the logs.

A few days later I dared to paint again.

Harold suggested we drive up to the foot of the White Mountains. He urged me to bring my art materials, to keep me amused while he fished. We set off early. Harold knew the country roads, the old tracks, away from the press of tourists. As soon as we turned off the main highway and the traffic thinned to an occasional passing farm truck, I took the wheel so he could rest. We drove through the vastness of the countryside, through gentle rolling farmland dotted with picture-postcard villages. Then the truck began to climb slowly through golden hills. Rivers gushed beside the roads, cresting with white foam as they collided with stones. We stopped halfway across a bridge to lean over railings drenched with spume and watch the water roaring beneath us.

'Used to come here with your grandmother. She loved the mountains.'

'What was she like when you first knew her? Before you were married, I mean.'

He looked into the distance, his eyes squinting at the morning sun. 'First time I saw her she was hanging out the library window feeding a squirrel. I dropped my pile of books down on the counter and the creature scampered away up the tree. "You've frightened him," she said. "Poor thing. I've been trying to tame him all summer. Oh, perhaps it's just as well — he's eaten half my lunch." She turned and smiled, and her hair swirled around her like a whirlpool and settled on her shoulders. I saw those green eyes and that was it. I was sunk! Miriam Delaney, she was then. So pretty she scared the life out of me. Library secretary. Worked for the university, but not a graduate. Not that she wasn't bright. Far from it. But her mind was different, not forced along a certain path. Free to wander anywhere she willed. Bit like that squirrel, I suppose. You'd think you had her eating out of your hand, then, at the slightest movement, she was off. It took me five weeks to pluck up the courage to ask her for a date. We found we shared a passion for history, although with her there was more romance than fact. It was like she took up where I left off. She'd take my dry lists of dates and names and breathe life into them. Three months later, we were married.'

'And that was in Salem, was it?'

'That's right. I'd been lecturing there. Then she persuaded me to apply for a post at Harvard. Never thought I'd get it, but *she* did. And she was right. We took a small house there, just on the outskirts of Boston, not far from my parents. They took to Miriam like a daughter. When little Hannah was born, they were over the moon. What a pair! You could see they were both of Irish descent, even though they looked nothing like each other. From somewhere way back in Miriam's ancestral tree, Hannah had inherited Celtic blood. Little thing, with that pale skin and her dark hair and blue eyes. She looked like a fragile china doll next to Miriam's red and emerald fire. I'd just sit and look at them both together and think they were perfect. Couldn't believe my luck. Thought I had everything. I *did* have everything. Should have quit there.' He turned away abruptly and headed back to the truck. 'Come on, girl, those fish won't wait all day.'

After two hours of driving, we rested by a wide stretch of meandering green river and scrambled over huge boulders to the edge. Harold cast his line, set his back against a grassy mound and immediately fell asleep. I set up a makeshift easel and board and studied the clear torrent bubbling over polished boulders. This time I anticipated the effect and first allowed myself to tune in and become a part of things. I was learning quickly. I ran with the water, ice-cold and free. Then I waited with the eternal patience of the stones. I felt the pull and the resistance between them, held it in my mind, then moved the conflict onto the paper. Again I would make the finished work a gift to Harold.

I had to wake him when his line caught and the rod bent over. I couldn't watch the catching and the killing. He cleaned and skewered the fish, and turned them over a fire. The skin shrivelled and scorched, and the smell conspired with the mountain air to overcome any scruples I might have had. We ate with our fingers, like primitive hunters, while wide-winged birds circled overhead, watching us. Harold said they were hawks, but I preferred to think they might be eagles.

We opened cans of beer, and he talked to me of the land and the people. When he returned to Boston he had resumed his career, devoting himself to the study of Indian culture and religion.

'Here? I always thought of Indians belonging to the Wild West, with wagon trains and cowboys.'

He laughed and shook his head. 'No, no, this is all Indian country. Or it was until the white man came and took the land. Some of the bloodiest massacres happened along the seashores of New England. They believed in the land, you see, that it lived, that the Earth itself was a living being.'

'You mean they worshipped the Earth?'

'They worshipped the Great Spirit. But they believed everything had a spirit, each plant, each animal, the rocks and the rivers. Everything lived and was part of the Great Spirit, yet had its own identity.'

'That's like what the Celts believed, wasn't it?'

'It's the way most human races see things, or at least they used to until the Christians put a stop to it.' He looked around, his old eyes taking in the stillness, sunlight glancing off water and the distant purple ranges against the horizon. He could sense it too, the energy and life in the land.

'The Indians, they practised shamanism, didn't they?' I asked. 'Isn't that something to do with spirit guides, like animals?'

'Kind of. It was like reaching out and joining with the Great Spirit by finding some aspect of themselves in the forces of nature. They'd put themselves through the most horrific physical and psychological tortures. Not a test of bravery, as some think. They believed it caused an awakening of a higher consciousness.'

'Sounds awful! They must have thought it worked, though.'

'They reckoned it did. Their higher spiritual self would appear to them in some recognisable form, maybe an animal or a bird. Through this totem they could regularly enter the other world. Act as an emissary for the tribe.'

'Did they believe in . . . other beings, then? I mean like spirits, things that existed independently of man?'

'Well, they believed in the Ancestors. Apparently these Ancestors were partly divine beings, like demi-gods. They had supernatural powers. Could change their shape from time to time to suit their convenience.'

'You mean like the ancestors of the Irish peoples, from the Fairie kingdom? Like elves and demons could disguise themselves as humans or animals?'

'Been reading Miriam's books, have you? Yes. It's the same concept. Pretty universal.'

'What was that song Miriam used to sing to me? It was Scottish, something about seals that change into men. Silkies, they called them.'

I searched my memory for the words. The tune drifted back to me.

'I am a man upon the land,
And I am a silkie in the sea,
And when I'm far and far from land,
My home it is in Sule Skerry.'
'It was not well,' quoth maiden fair,
'It was not well indeed,' quoth she,
'That the Great Silkie from Sule Skerry
Should have come and lain a child on me.'
'Well, thou shall marry a proud gunner,
And a right good gunner I'm sure he'll be,
But the very first shot that 'ere he'll shoot,
He'll kill both my young son and me.'

'It's so sad,' I said, a little embarrassed at my own singing.

'It's just a story, a folk tale. People need their folk tales. They justify the unfairness of life. Come on,' he staggered to his feet and crumpled his beer can, 'we should be getting back.'

I wasn't sure how much he knew. We still hadn't talked about Ireland and what had happened there, but we both knew we had to.

Time was running short. I had left it until two days before I was due to leave. Harold had suggested he take me to dinner at a restaurant on the wharf at the other side of the lake. Apparently some friends of his ran it and I was expected to be on display. I dressed up for the occasion in one of Miriam's swirling skirts and an open-necked silk shirt.

As we drove round the lake he brought the conversation around to my paintings. I'd noticed they were missing.

'Drove down here earlier to book a table. Thought I'd call in, see my friend Josh. Runs an art gallery just along the way. Took him your pictures. Asked him to knock up some frames for them.'

'Oh, I'm flattered.'

'You should be. He offered me a thousand bucks apiece for them.'

'What! That can't be right. He must have made a mistake.'

'You bet he made a mistake. Told him they weren't for sale.'

I was still reeling with disbelief when we arrived at the restaurant. There were the usual introductions and questions about England. Then we were shown to a candlelit table in a bay window overlooking the water, assured it was the best in the house for the occasion. As I slipped off my coat the candlelight glanced off the heavy silver at my throat.

'She gave you that?'

'Yes. Why? What's wrong?'

I had expected Harold to recognise it, maybe even to be angry, but I was not prepared for the look of dismay that darkened his face. He leaned across to me, his hands pressing down on the table.

'Get rid of it. You don't understand.'

I sat down and felt it sway against my skin. 'No, I don't understand. Tell me about it. Tell me about Ireland. What happened there? Why did you leave?'

He shook his head and lowered himself heavily into the chair. When the waiter came over, Harold said we needed some time and could we order later. I asked for some drinks. I thought they might be needed.

'Whatever it was, can't you forgive her?'

'I forgave her long ago. It wasn't her fault. You want me to tell you. So did she. She said so, in that letter you brought with you. *Explain to Cliohna*, she wrote, *tell her everything*. But I'm not sure there's anything to tell. It was all so . . . so nebulous. There was no reason to it all. Nothing I could see or touch. Only that pendant. That's why I lost her.'

'I need to know. I need your help.'

He reached out and wrapped his hands around mine. 'You're a gift. It's like having her back again.'

'Then tell me. Please.'

Sixteen

'I DON'T KNOW where to begin.'

'Ireland. Tell me about Ireland. What made you go there?'

Harold shrugged his shoulders. 'It was my subject, pre-Christian civilisation. The chance came up. I had to make a grab for it. It wasn't long after the end of the war, you see. I'd been over in Europe, Northern France. I was at university when America joined the war. But I had to go, we all did. Turned out to be the shortest war record in history. Lasted all of fifteen minutes. First time I saw action I got shot in the leg. Still bothers me when it rains. They shipped me straight home again, but I'd seen enough to want to go back there.

'I went to college and majored in European history. We married and I ended up at Boston, teaching, like I told you. There was a post-war upsurge of interest in all things European, particularly British. When Ireland came up, well, I couldn't pass up the opportunity. Not that Miriam would have let me. Back to the Old Country, she said. She didn't know the first thing about Ireland, but, like most Irish Americans, she had a romantic empathy with the place, a sort of homesickness for somewhere she'd never been. Though you'd think, with the stories they told of starvation and fighting, it would be the last place on earth anyone would want to go. Still, that's where we went, Miriam and I and little Hannah.'

The waiter arrived. I was impatient while he filled my glass with wine. Harold took a long gulp of his beer. When we were alone again, I asked, 'And what did you find when you got there?'

'It was everything and nothing we'd dreamt of. Stepping back in time. I know that's a cliché, but that's what it was. A small island after the vastness of New England. Yet there was wildness and rawness in the landscape that I'd not imagined, for all that it was cut through with roadways and neatly plotted out with dry stonewalls. Where New England was clean and untouched, Ireland was primitive and savage. It was still the Ireland Miriam's great-grandparents had left behind. She was entranced by the little stone houses with their earth roofs and the donkey carts bowling along dirt roads. Oh, there were the trappings of modern civilisation, cars and buses, shops and houses, but they were already outdated and dilapidated. The real things, the solid things, the castles and the standing stones, they were ancient. This was the Ireland I'd come seeking and,' he smiled, 'Miriam was bewitched by it all.'

'You were working on some excavations, weren't you?'

'That's right. A vast arena in the lower part of the mountains. Work was already underway when we arrived. Of course the whole area was steeped in legends. The Kingship of Erinn. You didn't have to learn about it. It was in the air all around you, it entered through your every breath, through the pores of your skin.

'The team worked out of Trinity College, Dublin. Of course I had no illusions about my position. I was the token Harvard man, international relations and all that. Working alongside wizards like Johansson and Dolby, I felt like the new apprentice. My first qualified field assignment, and I was determined to prove myself. And where we were going, what we might uncover! I would have worked as gopher for the chance to be there. There were others, of course — volunteers, students on vacation — but we three made up the main team. I was the only one with a family. That wasn't a problem. They were all enchanted with Miriam and the young one.'

'Hannah told me something about how you lived there.'

'They'd set us up in a village near one of the sites. I suppose we were both a bit shell-shocked when we saw the housing we'd been allocated. We could hardly complain. It was luxury compared with most of the villagers' homes. Miriam was like a little cork that bobbed back up on the water. She set about turning it into a home for us. She thrived there. Every day was an adventure. There was a glow about her, an excitement that was contagious.

'At first she was very involved with the dig, helping out when she could. She seemed to have an instinct for finding things, as if she could read the landscape. I got her to assist me with some local research, looking up parish records, that sort of thing. That got her interested in the social history of the area. She'd talk to the villagers and the crofters. Started to write things down. That was OK, too. In fact it was quite helpful to the work. Then she went off on a trail of her own, got sidetracked into folk tales and fairy stories. I was pleased for her. It was something she could do for herself but still share with me. She was finding her own role, a place for herself. It made us equals. Stopped me from becoming too single-minded.

'She was able to talk to the people, you see, relate to them in a way that we couldn't. Not that they were unfriendly, far from it. The Irish have a reputation for being warm and hospitable. That's true, they are all of that. But that's only the surface of it. They can fool you into thinking they're a simple, open, honest people. And that's true, too. But they have a breadth and a depth that can take you unawares. They're shackled to a land that breaks their backs and a religion that breaks their souls. And they rise triumphant over both. I don't know what it is about them. Maybe they cower before the priesthood because they have known darker gods. What was it Miriam said? "There are things lurking in the shadows of their psyche, with only the bread and wine to keep them at bay."

Whatever made them the way they were, Miriam could get them to talk, prise their secrets from them.'

As he spoke Harold had turned to the window and was gazing out across the lake. Then he seemed to remember I was there and turned back to me with an embarrassed smile. I had to keep him talking, keep him moving along the path.

'And what about Hannah, how did she survive?'

'Oh, she played, as children do. I guess she grew a little wild in that landscape. And that was no bad thing. It was good to get her away from the constraints of post-war, middle-class Boston. She was always a quiet child, gave little of herself away. Liked to play on her own. We tried to encourage her to mix with the local children, but she seemed to hang back. Preferred to be alone.'

'But you settled there OK?'

'Yes, we settled, worked out a pattern to live by. The seasons passed. The work was progressing. We uncovered a whole series of ring fortifications. And the burials, of course. Many had been disturbed before. In fact, it was unusual to find something intact. The Danes did a lot of damage. A rich tomb would have been ransacked. But also burials were a way for a tribe to lay claim to an area, generation after generation, and often layer upon layer. Then, for some reason, ancestors would be dug up and moved around. And the area we were looking at was old, really old.

'I suppose we were primitive ourselves. With today's technology we would have been able to do so much more. There was no carbon-dating, little in the way of chemical analysis. We didn't even have access to an X-ray machine on-site. But we were careful and methodical. Inch by inch, we uncovered the past.'

'Hannah said you were happy there at first, all three of you.'

'Yes. Yes, we were happy.'

'Something must have happened. Something that changed everything.'

Harold lowered his eyes to study the candlelight caught on the rim of his glass. 'Yes, something happened. We found that tomb.'

The flickering flame etched deep shadows in the lines on his face. Suddenly, he looked very old.

'You found a tomb? What sort of tomb?'

'There was a mound of earth set into the hillside and overgrown with bushes and small trees. At first we thought it would be another mass grave. There'd been several of those, some cremation burials, too. There'd been a lot of fighting in this area. Few people died of natural causes. When the portal stones were uncovered, we knew straight away this was something different. The set-up was all wrong. But it was more than that. You could feel it. We all did. Of course there was a lot of leg-pulling. Jokes about Tutankhamun and the curse of the mummy. We were whistling in the dark and we all knew it. Everything was . . . what's that phrase?'

'Out of kilter?'

'Yes, that's it. Things didn't quite fit.'

'How do you mean?'

'Well, it was obviously old. At the time we didn't realise just how old. And, miraculously, it was intact — no trace of previous entry. The earth lay undisturbed, the huge stone slabs at the entrance still bedded deep into the soil. This was a special place, saved for an important occupant. A deep cave in the slope of the hillside, carefully concealed and smoothed over by time and the cruel weather. A place fit for the burial of kings.

'Yet this was a burial without ceremony. The portal stones and the stone slabs lining the entrance passage were featureless. No carvings, no ornamentation, though it would have taken the work of many men to move everything into place. Strangely, the end of the passage was blocked with rubble. Not a rock fall. This had been carried there deliberately. The cavern, when we broke through, contained nothing. No artefacts, no weapons or jewels. No gifts for the afterlife. Just a lonely figure wrapped in a plain cloth. No finely worked burial robes, no richly embroidered cloak. Yet the winding sheet was of the finest linen. This was the tomb of a high-born noble, yet it was a place of secrecy. It was as if they did it in a hurry, as if they were trying to hide something.

'We were all caught in the mystery, Miriam as much as anyone. It was late afternoon when we cleared a hole in the rubble piled at the end of the outer passage. A torch beam pierced the small opening and touched the sad bundle resting on a raised platform. It was too late to move further that day, and we went away with plans for the next morning. When I got home, I was full of it. My excitement was infectious, and of course she wanted to be there too. But there was still a lot of work to do to clear the entrance before we could go in. I suggested she come down after lunch the next day and bring her camera. Of course we'd taken photos at every stage. Standard practice. But Miriam liked to keep her own records of the work.

'It was a fine day, full summer. I watched her striding across the grass towards us, camera swinging in her hand. She was wearing shorts — her legs were long and brown from the sun and the open air. She'd tied her hair back away from her eyes. Every time I saw her was like the first time. It never ceased to amaze me that she was my wife. When she arrived there was a break in the proceedings. We were all standing around drinking tea. I offered her some. She shook her head. She was anxious to see what had been going on, couldn't take her eyes off that opening in the earth. She felt it, too, whatever it was. But she waited patiently while I took a photograph.'

'Was that the one you showed me, the one from your wallet?'

'That's right. Last photo I ever took of her. I can still see her laughing and shading her eyes with her hands. Then I asked the others if she could look at the tomb. No one objected. She was almost part of the team. Besides she was so astounding that no one could refuse her anything.'

He became quiet, his eyes distant, watching the past. Don't stop now, please, I begged inside my head. I forced a calmness into my voice and said gently, 'So you both went inside?'

Harold took a deep swallow of his beer and wiped his mouth with the back of his hand.

'We had to duck down to pass through the entrance. For a moment she hesitated, as if on the edge of something and uncertain. Then she took a breath and stepped forward. I held her hand and we moved down the dark passage between stone walls and earth floor. The circle of yellow light darted ahead of us, guiding our way. I shone it back to watch her face as she gazed in wonder at the rough-hewn slabs. If anyone were to ask when I last saw Miriam, I think I would have to say it was then, at that moment, as she grasped my hand tight and steadied herself against the wall. The long loop of her hair fell over one shoulder and her eyes shone like cat's eyes in the dark. Yes, that was the last time I saw my Miriam. After that, she was a stranger.'

He fell silent again. The moon had risen and the surface of the water was skimmed with iridescent pearl. I counted the waves lapping on the shore, slower than a heartbeat. Harold took a deep breath and held it for an endless moment before he spoke again.

'We entered the tight little cavern. The air was still heavy and stale with that dry tang that makes an archaeologist's heart leap. Preservation! A chance the contents were still whole. No damp, no mould, no rotting. Even better, the body, if still there, could be mummified. And that's exactly what we'd found earlier in the morning.

'I flashed the light around the walls to show her the extent of that little world, then moved it on to that sad little bundle resting on its bed of stone. "There she is," I said, "let me introduce you to Peggy-Sue." Miriam wasn't amused. "Oh no, don't! Don't laugh at her," she said. "She deserves better than that." Then she knelt down beside the stiff folds of linen. The cloth was hard with age and a dull patchy brown, as if doused in stale coffee. At one time the shroud would have been creamy white. She reached out her hand, but I stopped her.

' "No, don't touch," I said. "It's all very fragile. Could crumble away at any moment. We have to go carefully."

'Then Miriam said, "I think you should call her Eriu. You know, after the daughter of one of the Danaan kings."

' "Now, don't start letting your imagination run away with you," I told her. "Yes, she's old and probably high-born. But that's all. We're not looking for proof of any ancient legends."

' "She seems very small," she said.

' "Yes," I replied, "but don't forget that people were shorter then. Even so, she would have been below average height. Look, we managed to uncover most of the skull and part of the left shoulder."

'I pulled back the sterile white cloth that Johansson had laid over the exposed areas. She stared up at us with hollowed eyes, her sunken, parchment skin pulled tight to her skull, teeth grinning in mockery of death.

' "And you do know it's female?"

' "Well, we won't be certain, of course, until the pelvis is examined. But from the curve in the cheekbone, I think we can make a fairly good guess."

' "Do you know how old she was?"

' "The plates in the skull aren't completely fused, so she would still have been a young woman."

' "I wonder how she died."

' "That's easy. Look here, side of the skull. See this deep gash and the bone all caved in. Looks like a blow from a sharp weapon. And the dress here, over the shoulder. These marks. They're not natural discoloration due to ageing and they don't seem to have anything to do with a design. Of course we'll have to carry out tests, but I'm willing to bet she was covered with blood when she was put in here."

' " What a sad and lonely way to die," she said.

' "It's also a very strange way. They went to all this trouble to inter her. Yet they didn't bother to clean her up, go through all the normal death rites. It's like they were in a hurry, trying to cover something up." '

My mind was in two places now. I could see the darkness of

the cave, and the shadow of Miriam leaning over the body, like a mother at a child's bed. But I was also in that candlelit room with my friends, gathered around the table. We were listening to a voice that was Malcolm's, and yet it was the voice of someone else, the voice of a young woman with blood on her dress. I forced my hands down into my lap, fingers gripping so hard that my nails tore at my own flesh. I could see the horseman and the flight of the axe. I forced myself to concentrate on Harold's words.

' "Is that hair, there?" Miriam asked. She was pointing to the scraps still clinging to the scalp, like dried seaweed on rock. "Yes, that's right," I said, "though naturally it's discoloured and brittle. But we can probably find out what colour it was."

' "It was red, like mine, but curled and wild. Her eyes were bright green."

'Something had crept into Miriam's voice. I'd been too involved to notice, but now I looked up, aware of how intense she'd become. She was staring at the body, hands hovering above it, as if she were trying to sense things from the air around it. She looked as though she were being drawn into something. Enthralled. That's the word. I know that sounds corny, but that's what was happening to her. I should never have let it go on,' he slammed his fist down on the table, 'should have got her out then, straight away! Instead, when she begged to be allowed to touch the face, I let her. She traced one finger gently, so very gently, along the withered cheekbone.

' "Such sadness," she whispered. "So lonely." And then, "What's this?"

' "What? I can't see."

' "Look here, at her neck."

'I tilted the lamp and illuminated the edge of a dark line tucked under the cloth.

' "Wait, I'll try and uncover a bit more," I said and I reached for the tweezers and took the edge of the shroud. "Probably a torque, a plain band of metal. It'll be the only ornament we've found so far."

'I eased the cloth back a hair's breadth, then another. Then the light caught the edge of something else, something bright. Miriam gasped. "There, you see! There!"

'Her hand darted out and snatched at the body. For a moment I froze. I was helpless and horrified.

' "What the hell do you think you're doing?" I said. But she drew back, clutching something to her. I had a glimpse of silver as her hand closed over it. The torque, from which it must have hung, had shattered, crumbling away into brown, dusty flakes. But the object in Miriam's hand was bright and smooth. It could have been brand-new.

' "Hand it over," I said. "Carefully now. Here, just place it in my hand."

' "No," she whispered, "it's mine." And the look in her eyes! I'd never seen... I think she would have killed me rather than let go of it. And then she was gone.'

As I listened my hand had moved to my throat. Now it was clasped around the talisman. Harold looked and nodded. Neither of us spoke. He drained his glass and signalled for another beer. The waiter came and refilled both our glasses, and it was a while before I was able to ask more.

'So what happened? Didn't you run after her?'

'Of course I did. By the time I reached the entrance she was halfway down the hill. Johansson and Dolby and the others, they were just standing there. "What's up with Miriam?" they asked. "Took off like a frightened rabbit. Didn't say a word." Then Dolby said, "She probably got spooked. Not her fault. Better go after her, Hal."

'What could I say? This was my career on the line. I just went along with it. Said she got scared by the body. Then I made some excuse about equipment so I could go back inside. I rearranged the shroud, eased it back into place, hoping it would look as if the torque had just disintegrated beneath it. Covered it all over. Then I went down to find her.

'By the time I reached home, she'd shut herself in the bedroom. I tried to reason with her. I pleaded, threatened. When she eventually came out, she had that thing on a chain round her neck.

'After that she'd have none of me. It was like she couldn't hear me, like she was tuned into something else. I'd lost her. Time after time I tried to talk her into handing the ornament over. At first I was concerned about the morality of it. The threat to my career. What if anyone saw her wearing it and put two and two together? Then, gradually, I grew to be afraid of it. I know it sounds crazy, but it was that thing that caused the change in her. It was like it had some hold over her. Of course that's nonsense. But, maybe, if *she* believed it, that would be enough.

'Oh, we went on for a while. Barely civilised. We talked when necessary, but we had nothing real to say to each other. She wouldn't let me near her, wouldn't let me touch her. That thing round her neck, it was like an invisible hand, pushing me further and further away. I felt like an intruder in my own home. Spent less and less time there. Threw myself into my work. Miriam immersed herself in her story-collecting. Spent all her time with the local people, going around the villages, delving into this magical stuff they all believe in. It became like an obsession with her. At least she was still taking Hannah with her. Then she'd spend hours alone, reading and writing. Walking. Wherever she was, whatever she was doing, she was . . . absent.

'Then, suddenly, it was time to go back to the States. I was almost relieved when she refused to go with me. Our marriage was dead. There was no point in dragging its corpse all the way back to Boston. Somehow she'd persuaded the authorities to let her stay. The worst part was leaving Hannah. I told myself that in the long run it would be easier for the child if the break were permanent, that it was right she should stay with her mother. There was nothing I could I do for her. That's what I told myself. But there was also that invisible hand, pushing me away, pushing me out.'

'So you went back alone.'

'Right. And in no time her work started appearing on the bookshelves and in the bestseller lists. Of course I bought the first one, read some of it. A romanticised blend of historical fact and mythology. I didn't bother with the rest. But others did. Seems she could hit the nail on the head, led researchers along all the right paths. By then I was looking in other directions. I'd had all I wanted of Celtic history.'

'But you kept in touch.'

'I wrote often, to begin with at least. I suppose as time went by the letters got fewer. But, like I said, I always sent a card and a letter to Hannah on her birthday and at Christmas.' He looked down at his hands, twisted together on the table. He scratched hard along his finger with the nail of his thumb. His skin was purple with age, the nails yellow and cracked. I laid my hand on his. Mine looked tiny, like a child's.

'Hannah and Miriam were never close,' I said, 'and I think Hannah's very lonely. Perhaps it's not too late.'

We both fell silent for a while. Then I said, 'Greg told me about you and Miriam keeping in touch.'

'She wouldn't write back, not at the beginning. I was surprised when the first letter arrived. It was several years later and it came from a firm of solicitors. She'd moved to England by then. After that she wrote every year. Just a brief update and a few photographs. Always via the solicitor — I never had her address. I wrote back to her, but I never made any attempt to return. God knows I should have done, for Hannah's sake. I'd thought about it often enough, but time falls away and it becomes more and more impossible.'

'You never thought to divorce or remarry.'

'No, never had reason to. I expect you're going to ask if there was a man in Miriam's life, if that's what drove us apart. There were times when I wondered myself. But there was nothing to go on, no one who would make any sense. Although, when I think of those times, there are things I can't quite seem to remember. Like shadows at the edge of my mind. I don't know. It all slips away before I can touch it.

'It's like I said, I can't tell you what happened. There's nothing to tell, nothing real, nothing solid. Only that thing you're wearing. If I never did anything for Miriam and Hannah, at least I can warn you, Cliohna. Get rid of it!'

I knew he was right. I knew everything he had told me was true. But I also knew how Miriam had heard it call to her. I knew how she had knelt beside the body, her eyes searching, her hands sensing the air. How she had to possess it. How she wore it every day until she died. How she made me promise never to take it off.

And now it was mine.

Seventeen

I THOUGHT THE FLIGHT home would never end. Like some forsaken astronaut, I was doomed to circle the Earth forever. The cabin had become oppressively familiar. My armchair capsule existed in its own time—space continuum, divorced from a world where real things happen. Or perhaps they only seem real, or they only seem to happen. And all the while my hand moved to my neck, my fingers tracing the silver form of a bird, caressing the lines and curves.

I must pull my head together, I told myself. I needed to think clearly, evaluate everything objectively, examine the new facts and fit them into the overall picture. Then I'd decide upon a plan of action.

As if I could do that. As if it were that easy.

I kept seeing Harold. We had found each other and he said that was enough for him, he was content. I promised I would be back very soon. He held me tight until the last moment and his eyes were red. When I looked back, he was blowing his nose on a grubby handkerchief. I boarded the plane feeling wretched, trying to hold the breaking threads together as long as I could.

The engines droned on. How many hours do I have left? I

wondered. A film projector splashed colour on the screen in front of me, and two men with guns ran from each other in meaningless silence. I must work this thing out, try to understand what was happening before we landed and it started all over again. If I concentrated I could figure out a way through it.

The attendant brought supper. It was all set out on a tray, neatly divided into compartments, all the components of a feast neatly wrapped in transparent plastic and clearly labelled so one knew exactly how to handle them. But my situation wasn't like that. I tried laying all the pieces out in front of me, each in its appropriate slot, all hermetically sealed and emotionally sterile. And still no sense could be made of it. When the attendant returned, I found I'd opened all the little packets, tipped them out and shuffled them around. I handed her the tray, demolished and uneaten.

Already I was missing Harold. I resolved to call him as soon as I got home. Of course I never did. Other things intervened. I must speak to him now, perhaps today, when the sun comes up. I must tell him what has happened, or at least as much as can be told. At the very least I must let him know where I am now. But then, sitting there in the sky, the plane taking me further and further from him, I needed the substance and the safety of my grandfather, the solid strength of his hands.

I have to think, concentrate on what I *do* know, I whispered to myself. Above all I knew he had come to me and it was not against my will. Therefore, as long as I was capable of making choices, I would hold some responsibility for whatever happened. But how do you cope when a fantasy lands in your lap? Herewith, one unicorn, handle with care. Knowing my luck there would be no instructions. I wouldn't know how to feed it or what it was capable of. It could tear the universe inside out. I had to stop this nonsense. It was getting me nowhere.

Every moment, every hum and throb of the engine, was eating up the distance between us. That was the only thing that mattered, to be home. To step on creaking, wooden floors through shafts of dusty sunlight. To wipe mist from the window and see the orchard, the trees with moss on their bark and spider webs strung with silver rain. To feel him there, to know he was moving closer. To feel his breath among the loose strands of my hair, the strange webbing of skin between his fingers.

Oh God, his smile, I thought, I've forgotten his smile.

I'm in turmoil, scrambling among layers of memory, desperately grasping at images. No, he's there. I breathe again. He's in the kitchen, hunched on the counter-top, his fingers twirling the stem of a wineglass. His smile is lazy. It starts at the corner of his mouth, just a movement of the cheek and the crinkling of the corner of his eye. It spreads slowly and his lips part; the darkness of his face retreats like the shadow of a summer cloud chased across the meadows by the emerging sun. His teeth are small, not white but a pale ivory, and the edge of one tooth overlaps another. He's not perfect. I have him now. I can rest easy. But I'm not easy. There's heaviness inside me, a vast iron hollowness that engulfs my solar plexus. It's the space where he should be, where he will be if I can ever reach him again.

I had to see Hannah when I got back, spend some time with her, try to make things right between us. I'd tell her about Harold. Even if she didn't want to hear, I'd make her listen. I'd tell her about the box and the letters and about the photos in his wallet. I needed to make her understand that it wasn't his fault. Or Miriam's really. But someone had to take the blame for what they did to Hannah.

My hand was at my neck again, touching the silver. For a while I slept. I dreamed of the rushing of wings.

The plane landed at 10.30 in the morning, right on time, then spent an eternity manoeuvring on the airfield before it finally docked. I watched suitcases going round and round on the carousel.

Several times I abandoned hope of mine and turned to run to the exit. But it would do no good. They would only call me back, force me to wait.

Even though I had some priority, the line through Customs crawled. It was there I remembered Paul. He would be waiting for me, impatient, disapproving. He would moan about inadequate services and the lack of facilities for the public. I would have to endure the journey, the pointed questions, the begrudging acknowledgement of my survival. Perhaps I could get a taxi instead. No, that would take much longer. Paul was the quickest route home. Besides, he would be bound to see me. Unless he was late, unless he had forgotten. No, never, not Paul. He would see this through to the bitter end.

I stacked my belongings on a trolley and a steward directed me to the gate. There a tight crowd pressed forward, straining over the barrier, reaching out hands to loved ones, smiling, calling their names. Paul was not among them. Could he be waiting in the café area, expecting me to go to him? The wheel of my trolley squeaked over the tiled floor, echoing through the vast space.

Then, suddenly, there he was.

I saw him across the far side of the hall, a crowd of people between us. But I knew him. He stood with one foot raised and braced against the pillar on which he leaned, arms folded across his chest. The angle of his raised knee parted the folds in his long black coat and I saw he was wearing . . . yes . . . he was, and I laughed out loud. He was wearing red shoes! Bright red, glossy leather shoes. He couldn't have heard me, but he turned his head, very slowly, and frowned. And then he began to smile and the sun came out, just as I remembered.

I was running across the floor. Perhaps people were in my way, but if so I wasn't aware of them. I dropped my bag and papers; my luggage stood abandoned. He was there and I was drinking in the smell of damp moss, grasses crushed on a hot summer's day. I was wrapped in darkness, the embracing warmth of soft earth, a cavern in which to bury myself. His mouth was on my face, in my hair, whispering words, strange words I couldn't know the meaning of, yet I understood. His arms so tight around me I could scarcely breathe. After a long, long while he let me go and we were both laughing.

'So you decided to come back to me then? Has my Little Wren had enough of flying round the world?'

'I had to go. I had to find out . . .' I stumbled for words.

He was suddenly serious, and very tender. 'Yes, I know. It's all right. Shall we go home now?'

I nodded. 'Oh, my things, my suitcase.'

I stepped backwards across the floor, reluctant to leave him, thinking that if I turned my back he might disappear. But he didn't. He just watched me, smiling in wonderment, as if I were the most fascinating creature on earth. His eyes were softer than I remembered, gold tinged brown, like warm toffee. He continued to watch as I retrieved my bag from an amused airport official and struggled to lift my case off the trolley.

'Look, do you think you could . . .'

'What?' His expression changed to quizzical frown. Then realisation dawned. 'Oh, your luggage. You want me to help?'

'Yes, that would be nice.'

With the swiftness of a chameleon snatching a moth, he scooped up my belongings in one hand and took me in the other. We were heading for the short-stay car park.

'Do you like my shoes?'

'Yes, they're wonderful shoes.'

'I chose them in your honour. A fanfare of colour to welcome the return of the traveller.'

Then I remembered. 'Oh, what about Paul? He was supposed to meet me.'

Iolair turned and paused for a moment. 'Paul couldn't come.' He grinned at me, that mischievous schoolboy grin of wicked innocence. 'You didn't want to see him anyway, did you?'

'What do you mean, he couldn't come? How did you get here, then? And how are we going to get back?'

'It's all right. I brought your car.'

'I didn't know you could drive?'

'No, neither did I. Miriam would never let me try. She said that life was perilous enough as it is. I don't know what she was making all that fuss about. It's quite easy, really. Though we loved each other dearly, there were times when she displayed a distinct lack of trust in me.'

As if to justify himself, he pointed to Fifi, who appeared to be unscathed, although parked at an uncomfortable angle. The keys were still in the ignition. Iolair deposited my belongings on the back seat and then turned to hold me tightly again.

'You won't go away again, will you? You must never leave me.'

'No, I'll never leave you.'

'Until you have no choice.'

I knew he was thinking about Miriam.

He turned the engine and yanked the gear stick into reverse. I was still fumbling with my seat belt as the car jerked out backwards across the aisle. Then we were moving forward and down the slope towards the exit.

'Oh, just a minute. You need to pay. We have to go back and get the ticket stamped to let us out.'

Iolair turned to me and winked, urging the car towards the barrier. The red and white bar zoomed straight at us. I gasped and ducked, but it lifted lightly into the air and we slipped under it. Twisting around to watch it retreat, I didn't realise the lights were about to change at the junction. I turned in time to see a flash of red and the look of horror on a lorry driver's face.

'God, what are you doing?' I clung to the dashboard, shaking. For several moments I forgot to breathe. 'I think it might be better if you let me do the driving.'

'Nonsense. Do you think I can't do this?' He turned to me, reaching out to stroke my cheek with the back of his hand. 'You must not be afraid. You're with me. Nothing can hurt you now.'

'I'm trying to believe you.'

'Oh, but you must believe. Belief makes anything possible.' He grinned and his eyes shone with delight.

I could not help but laugh with him. Like a child on a bumper ride, he swung the car back and forth, jumping ahead of one car then another. Should I explain what the indicators were for? No, that would just complicate matters. Instead I held on in silence, my heart kicking against my ribs. Then we moved into a dense stream of traffic.

'Oh, this is no good. I want to show you what I am capable of.'

For once I was thankful the M25 was jammed. Whatever he did, at least he would have to do it slowly. There was stillness before he spoke again.

'I'm glad you decided to keep the cottage. I wouldn't want to go away from there.'

This came at me suddenly, taking me unawares. I had to think for a moment before I realised that it was his home, had been for a long, long time. There were many things from the past I would have to get used to.

'No, I won't part with it. I think I'm in love with it, too,' I said. 'Ever since that first time I went to see Miriam.'

'Ah, yes.' He smiled wistfully, as if remembering. 'But if you did want to go, if you really wanted to be somewhere else, that would be all right too. Anywhere in these islands. Whatever you wanted.'

'Was that how it was with Miriam? Whatever she wanted?'

I'm not sure if it was curiosity alone that prompted the question. Was it possible that I could be jealous?

'Yes, whatever she wanted. And whatever I wanted. We had to compromise sometimes. I didn't always win.'

'Is that where all that money came from? From you? Greg said she made good investments.'

'She liked to play the stock market. She wasn't very good at it, really, made some bad choices. I had to readjust things sometimes, that's all. It was just to please her.' He looked at me very seriously. 'We can always make some more money if you want. I'm quite a skilled financier now.'

'Oh, no. No thank you. I think I've got enough.'

'We can enjoy it, you know. There's so much we can do, Cliohna. So much I want to show you. Anything is possible. You understand that, don't you?'

'I think I'm beginning to understand.' Who was I fooling? Of course I understood nothing.

The car lurched forward and veered left on to a slip road.

'Ah, that's better, some space. Now I can show you some real driving.'

He turned the wheel and we joined the M11, sliding across to the outer lane amid a blaze of flashing headlights and blaring horns. Iolair responded by pushing his foot down hard and my little red car shook as the needle climbed up to ninety.

'There is a speed limit, you know!'

'Don't be silly, Cliohna. There are no limits.'

I clung on tightly, my feet braced against the floor, and found that I was laughing. He caught my hand in his. I was aware of the coolness of his fingers.

'I would never let anything, or anyone, harm you. I promise you that.' Then he looked back to the road again, sparkling with excitement. 'Come on, relax. This is going to be fun! I want you to enjoy it.'

The speedometer swung right over. Ahead of us a blue van loomed closer and closer. I clutched his shoulder and squealed as he lurched to the left and overtook on the middle lane.

'You can't do that! You can't overtake on the inside!'

He looked at me intensely and reproving. 'This is my game. My rules. Watch this.'

He moved into the outside lane where, ahead of us, a coach was trying to overtake two lorries. Children jostled and waved from the back seat as we sped towards it. There was nowhere to go. I braced myself against the headrest. The window bore down on us. I think I screamed. And then the road ahead was clear — the coach had gone. Vanished! No, there it was — a miniature reflection in the wing mirror, far behind us and still overtaking the lorries.

'What happened? How did you . . .'

'I'll show you. Watch closely. I'll go slower this time.'

Iolair gripped the wheel, heading for a red sports car. The driver was obviously determined to stay ahead of us. This time we drove straight through him — not around or under, but straight through. There was a whoosh of coldness and a blur of colour, like driving through a waterfall. Then we were ahead. I twisted around and caught the terrified eye of the young man at the wheel in his Armani suit. I couldn't resist giving him a wave.

It was a fairground ride, furious and terrifying. We overtook one of those space cruiser things, by driving through the crash barrier: the grey metal strips ran straight into Fifi's engine and down between the front seats. Then, suddenly, inexplicably we were bumping along the hard shoulder. It was like a film cut and rejoined in all the wrong places. We would be in one lane then, suddenly, we would be in another, or driving up the embankment. A dozen times he took us to the edge of destruction, turning the world around at the last second. Cars were coloured streaks that vanished in our wake. Iolair was electric, his nearness intoxicating. I was drunk on the danger and the outrage of it all.

Eventually it came to an end. Fifi spun onto a slip road and slowed to a modest seventy. Tears streamed from my eyes and my head swam. I don't know if I was relieved or dismayed that the journey was over. As my heart slowed to a steady pound, Iolair looked smug.

'I think we're nearly home,' he said.

He drove sedately through the village, demonstrating the skilled precision of a driving tutor conducting a master class.

It had been less only a week, but the landscape had changed. Most of the autumn colours had fallen. Bare branches threw lace netting against the sky and birds jostled for places along the telephone wires and made sudden, wheeling forays into the still air. The cottage looked bleak, the windows dark and the pathway blocked with heaps of wind-blown leaves. But the ivy was still green, intensely dark and lush, binding the walls against the winter. As we opened the front door there was a faint mustiness. The rooms were cold, but a fire would soon warm them. The stairs creaked in protest at our invading feet. Sunlight, still strong in the noonday, found its way through the upstairs windows to light the white bed covers and draw lattice diamonds on the walls.

Was it such a short time ago? I can count the hours, and yet it could have been in another lifetime. Perhaps it was. I still taste the salty sweetness of his skin; feel the coolness of his hands moulding the curve of my back. I touch the delicate nodes of his wrists and the shining sweep of the bone in his calf. His shoulder blades, white and angular, are the budding promise of wings. Long, velvet lashes brush my cheek, our faces secluded in darkness by his hair, let loose and falling around us. The only light is the amber glow of his eyes. I feel the tautness of his arms and the force of his hands and the lightness of his fingertips, soft as the brush of feathers. The beat of one wing follows upon another, then another. A rising, a lifting, a tender flight, borne aloft upon gentle air. I am carried against the sky, held on high amid the sudden rushing of hot winds and the piercing sweetness of sunlight. And still the throbbing of wing upon wing.

Yes, that is how I remember it.

And when it was over he spoke to me in that strange language, or perhaps it was to himself that he spoke. It didn't matter that I couldn't understand the words. The sounds were sweet notes, tender as a lullaby. I curled into the curve of his body listening to the murmuring of his voice until it was lost in deep waves of warm breath and I saw his eyes closing. His eyelids were the soft purple bloom of dusty grapes upon the vine.

'My Elven Lord,' I whispered. 'My Faerie King.'

For a while, as afternoon light crossed the floor, I lay and watched his stillness. Then I, too, drifted away. In that last moment, between waking and sleeping, I heard a sound. An earthly sound, it was, a sound from that other world of everyday. It had an urgency that would once have summoned my attention, but that was before everything changed.

Eighteen

I DIDN'T DREAM, yet some part of me was aware of the movement of time.

That sound again. It cut a jagged line through the hushed house. I woke instantly. The noise stopped as abruptly as it had started.

There had been no transition from sleeping to waking, no gentle amnesia to hold back the tidal wave of memory. I was fully aware of the man who slept beside me — that is, I was aware of his presence. I knew little of him, or of myself for that matter. I knew I was no longer a shadow-puppet, jerked on a stick against a two-dimensional backdrop: a flimsy paper cut-out thing of no consequence. I had been transmuted into a golden stranger by the alchemy of this child of air. We lay in our crucible bed, his arm heavy on my shoulder. I could feel his breath against my ear, like the familiar sighing of the sea echoed through a shell.

The room was moving towards darkness now, the walls washed in a softer, blue-grey light. I was surprised to find myself feeling both thirsty and ravenously hungry, then realised it must be hours since I had last had a meal. I rearranged his arm and slid gently from the bed. Wrapping something warm around my shoulders, I padded across the landing and down the darkened staircase, taking care to avoid the familiar pattern of creaking floorboards. I would surprise him with something to eat. Did he eat food? He certainly drank plenty. Anyway, I bet there was nothing in the house. Passing through the sitting room I glanced at the culprit, the cause of my rude awakening. The telephone crouched in the corner, the message recorder winking at me with its one red eye.

There was a sealed carton of orange juice in the fridge. I filled a glass and carried it through to the sitting room where I stood by the window looking out over the orchard. The sun had tipped below the horizon, embossing the sky with brash streaks of gold leaf against heavy, hanging curtains of dark purple. There was no rosy afterglow, no promise of a bright tomorrow.

From the corner of my eye I could see the little red light, insistent, demanding. It wouldn't be ignored. Perhaps if I let it run it would go away and leave me in peace. I pressed the button and returned to the window, sipping from my glass, the juice ice-cold and sharp in my mouth.

There was a stream of messages, most of them expected. I recognised Greg's voice, something about dividends. The orchard was almost bare now, the grass overlong and strewn with wind-fallen apples, brown where the wasps had gorged themselves. Then Hannah was speaking. I should have phoned her, let her know I had returned. I promised myself I would call her back. But not now. It occurred to me that I knew nothing about gardens and gardening. I wondered if Iolair would know. Doubtless he could make flowers grow in extraordinary, unexpected ways. I couldn't imagine him mowing the lawn. I became aware of Marcus's voice. He sounded excited: the little leather book I'd left with him, a translation, things I no longer needed to see or hear. All that was irrelevant now.

Then there was Angie's voice. *It's half past two now. Did you manage to get home all right?*

That must have been the call I had heard as I fell asleep. I wondered how long he would sleep for, if I should wake him.

Angie sounded agitated, unlike her. Was she saying something about Paul? The machine clicked off. A word hung in the air. *Injuries*, her voice had said.

'Injuries.'

Then silence closed in, smothering it. I wished the room would remain silent forever. There was something malevolent about that machine, the way it squatted in the corner, a fat little toad with a spiteful red eye. It wasn't to be believed, the malicious little liar. Ignore it. Dangerous even to touch the thing. I would have to force myself to cross the floor, make my hand press the button and rerun the last message; will myself not to listen.

Hello, Chloe? Angie here. It's half past two now. Did you manage to get home all right? They said at the airport they'd get a message to you. I've just got back from the hospital. You're not to worry, Paul's going to be fine. The injuries aren't too bad. Well, nothing that won't mend. They're going to keep him in for a few days. Call me soon as you get back, won't you? I'll be at home.

I knew.

Even before I rang Angie back, I knew what had happened. Oh, not the details of course, but I knew who was responsible and why. I was as much to blame. I should have asked, should have made him tell me where Paul was, why he hadn't come. Instead I just went along with it all, enjoying the ride. My hand shook as I lifted the receiver. She answered straight away.

'Chloe? Oh thank goodness. I've been ringing all afternoon, left messages all over the place. Where have you been?'

'I'm at the cottage. Fell asleep. I'm sorry. I didn't know.'

'You didn't get my message? Oh, no! The stupid woman. She promised. How did you get home?'

'Never mind that now. What's happened to Paul?'

'Look, you're not to worry, he'll be fine. There was an accident. It's not serious. Well, it is, I suppose, but he's going to be all right. I feel awful. It was my fault really. You know what I'm like with animals.'

'Angie, just slow down. How badly is he hurt?'

She drew a deep breath.

'One ankle's broken, the other badly sprained. Dislocated shoulder. Concussion. Cuts and bruises. There's a nasty gash on his head.'

'What was it? A road accident?'

'No, he fell.'

'Fell? OK, tell me exactly what happened. Start at the beginning.'

'Well, it was this morning when he came around to collect the car. I'd just got out of bed and put the kettle on. He was very early, so I said I'd make us a quick coffee before he left. Anyway, he followed me through to the kitchen and we were just standing there talking and there was this noise. Sort of scuffing and thumping. It seemed to be coming through the kitchen ceiling. At first I thought it was a burglar. I said we should call the police. Paul went outside and saw there was something on the roof and told to me to come and look. You won't believe this, but it was a bird! It was on the low part where the kitchen extension is, sort of hopping along the ridge trailing its wing. It was still fairly dark, but we could see it was enormous. I'd swear that it was six feet across. Obviously it had escaped from somewhere and got itself hurt. Well, I couldn't just leave it, could I?'

A heavy feeling, like a pool of lead, was growing in the pit of my stomach. The weight of it dragged me down into a chair.

'So what did you do?'

'Well, I told Paul to just keep an eye on it while I went back inside to ring Kevin. He's one of the practice vets, knows a lot about birds of prey. By the time I got back outside, Paul was already on the roof. I'd told him to wait, but you know what he's like— Oh, sorry.'

'Then what happened?'

'Well, he'd put the stepladder up against the guttering and climbed up. You know how steep the roof is there and the slates were all wet and slippery. I begged him to get down, but he wouldn't take any notice. He said the bird had broken its wing and he was going to try to hold onto it until Kevin got there. He insisted that the bird was tame and he could handle it.

'Then, all of a sudden it took off. Swooped down on him. I'd swear it went straight for him. Paul lost his balance and slid down the tiles. He managed to get his foot on the guttering and steady himself, and for a moment I thought he was OK. Then the bracket gave way and next thing he was on the ground. I did what I could, then called the ambulance. Fortunately it was quick — it turned up the same time as Kevin. All a bit chaotic.'

'And what happened to the bird?'

'The bird? Oh, I don't know. Flew off somewhere, I suppose. I went with Paul in the ambulance. They did no end of X-rays and tests. Took ages. They seemed to think the gash on his head was where the thing attacked him so they gave him tetanus jabs and stuff. Anyway, while that was going on I rang the airport to let you know you wouldn't be picked up. I didn't know what else I could do. I thought you'd get home somehow. Then I waited until they found him a bed. They said he's all right to have visitors. Just a moment, I'll get you the number of the ward. I've got it written down . . . Oh, yes, and there's more bad news. I'm afraid it's your car. When I got back from the hospital, well, it just wasn't there. I've rung the police and reported it. They said they'd send someone around, but that was a while ago now and—'

'It's all right Angie, I've got Fifi.'

'*You've* got it? But how? I mean . . . Oh hell, Chloe, you could have let me know.'

'Look, I'm sorry, I can't explain now. Tell the police it's a mistake. I've got to go.'

'Hang on, you'll need to know which ward—'

But the receiver was down and I was back at the window. The orchard was in darkness now. The branches creaked, shadows moving upon shadows. There had been no message. He hadn't exactly lied to me. Would he know it was a lie? Did he even know what a lie was?

The machine reran the message from Marcus. I listened to it twice through, then lifted the receiver off the hook and laid it down beside the phone. I don't know how long I stood there or what I was thinking. I wasn't even consciously aware of making a decision. I trod each stair as gently as I could, not daring to wake him. I could see his outline against the whiteness of the sheet and I wanted to cry. I wanted to go to him, to curl up in his warmth. If he spoke to me, if he touched me, then I knew I would stay with him and I would never know.

Snatching some clothes and shoes, whatever came to hand, I crept from the room, and dressed downstairs in the dark. If I moved quickly I would be back before he even realised I had gone. My handbag was lying on the hall floor where it had fallen when we came in. The car keys were still in the ignition. I must speak to him about that, I thought. I kept the revs down as I pulled away, praying the noise did not disturb his sleep.

God, was I so naïve as to believe he hadn't heard every word?

The doorbell echoed through the house. A hollow sound, then silence. The hallway was in darkness. They must be out. I was about to press it again when a light sprang up through the stained glass panel.

'Oh, Chloe! Heavens, child, come in, come in. Janet, it's Chloe!'

'I'm sorry. I should have rung. I hope it's not a bad time. If you're busy . . .'

'No, no. Not at all. You know you're always welcome. You got my message then? Good, good. We weren't sure exactly when you'd be back. Look dear, look who it is!'

Janet appeared, fumbling for her glasses. She held her arms out and I felt an urge to rush into them. I needed someone to cry onto. Instead I gave her a formal peck on the cheek.

'Now, would you like some tea or coffee, dear?'

'Would you think it awful if I asked for something stronger? A scotch perhaps?'

'Of course not. Rough journey, was it? Have you eaten?'

'No, but please I don't want to be a bother. It's bad enough me turning up unannounced like this.'

'Not at all. Marcus has been like a cat on hot bricks for two days now, waiting to talk to you. Come through to the kitchen — I'll make you a sandwich.'

I sat at the kitchen table while Marcus poured us all a drink and Janet stripped the remains of their lunchtime chicken. There was a large brown envelope in the centre of the table. Marcus pulled it towards him, holding it in both hands.

'So, how was your journey? I want to hear all about it. And what about Miriam's husband? Did you find him?'

Janet laid a plate in front of me and I felt obliged to take a bite for the sake of politeness.

It was the first time I'd actually spoken to anyone about Harold. It brought him back to life. Janet asked the questions. Marcus listened. He sat on the edge of his chair, his knees pressed close together, fingers running along the sharp edge of the package. I told them about the countryside and the lodge and the lake and Harold's woolly hat. I talked and bit into the bread, then talked with my mouth full. I told them about the pick-up truck and the fishing and the way he fell asleep all the time. I wanted to be with him so much it hurt. And I wanted to get it said so that we could talk about other things. My eyes were on the envelope. There was nothing written on it. It gave nothing away.

'There, I knew you'd be hungry.'

The plate was empty. It took a moment to figure out where the food had gone.

Marcus coughed a little and fidgeted.

'You said on the phone that you had something to show me. A translation.'

'Yes, that's right.' He settled his glasses on the bridge of his nose. 'I have a connection at Oxford, George Benson, professorship in ancient languages. I doubt you'd know of him. He and Miriam met only a few times. Anyway, I rang him the morning after you came around, and he invited us down for a couple of days.'

'Oh, I didn't mean you to go to so much trouble.'

'It was no trouble, I assure you. He lives in Brighton and we welcomed the excuse for an unexpected holiday. Besides I was intrigued, and so was George, as it transpired. Obviously, from the way it was presented in its own binding, it had to be something special. As I anticipated, it didn't prove too difficult for him. The actual handwriting is Miriam's, of course, therefore modern and clearly written. George said that was half the battle, so to speak.'

He opened the envelope, drew out the little brown leather book and passed it to me. I held it with fearful reverence, as if it were a time-bomb about to explode in my face.

'What is it? A story?'

'It appears to be something written for you. Yes, he said there was a story in it, one with an unusual theme. He'd never come across anything like it before. But it's interspersed between a personal message. I have to confess that temptation overcame me and I asked him to let me take a quick peek at the passages concerned with the folk tale. I hope you'll forgive me.'

'On the phone you said something about the pendant.'

'Yes. Now, that was the really extraordinary thing. You'd asked me about it, hadn't you, that very evening? I told you, didn't I, Janet, how we'd looked at it?'

'That's right, dear. I remember because I noticed myself that you were wearing it, Chloe, and I was going to ask you about it. And that was really strange, because for years I'd admired it on Miriam but always forgot to mention it. And there I was doing the same with you.'

'Marcus said it's an eagle: Iolair. That's right, isn't it? How does that connect with the story?'

'Here, you must read it for yourself. But I should warn you, George said that the whole thing is rather . . . Well, to be blunt, he said Miriam may have been becoming a little confused towards the end. She may have lost the boundaries between myth and reality. I don't know. I haven't read all of it: it was obviously intended for you. You'll have to judge for yourself.'

He pulled out a folded wad of creamy paper, several sheets thick, and smoothed it flat on the table. He was almost bubbling as he handed it to me. The centres of the pages were covered with a neat handwriting in clear blue ink. A wide margin on all sides was dotted with reference notes and remarks, alternative translations and general comments, all in red and green, which I supposed held some significance for George Benson. It was the central text that filled my attention. I read the first line:

IN TIMES LONG PAST, before the dark shadows were cast along the borders of the worlds, the realms of Faerie and of Erin were but a footstep apart . . .

This was it. This was the key, I knew it. I was suddenly conscious of Marcus and Janet watching me, smiling and eager.

'I'm sorry, you must think me very silly, but I think I need to read this on my own.'

Marcus looked confused and disappointed.

Janet stood up. 'Of course you do, my dear.' She patted her husband's shoulder and spoke in a loud, theatrical whisper. 'It's her grandmother's. With her so recently . . . naturally she wants to be alone with it.'

'Yes, you're right, of course. I'm sorry, Chloe. I wasn't thinking. I was so excited about the document that I forgot— I mean—'

'Why don't you take her down to your study? It's quiet down there.'

We descended into the darkness. Marcus snapped on the desk

lamp, creating a pool of light against the shadowed corners. As I sat down, he backed away, fumbling with the buttons on his cardigan.

'Just call out if you need anything.'

Then I was alone, although I still felt as if there were eyes watching me from the hidden corners of the room. My hands were trembling. I laid the pages out on the desk and began to read. I have the book and the translation with me now, but, even without looking, I can remember most of it word for word.

Nineteen

IN TIMES LONG PAST, before the dark shadows were cast along the borders of the worlds, the realms of Faerie and of Erin were but a footstep apart. The immortals dwelt alongside the sons of men, and each was known to the other. Greatest of the Faerie were the Elven people, for they were a mighty race who towered above humans in stature, strength and knowledge. Despite the many blessings bestowed by those magical beings, the bonding of friendship between our kind and theirs was never easy. For they were different in their ways, inconstant and capricious, and men would forever look to them with caution, even fear.

These are the words that opened my first published book. They are also the words I will use for my last book. This one I write for you. It may be shorter than my other works, a few pages, that is all, but I believe they are the most important words I will have written. And it is for you, Cliohna, you alone. If everything has happened as I plan, it will find its way into your hands. So read these words as if I were speaking to you from the other side of the veil.

I have lived an enchanted life. Oh, that sounds such a cliché, but for me it is a simple truth. Some things you will have discovered by now. There will be more, so very much more, and it is all a gift for you.

By now I will be buried and he will have made himself known to you. At first he will have asked for the talisman and you will have resisted. Very quickly he will have lost interest in it. He will have shown you something of his nature, and others will have told you about the past. You will have drawn your own conclusions. Trust your intuition: it is your best counsellor. There is a little more you need to know, and that I will tell you now. I had better begin in Ireland. Or maybe even before then.

I have always known there was more happening around me than my mortal senses allowed for. My mother used to say I was a little 'fey', that I was somehow in tune with another world. It is true I have always had an instinct for things. She said things always fell into my lap. Not exactly second sight, but often I could feel when something was about to happen, which path to choose, which move to make. Not always, though. There were heartaches. You were one of them.

I think by now you will have found Harold, and, if he has heeded my letter, he will have told you everything as I asked. He is a good man, much better than I, and stronger too. I think he will outlive me by a few years. And I did love him once, although it is only a memory now, a passion that evaporated like mist clearing when the sun comes out. And there was my child, Hannah. And we were all happy together in our little house in Boston. Except that there was always something else tugging at the edge of my mind, drawing me away. As if there were something I had lost before I had even found it.

It was not until the letter came with the offer of Ireland that I knew that I had been born in the wrong country. I would have bullied poor Harold into it, but he was already as excited as I was. He had always dreamed of going back to Europe, and when they said Ireland and three years there was no holding him. It was a magical place and a place of magic. The very air sang with it. Harold, naturally, threw himself into his work and I tried to help as best I could while making a home for us all and looking after little Hannah.

The people fascinated me with their strange mixture of religion and folklore. They worshipped the Earth Goddess, of course, only they called her Mary. I started listening to the stories. It was like I was looking for something, even though I knew not what. I became absorbed with the legends, the ancient kings and their tribes, the people who had lived, or those they believed had lived. And then there were the other beings, those who were not mortal, and how the two existed in harmony or in conflict.

Whoever I talked with knew something, a scrap of another tale, or the same tale with a variation: stories within stories. A different history from the one Harold collected, but I thought mine was better; at least mine was still alive. Yes, I started to collect the stories and I had some plan of putting them together, maybe having them published. Harold didn't seem to mind. He was full of his own research. Much of the time he was at the university, and when the weather allowed there were days on end spent at the digs.

I used my time going from one croft to another, or travelling between the villages, seeking out the old ones who remembered what their grandparents had told them. Often I suspected they had made it up, eager for the few pennies I made them take, but if you could have seen how they lived you would not have begrudged them either. But occasionally they had something worthwhile to tell me. And I knew that time was running out, you see. Soon the modern world would find its way there and the ancient voices of the bards would not be heard above the scorn of the young people and their transistor radios.

I used to take Hannah with me when she was not at school. I thought it might stimulate her imagination. She was always such a serious child, so pragmatic, as if she were too old for her years, not from wisdom, but from lack of frivolity. I was the frivolous one. I would tell her that we had come home, this was the land of our birthright; the blood of ancient kings ran in our veins. And I know that is true for me and for you, Cliohna, and blood will out, as they say. But occasionally it skips over a generation.

Poor Hannah. She was always small and frail-looking. But she began to thrive in that clean air, and she ran free as a bird, at least at first, though she was always an awkward child, closed in on herself, her little face pale and pinched. She seemed resentful of me. I did my best to be a good mother to her, yet nothing I did was ever right. I hoped she would make friends with the other children, but she would always shy away from them. I don't know why. I could see she wasn't happy. Perhaps Harold should have taken her with him. But then there would not have been you, my Cliohna, my Little Wren.

So, one day I went to visit a woman who lived on the edge of the next village. She and her grandmother wove shawls on an ancient loom, then sold them to a buyer from London. It earned a few coppers to eke out her husband's pittance. I had an idea how much those shawls sold for in Bond Street shops, so I always made sure they were paid something for their stories, not that I could afford much. I suppose I felt guilty about how they were exploited without me taking their time and their trouble too.

Anyway, I had called later than usual and the woman was busy preparing the evening meal when I arrived, so it was her grandmother I talked with. The younger one looked haggard, so God knows how long the old woman had lived. She sat in the inglenook, urging life into the fire with a charred stick. The peat was damp and smoked the room out, and her skin was dried and cracked like yellowed paper, as if from years of tending the hearth.

She spoke the name Eriu and I held my breath.

Eriu was one of the daughters of MacGrene, a legendary chieftain, and her name is woven into the fabric of many tales. And of course I knew of the goddess Dana and the Tuatha de Danaan, the Children of Dana. But I had never heard this version before. This is what I wrote down that afternoon.

It was during the fourth age, when the Children of the goddess Dana had grown strong upon the land. Many gathered about MacGrene, being one of the three brother kings who ruled over Erin and chief of a powerful clan. And MacGrene took to him a wife whose name was Eriu and she bore him two fine sons, Elwyn and Fahran, who grew to be great warriors and leaders of their people. Then she bore him a daughter, who was also named Eriu for her mother.

The young Eriu grew to be exceedingly fair. Small and sprightly she was, like a dainty bird, though she was headstrong and defiant. For this reason she was often named the king's Little Wren. There were many who sought to claim her in marriage but she would have none of them. Her father and brothers could have no sway with her, being in fear of the power of her immortal lover. For she had come to love an Elven Lord, and he, in turn, bestowed his love upon her.

It was the names, you see — Eriu and Elwyn and Fahran — it was as if they had awakened something inside me, some long-lost memory. I knew I had to find out more.

The shawl-makers lived in the last house of the village, set a little apart from the others, on an unmade roadway that tapered, coiling around itself, as it fought its way around rocky outcrops. Not high enough to be called mountainous, the terrain was nevertheless not easy and few used that path even though it led over the crest and down into the next village. Less exhausting, they said, choosing to go the long way around, but that was more to cover their fear.

The professors believed that there had been a ring fort on the higher ground. They started excavating the area, much to the disapproval of the villagers, who, nevertheless, continued to make us welcome and fed us on tea and scones with lavish helpings of dire consequences should 'the lady' be disturbed.

The villagers said the hillside was full of ghosts: they believed that their ancestors walked the rocky passes. There were tales of a hard battle and many dead; their bones frequently turned up when fresh fields were ploughed for planting. There were stories of a noble girl named Eriu, who was buried there somewhere, although no one was sure exactly where. Eriu is not an uncommon name in their history, but this was a local legend, and now, from the old woman, I had found more pieces of her story and was determined to put them into place.

When they found the tomb, Harold came home full of excitement. How old was it? Would there be artefacts? Human remains? Naturally, there was academic argument and speculation, especially as there were some things about it that did not fit into the expected pattern.

But I had already been told the secret of who it was, and I felt dizzy with the knowledge, although I said nothing to Harold and his academics. You see, a few days before I had returned to the shawl-makers and the old woman had told me more about 'the lady'. This time I had the impression she was expecting me, and her granddaughter left almost as soon as I arrived, as if by prior arrangement.

'So you want to know more about her, do you?' the old lady said.

'Yes, that's right. I was told there is a woman buried somewhere near here. Is it the same one? Is it Eriu?'

'Well, who's to say? I only know what I was told when I was a girl. I'll try to remember, if you wish to listen, that is.'

'Yes, please go on,' I begged her. And she told me. This is what I wrote down afterwards.

Eriu was not content. For, although she loved her Faerie Lord dearly, she knew his adoration of her was but a passing diversion. No mortal woman could ever truly win the heart of one of his race. Eriu feared that he would soon grow tired of her.

Determined not to lose him, she sought the counsel of the Filidh, one by name Ruad Ro Faessa, meaning Lord of Surpassing Knowledge, he being the sorcerer of her tribe and skilful in the magical arts. Eriu came to him in innocence, not knowing he was both jealous and fearful of the Elven Kings who had scorned his human sorcery. He saw here a chance to avenge himself. Feigning naught but concern for her distress, Ruad Ro Faessa persuaded Eriu that he knew of a way to bind her lover to her for all time.

'First,' he said, 'you must discover the nature of his name. For, although the Elven language cannot be spoken by human tongue, his name would have some meaning that you can comprehend. Then you must, without his knowledge, take from him some possession, some object that he keeps about him and which is made of the silver that is mined beneath the mountains of his homeland. This you must bring to me.'

And so, when next she and her lover lay together, she fed him upon honey wine until he became intoxicated and his thoughts confused. She asked him his true name, and at first he laughed and said that she had not the voice to speak it. But she so coaxed him and cajoled him and teased his befuddled mind that, at last, he agreed that he would show her.

He broke a branch from a hazel tree and fashioned it into a wand and took it to the water's edge. The moon was well risen, and where its silver light mirrored the water he reached out and drew the wand across the surface. When she looked into the lake, Eriu saw within it the form of a great bird, an eagle.

Then, as dawn came and he rose to leave her, and as he held her in a final embrace, she slid from his scabbard a short dagger. The hilt was carved from blue crystal, but the blade was of the Elven silver, which would never tarnish nor wear away. When the sun had risen, she returned to Ruad Ro Faessa, who told her she had done well.

The Filidh set to work. First he calculated the days and the seasons and the rise and fall of the planets. Then, when the waxing moon was past its first quarter, he kindled a furnace among the rocks in which to melt the blade. Uttering spells and incantations and drawing secret signs upon the air, he reshaped the strange metal into the form of an eagle. And lastly, in a circle of oak trees, and amid the heady smoke of incense, he fastened the talisman around Eriu's neck.

'Wear this always and his love for you will never falter,' he commanded her. 'For unless you choose to return this talisman to him of your own will, his heart is forever bound by my enchantment.'

Of course it was just an old tale, one that had become more fanciful with every telling. Woven through it, as always, were elements of other stories I had gathered, but an interesting variation nonetheless. And that was all I knew when they opened the tomb.

All morning I waited, counting the minutes until I was allowed to join the men at the site. When the sun reached its height, I started out, walking the main road that skirted the hill. A pleasant walk on any other day, but that day my whole body felt alive with eagerness. It was as if she were calling to me, impatient for what would come.

I knew, when I set foot over the threshold, that I had crossed a line in time and that I could never be the same. As I walked down that tunnel between the stone-slab walls, I could feel her all around me, as close as her breath on my skin. The lamplight pierced the darkness, and there she was.

I asked questions, but I already knew the answers. I knew the name of the tight little body bound beneath the shroud. I knew how her hair twisted into curls the colour of copper and rusted iron. Harold showed me how she had died with the fall of the axe and the blood that stained her winding sheet. I could sense the haste in which she had been hidden. But why? Why had they hidden her?

And then I saw it. A glint of silver, the only bright thing in that dark grave. It screamed at me as if it had a voice of its own and it were pleading for its salvation. I knew why I was there: it was because she wanted me to have it. My hand was pulled towards her. Harold probably tried to stop me, but if he shouted or swore, I did not hear him. All I knew was my hand closing around the silver light, and if I had had to pass my fist through white-hot fire to reach it I would have taken it just the same.

And then I was running. I saw no one, heard nothing. There was only me and Eriu and what I held in my hand. I locked and bolted the door, looking desperately for some way to keep it safe. Then I knew it was simple. All I had to do was to put it on, to wear it around my own neck, and we would all be safe. So that's what I did.

Naturally Harold was furious. We argued for days: in fact we never stopped arguing about it. I only half heard him. He must have told you the rest.

I went back to the old woman of course, very soon after. The talisman lay hidden beneath my clothes, but she knew. She poked the damp peat with her stick until sparks rose like a bonfire on a frosty night.

'So you found her, did you? Well, she was never at rest. Perhaps now she can sleep, now that you have taken the burden from her.'

'What do you mean?' I asked.

She told me more of the story — not all of it, but enough.

And thus the Elf was bewitched, and Eriu had bound his heart to hers all the days of her life. They both found great joy in each other and their life together. So enamoured was he of his lady that he would see her neither age nor change with time. He did not mourn the loss of his freedom, for the span of a mortal lifetime is but the passing of a season to one of his kind.

He still moved between the worlds and would journey to be among his kindred. But always he would return swiftly, for he could not bear to be parted from his Eriu. Furthermore, he could never be completely free of the mortal lands until she released him, as she had sworn to do, when her own life neared its end.

But alas, a great tragedy was to befall Eriu and her clan. Despite treaties and agreements negotiated by their father, her brothers could not maintain peace with the neighbouring tribes. Being proud and hot-headed they had, by some act of impulse, offended their former enemies. In retaliation, a raiding party was sent to attack their village.

They came at dawn, rising out of the mist and taking the tribesmen unawares. Elwyn and Fahran were quick to rally their men. After a long and bloody fight, they forced the raiders to flee, driving them back across the borders into their own territory.

The brothers and their men returned in triumph, but their joy was short-lived. For they found their village blackened with smoke, and the sweet meadow around their stockade strewn with the bodies of their dead. Worst of all, they found their beloved sister lying upon the battlefield, her body soaked in her own blood and that of her kinsmen.

For this they were heartbroken, but also mightily afraid. They knew that the Elven Lord would soon return seeking his lady. Fearing to bring the wrath of the Sidhe down upon the survivors of their clan, they hastily entombed her body and sealed the chamber. She still wore the robes she had died in and the talisman was about her neck.

'So, what happened to him?' I asked her.

'Have patience. You may come back here once more, but not yet a while, you will know when. For now, let our lady rest in peace.'

It was after that that I began to see him. It was in a little wood near where we lived. I thought at first I had caught sight of a bird, an eagle. Then he was there. It was as if he came from nowhere, stepping out from behind a sapling that was no thicker than my arm. At first he asked about the talisman, but I held it fast.

After that I saw him often, but did not make the connection. It was too easy to make rational excuses. But then there were things that happened, things about him that I could not continue to ignore. You will know all about that by now.

Harold left and I remained in Ireland. We were together.

I said I have had an enchanted life, and that is literally true. He showed me things, wonderful things, took me to places where mortals never go. And he told me stories and how to read the languages they were written in. With his aid I learned Gaelic in one night. I dreamed I was reading it from a book and I woke with the letters and the language in my head. He told me things about the history and the land, how they came about and where things would be found. I started to write down more of the stories, and my books were published.

It was not long before he grew impatient. Not with me, you understand, but with the life there. He listened to the radio and then he wanted a television set, which he watched for hours. He found that the world had changed and Ireland had not. He wanted to see more. So we made the journey to England. It was painful for him, but he was determined. I told myself it was for Hannah: she was unhappy in Ireland, and besides it was no place for a teenager. But that was a lie to myself. It was for him that we came to the fenlands and the cottage, and later, after Hannah had left home, we travelled Europe. By that time there was plenty of money to play with and we chartered a small aircraft to cross the Channel at the narrowest point.

He was like a child in a toy room. As you will learn, he loves wine and good food, the theatre and the arts. He also loves gambling, but always cheats. He was shocked by the level of technology, communication, jet planes, computer technology. No wonder people ceased to believe in our magic, he would say, they have enough magic of their own now. But that never stopped him from showing off with his.

Mine has been a strange life, but I would not change one day of it. My only regret is that I could not love Hannah the way I love you. She is my blood and bone, but there is none of my spirit in her to bind us. Eventually she married and David was born. And then you came.

He saw it straight away: the green eyes, the red hair. Our Little Wren, we called you. Though I must tell you that there were times when he seemed confused, as if the threads between him and his Eriu were not completely broken, and that she and I were one and the same. When he saw you, it was as if he had found her all over again.

And when I thought I had lost you, that Hannah had taken you from me, I vowed that you would take my place. I swore that I would make it up to you, Cliohna, and I will.

I have.

There is one more thing you must know.

Before we left Ireland, I went back to the old woman for the last time. What she told me that day I must tell you now. She still sat by the fire, and I wondered if she ever moved from there. Perhaps she would die if she let the fire go out. She did not look up when I came in. I thought she had not heard me, but she said, 'So, you understand now, do you?'

I nodded and there was silence between us. Only the fire crackled and, somewhere outside the window, a raven called to its mate.

'You said you had more to tell me. What happened to him when she died?'

She turned and looked at me for the first time. Her eyes were covered with the milky white of cataracts, yet I swear she saw right through me.

This is what she told me that day.

Hardly had the stones been set over the entrance when the Elf returned and discovered the death of his love. He had not known that life could hold such pain. In his grief he smote the trees and tore their roots from the earth and caused the rocks to split asunder. No creature would dare come nigh to give him comfort.

But that was only the beginning of his torment. For he had also lost the talisman, which Eriu could never now return to him. Even had he opened her grave and taken it from her body, the spell could not be broken. Only if it were returned to him freely would he be released.

Now the full force of Ruad Ro Faessa's curse fell upon him. Unable to dwell in this world, yet unable to return to his own, he is doomed to wander the Shadowlands forever. He knows neither day nor night, neither the comfort of another's voice nor the touch of a hand. He marks not the passage of time, yet every moment is, for him, eternal. Thus he has remained down the years and the centuries, grieving for the loss of his love who can never return to release him.

Despairing of finding salvation, his only hope is for the final peace that lies in oblivion.

'Only if it were returned to him freely would he be released.'

I have often wondered what I would have done if I had known all this when I entered that tomb. Would I have acted differently? But by then the spell was upon me also, and there was no turning back. I could never let him go. He was my life.

And now, my dearest granddaughter, I commend him to your love and care, and you to his.

I reached the last word on the last page and continued to stare at the inky trails swimming in front of my eyes. I was aware of the silence in the room and, beyond, the murmuring of voices from a distant part of the house. No doubt they were waiting for me, expecting me to share their innocent pleasure.

But I was far away in that antiseptic room with its unremitting light. Miriam lay against harsh, white sheets. I could feel her hand tight around my wrist, her nails biting into my skin.

Never take it off, she pleaded. *Never give it away. Promise me.*

I don't know how long I sat there, held tightly in my own arms, rocking myself back and forth, and whispering the same words over and over again. 'Oh, Miriam, Miriam. What have you made me do?'

Twenty

I FOUND MY WAY back to the village. By then it must have been nearly midnight. As I approached the cottage I heard music. It was that same tune, that sweet lament that Miriam loved so much. It reached out, gathering me into its shimmering web. Each note hovered above me, clear and pure, a single droplet hung upon the night air, living for a moment then turning to vapour as its successor was born. I don't know how long I listened. I could have waited there forever in the stillness, flecks of dew gathering on my hair. But, of course, he would know I had returned and there were so many things that we needed to say. A warm glow of light at the window beckoned to me, and, as I opened the door, the music billowed and fluttered around me, carrying me towards him.

I found him seated in the centre of the dining table, cross-legged, his bare feet long and graceful. Flames skipped over logs in the hearth, casting a red glow on the white plaster walls, like sunset staining undefiled snow. He leaned forward, his head slightly angled and his lips drawn tight as he blew across a flute, its dark, wooden curves as warm and mellow in the firelight as the notes that tumbled around it. I stood before him, waiting. He raised his eyes to welcome me, but continued playing until the tune had ended. Then he laid the instrument down.

'So, now you know everything.'

I didn't move. I tried to smile, to keep things light. He smiled in return.

'I know some of it. That was a fine chase you led me. Halfway around the world and back again. Why couldn't you have told me?'

'Oh, yes? And you, of course, would have believed me, wouldn't you?'

I faltered. He stretched his hand out towards me and still I could not move.

'I don't know,' I said. 'I don't know what I believe any more.'

He shook his head. His hair fell loose each side of his face, black as raven wings. The firelight turned his eyes to molten amber. I had never thought of beauty in a man before, but he was beautiful. One day, I thought, I will paint you like this.

Aloud I said, 'All that time, all those years. How could you bear it?'

'I knew you would find me. I knew that if I waited you would come for me. You always do.'

'What do you mean, I always come for you?'

He looked away, turning toward the fire. 'That's how it has always been. I knew you straight away, even when you were newly born. You knew I was there, you could see me. You smiled and lifted your arms to me as if you would have me lift you up. I was almost afraid to touch you, so small and fragile you were with your bright hair. Like a tiny bird.'

'Like a wren you mean, like the king's Little Wren?' I felt as if something had entered me, a cold, white hand, clutching deep inside where I could not resist it.

'Yes, like a little wren. But I knew you. I could see her in your eyes.'

'Who? Who did you see?'

'You came back for me. You saved me.'

The cold hand squeezed tighter. 'It was Miriam who saved you. She brought you back.'

'Yes, that's right. Miriam. She called me back. There was nothingness. Endless and forever. No beginning, no ending. On and on and never moving. And then I sensed something, like the faintest breath of wind touching my mind. It became stronger, firmer. A feather-light sound, as if she were calling me from far, far way. Then there were colours and taste and smells and light. And it was her, Miriam. And she was so bright and clear. I had thought never to see those green eyes again. But there she was and we were together again.'

'No, surely . . . you were mistaken. Miriam wasn't the same as . . .'

He looked at me, but there was confusion in his face. His mouth moved, as if he were struggling with the words. 'Of, course it was her. She was mine again. Do you think I would not know her?'

There was no point in pursuing this; he was beyond logic and reason. I tried another path, my voice still gentle. 'Miriam had a husband. And a daughter. She cared about them.'

'No, we cared for each other. It was as it always was, as it always will be.'

We fell silent. Logs cracked and fell in the hearth. The icy hand lay heavy, as if something inside me were dying. I moved around the table to the bookcase, to the row of green leather covers embossed with silver, her name, her work.

'You taught her to write, didn't you? As you showed me how to paint?'

'There were so many memories of my people and hers. I unfolded the past for her, opened up the gift of seeing and telling.'

I stood almost behind him now. 'And then you both left Ireland.'

He tossed his hair and looked at me over his shoulder. 'Oh, everything was new. It was amazing how the world had changed in that time. As if the whole human race had learned the secrets of magic. So many things I would never have dreamt of — electricity, music and pictures travelling through the air . . .'

'And fast cars?'

That made him laugh. It rekindled some of the sparkle there had been earlier, and we both laughed longer than was justified.

'But somehow Ireland itself had not changed. There was talk of these new wonders, but often it was with frowns and whispers as if they were afraid to let the new world in. I wanted to see it all. And, of course, Miriam's name was known. Demands were being made on her to visit places, talk to people.'

'So you made the journey.'

'Yes. It was painful but swift. As you see, I survived.'

I walked around to face him again. 'And Hannah. What about Hannah?'

'What about Hannah? She was nothing to me. A very strange child. I never could understand her. I don't think her mother understood her either. Her . . . essence . . . it was so different from Miriam's. She had no sense of mystery. But the girl had strength and self-discipline, I suppose. She was given the space and freedom to be herself. I think Miriam was relieved when she went her own way.'

'Didn't the pair of you know how unhappy you had made her? Didn't you care? And what about David and me?'

'Ah, with you it was different. We leaned over your cradle and you smiled at me and I knew you. I thought I'd lost you when those men took you away to that evil place.'

'What evil place? You mean when they put her in the tomb?'

He shook his head, frowning as if he were grasping at something half-seen. 'No. It was an ambulance. You were so ill and there was nothing I could do to make you better. They took you away from me.'

'It was Miriam they took away. Miriam! It wasn't me.'

He looked up and tried to smile. There were tears in his eyes.

I struggled to hold my voice steady, to move so carefully. 'Do you know how badly you hurt Paul?'

'Not nearly as badly as you hurt each other. At least the injuries I inflicted will heal.'

'Don't you know you could have killed him?'

'But I didn't. Besides, all that doesn't matter now. You are here. We have each other.' He held his arms wide, his hands open, submitting, surrendering. 'And I love you.'

'No. No, I don't think you do.' It was at that moment I knew I loved him. It was the heart-tearing love a mother feels for her broken child, the brittle, biting love born of pity. 'It's all an illusion,' I said. 'Can't you see that? Whatever it is that you're feeling, it's not real. I don't think you even know who I am.' Hot tears swam in my eyes, cruel prisms that split the firelight and filled the room with flashes of red and gold.

'Of course it's not real,' his voice rose in anger. 'And do you think your mortal love is more real than this? Do you think any love is more than illusion?' His hands were gripping his thighs, digging into flesh. 'Do you know what human love is? It's a ragbag of hopeless wants and needs that you tie into a bundle and throw at anyone you think might wear it for you. And if you're lucky they'll do the same to you. Then you cling to each other out of loneliness and desperation until one of you changes so much that you can no longer bear the pretence. So you strip off your disguise, show who you really are, and the whole damned game is blown to pieces. Isn't that what your love is?'

'No. It wasn't like that.'

It was a feeble protest. It *had* been like that. Exactly like that.

'Is that the reality you want from me, Cliohna?' There was no way I could answer him. He softened, moving towards me. 'I will never pretend to be anything other than I am. I will love you whatever you are, whatever you might become. I will always love you. I cannot do anything *but* love you. No one else can give you that.'

'But you have no choice.'

'Does any lover have a choice?'

'Can't you understand? It makes you my prisoner.'

'Is not everyone a prisoner of something? Is it not the very nature of humanity to give away your freedom? We will make it our gift to each other.' He held out his hands to me again. 'Trust me. It will be all right between us.'

I knew that every moment of my life had brought me to that time and place. Every thought that I had ever known was held within the silence of that room. His hands were so close to mine. I felt his breath stir the air between us. But for all that I dared to touch him, he might well be on the far side of the moon.

I turned away. 'I need some time. Please, can you leave me for a while?'

'Leave you?'

'Yes, go . . . Wherever it is you go to when you're not here. Just for a while. I have to think. Please.'

He sighed.

'Please?'

'If that's what you truly want.'

'Yes, it's what I truly want.'

'Very well, then. Just for a while?'

'Yes, just for a little while.' I wiped the stinging wetness from my eyes, and when I looked up again he had gone. The wooden flute lay on the table, rolling gently from side to side.

I shivered. Despite the heat of the fire, the room felt suddenly cold. Crossing to the fireside I curled into Miriam's chair and wrapped my coat over me like a blanket. I did try to think, but there was too much to think about and my head was aching. All I could do was watch the flames split the blackened logs apart and open the red-hot heart of the wood. Warmth stole up my body and I gave way to the comfort of insensibility.

I was in an empty place, a barren place, cold and desolate. Heavy clouds hung over black mountains against a charcoal sky, shadows upon shadows upon shadows, until there was no discernment. I stumbled over cold rocks whose knifed edges cut my bare feet. Leaden pools of water barred my way at every turn.

At the edge of one of the pools I knelt and bent over the water. A sallow moon shed no light upon its surface. Instead I saw my own reflection, skin as white as the sickly orb above me. Only my eyes gave light, flashes of green ice. Unruly hair curled around my head like the red serpent-tresses of some pale Medusa. In the measureless depth I could see a face beside my own. As it rose towards me, I knew that it was Miriam, her eyes smiling and warm, her face my own face but finely moulded and graceful, her hair a swathe of red satin. And then there was another face that rose on the other side of mine. She was like Miriam, but more like me with her serpent hair and her worried eyes. There was something on her cheek. Something dark that oozed and trickled down from her forehead, matting her hair and staining her skin. Then the surface rippled and our three faces merged together, making us one. I was overwhelmed by a surge of fear and loathing.

'No, I'm not you!' I cried. 'I am not you!'

My hands pounded the water's surface. The trinity shattered into a thousand shards, flying away from each other on concentric waves.

Then, suddenly, the world tilted. I screamed and snatched at the edge of the pool as the ground fell away beneath me. I was sliding over sharp-edged rocks, wet and slimed with moss. Only they weren't rocks, they were slates and I was sliding down, tumbling into emptiness. My hands clutched at something hard and cold, and I was hanging over the edge of a roof with no ground below me, just an empty, endless pit of darkness. Rotting metal flaked beneath my hands. It creaked, then jolted and swayed. Then all was still. I held on, the sinews of my bloodless fingers taut and cramped with pain. Then I was jarred and shaken again. This time the gutter gave way in a shower of dust and I was falling down and down and down . . .

My whole body jolted awake. It took a moment to realise where I was and for the terror to subside. I was still alone. The fire had died in the night, and morning light was seeping into the room, cold and grey as the spent ashes in the hearth.

Twenty-one

I CAN'T STOP SHIVERING. The mist is still quite thick. It swirls around me, wet and clinging, its coldness seeping through my clothes, my skin, invading every fibre of my body. I welcome it. It tells me I'm alive.

There's no one else to be seen. Perhaps I'm the sole survivor on an abandoned ship. No, that's silly. The other passengers are inside, either asleep or hanging around the bars getting steadily drunk. But I'm determined to stay on deck, even though there's nothing yet to see. My legs throb with the pounding of the engines. Somewhere out of sight, back in the mist and the darkness, water is churned into creamy trails to mark our passage. I think, at long last, it may be growing lighter, the palest whisper of dawn diffused through clouds of sea vapour. If I lean over I can make out the sea, a sheet of black glass far below me. The railing is the only colour in this cold world. They have painted it bright yellow, and there are patches of scabrous rust where the salt has bitten into it and flecks of paint speckle my hands. I'm holding on tight to this railing. It's hard and cold and wet and very, very real.

I drove all the way across-country. Motorways must have been invented by sadists for the exclusive use of masochists. My back feels like someone has drilled iron bolts through it. The journey took hours, with just the occasional stop for petrol and sludgy, service-station coffee. I suppose I should have eaten something. I did manage to catch a few hours' sleep before I came on board, but I still feel exhausted. My face is stretched tight and my eyes are red-raw as if I've been rubbing grit in them. I'd sell my soul for a hot bath.

It was only yesterday morning when I awoke in Miriam's chair, but it could have been in another lifetime and in some far, forgotten century. I sat in the cold morning light, watching the dead fire, waiting for something to happen, even though I knew nothing would. The responsibility was mine. I was the one who had to make things change. I uncurled, stiff and aching, and walked through the dim hallway to my studio. This was my territory — the only part of Miriam's world I could honestly own. As I stood in front of her portrait, she looked down at me, seemingly unchanged. Oh, but she *had* changed. This was no longer the woman I had painted.

'Who are you?' I spoke out loud, startled by my voice reverberating through the hollow house. 'Did I ever know you? Were you ever my Miriam?'

There was no answer. Her eyes were my eyes. Yes, all three of us, we have the same eyes, the same genetic pattern carried over the centuries. Perhaps that explains a great deal. Those eyes looked at me and into me as if they knew I was there. I think she loved me — yes, perhaps in a way she did. Whoever she was.

'And you loved him too, didn't you?' I whispered. 'You loved us both. You wanted to show me what real love was, or so you said. Oh, what a wonderful bequest. What a grand and noble gesture.' I was suddenly hot, blood flushing my face and my heart racing, pulse pounding in clenched fists. 'You made a gift of us, each one to the other. Didn't you? I suppose I was the consolation prize, wasn't I? A sort of compensation for your mortality. You thought you could go on owning him through me.' I remembered how he was on the day of her burial. I saw him, standing there, in that very place, looking at her just as I did. Then later he had turned to me for help.

Give it to me, he had begged. *Give it to me now, while I can still ask it of you. Give it to me. Before it is too late.*

And I had failed him.

'Did he plead with you like that? In that brief release, when he could still think for himself; before the trap closed in on him again?'

She gazed at me, unmoving and unmoved.

'You may have loved him, but you didn't love him enough, did you, Miriam? Or is it Eriu? Whoever you are, you had no right to do this to us. *You had no right!*'

It wasn't something born of impulse. It was a deliberate, calculated act, all fury channelled and compressed into a fine edge. I walked to the kitchen. The flagstones struck coldness through my feet and I remember thinking that I must have slipped my shoes off by the fire and shouldn't forget them later. I knew which drawer to open. They lay there, a dozen or more, bright shining steel and the wood worn pale in patches by years of familiar touch. I tested each one, scraping it across the ball of my thumb. The one I chose was large and broad, like a bright, silver fish, the handle rosewood and curved to fit the palm of my hand. I carried it back to the studio. A pale wash of sunlight had entered the room in my absence. It glinted off brush handles and metal tubes. I noticed that I had left the top off one and there was a crusting of crimson paint sticking to the tabletop.

I turned to the portrait, not sure exactly how to go about the task. Grasping the frame firmly with my left hand I pressed the point of the blade into the top corner. The canvas moved but resisted the pressure. I lifted my wrist away and thrust down, stabbing the surface. This time it gave in a jagged tear. The knife dragged down and down, each thread of the weave resisting then breaking, stopping and then moving. Where I cut through dry paint, it came away like a shower of confetti-coloured petals. Other patches were still soft, and rippled against the blade in plastic ridges. The knife reached the opposite corner and the canvas flapped loosely in the middle. I moved the knife to the top, the other corner, made a second cut to cross the first; turned the knife to the side, another gash.

Hold the frame. Stab, pull. Turn the knife.

Stab, pull.

Slash, tear.

Cut, and cut again.

Again. And again. And again.

Then it all stopped. There was nothing left to destroy. Shreds of canvas hung from the wood like the tattered remnants of a battle flag. I stepped back, gasping, the energy flowing out of me like blood from a wound. Then I placed the knife carefully on the table among the empty tubes of paint, turned, and left the room.

My feet twisted into my shoes while I searched for Greg's phone number. He wouldn't be at his office on a Sunday. That was a good thing. It would make everything easier if there were no questions, no convoluted explanations. I pressed the numbers. The secretary's voice, a polite apology, detailed instructions, bleeps and buzzes that gave me no space to speak. Eventually, when there was silence, it took me by surprise.

'Er, Greg? It's Chloe. Look, I'm going away for a while, a few weeks. I've decided to sell the cottage.' Intention crystallised from the words as they tumbled out. 'Can you do that for me? Sell the house, I mean. Get an estate agent or whatever one has to do?'

I looked around at the low room with its crumbly walls and dust-silted shelves, paintings barely discernible through tar-thickened varnish, graze-cracked porcelain and threadbare rugs — the battered relics of extinguished lives.

'And everything in it. There's nothing here I want to keep. Get rid of it all.'

Sweet relief washed over me like cool, cleansing rain.

'I'm not sure exactly where I'll be yet. I'll ring you in a few days, as soon as I have an address. I suppose you'll want the keys? I'll drop them in the post, I won't be needing them again. Oh, and thank you, Greg. Thank you for everything.'

Another assault on the studio, this time armed with boxes. I tried not to look at the wreckage on the easel. There were paints and paper to be gathered, pencils and brushes. A few small canvases, all that I could sensibly carry. Through the house with them and into the boot of the car. My suitcase was ready: there'd been no time to unpack it. There it lay in the hall just as we'd left it yesterday, but I mustn't allow myself to think about yesterday, just pick it up, take it to the car. Then my coat, thrown on the front seat. I stood in the roadway. I had taken everything I wanted from this place.

No, there was something else. Back through the hall and up the stairs to Miriam's bedroom and the chest of drawers. It was in the bottom drawer, right at the back where I had covered it over, reburying the secret. I pulled out the shoebox with its silly yellow ribbon. One of the corners tore as I yanked it free, splitting the cardboard. No matter, it would hold.

Then down the stairs again and across the landing. That's where I had thrown Paul's jacket button out of the window. It must be still out there somewhere. Oh, God, Paul. I had forgotten all about him. I should have gone to see him. No, I couldn't face that. Not in the hospital. Not knowing that it was my fault. Could I tell him that? Perhaps I should ring? And say what, for heaven's sake? Tell him everything? Tell him the truth? Oh, right, yes, and he'd have a team of psychiatrists around here before I put the phone down.

Perhaps I could simply write to him, apologise for the way I'd behaved? But what does an apology achieve, anyway, apart from comforting the perpetrator and paralysing the victim? No, contrition was too cowardly a weapon. Paul would forgive me, of course; it was the right and proper thing to do, an act of chivalry. Then I could run away with a clear conscience and leave him to stifle his resentment beneath his stuffed shirt. No, I wouldn't do that to him. I'd leave him with his anger intact, that'd be the least I could do. God knows he'd earned it. Could I bear the thought that he might grow to hate me? Well, let that be my penance.

The engagement ring was still in my purse. I dropped the shoebox on the table while I searched for an envelope, slipped the ring inside, wrote Paul's name on the front and propped it on the mantelpiece. Someone would find it. Someone would give it to him.

I turned to retrieve the box and saw the flute on the table. It must have been there all the while, the two woods blending together and making it almost invisible in the early light. Only then, with the sunlight dancing off the keys, did it call to me. Instinctively my hand reached out to the deep, warm glow of its body and to any trace of him that lingered there. The tune he had played surged through my head as if it would burst through and flood the room. For a moment my fingers glanced over the instrument, almost touching. For a moment I almost gave way.

I stepped back, snatched up the box of letters and ran with it to the car.

I won't let this coldness beat me. The sky is definitely lighter now, endowing the layers of fog with a phosphorescent glow. I don't think it's my imagination — yes, I can see a smudge of darkness where the horizon would be. We should be nearly there by now. I wonder how it was for those first travellers. The Tuatha de Danaan came out of the misty seas, it is said, from some mysterious land far away. They came with their swords and their songs and their magical arts. They came in their wooden boats with the sails slack in the windless air and their oars silently dipping the water. Is this how they first saw the land of Inisfael? All I have is my paints. And some money, and my car. I suppose I'm comparatively well-off. But they had each other, and I'm alone. For the first time in my life, I'm completely alone.

Hannah. I suddenly miss her. How strange, I never thought I could. I must ring her as soon as I can. I really will this time.

Things have changed between us and we need to talk Oh, I don't suppose we can ever get to understand each other, but there must be some way of reconciling the past. I wonder if I should invite her to join me here? No, she'd never set foot in Ireland again. But what about the New Year? Would she go to Boston with me? Maybe. I have that box of cards, all those unhappy birthday wishes, all those uncarolled Christmases, all clamouring to be heard. Between us, Harold and I might be able to persuade her.

Hannah was right, of course. So, why didn't I listen to her? Well, she's my mother, isn't she? The last person I'd listen to. But she does love me, I can see that now. In fact, of all of them she's the only one who ever did. So why does she have to be so bloody irritating? Yes, I'll have to call her soon.

Something is happening. There's a break in the rhythm of the engines. The pulse of the ship is slowing and the throbbing deck picks up a deeper, richer note. There's a barely perceptible tilt as the stern slews sideways. I cling tightly to the rail. The darkened skyline has taken on shape and form, squares and angles, a jumble of roofs pinpricked with electric light. Men's voices carry across the water, vibrant in the empty air. It won't be long now. I'm not simply running away; there's some purpose in it. You can't run away from something without running towards somewhere else at the same time, even if that's not what you intended. We have a history here, Miriam Delaney and Eriu and me. Our roots are buried deep in this land. And I will paint. That is his gift to me. I will paint and make it my gift to him in return, the only way I have of saying thank you. I will paint because that's all I have left of him now.

It was the hardest thing I'd ever done. It's still with me and it always will be, cut sharp and clear into my mind where I relive it, second by second.

I stand by the cottage gate for a few moments, holding myself steady. Then I walk, for the last time, the length of the path and through the ancient door, on through the rooms, then out again, into the garden and the orchard. The sun, still barely above the hedgerows, dazzles my eyes through a veil of mist. I hardly notice the chill in the air. A frosting of dew blanches the lawn and the tender blades are crushed beneath my feet. Autumn has taken a fast hold and winter will be swift to follow.

Harvesting is over. It's time to give back to the earth.

The trees are all but bare. Here and there a tenacious leaf holds on in hope. Strange how the trees were so much taller when I was a child. Which was my favourite for climbing? I can touch the lower branches now without stretching. Why does it have to be so near, so effortless? Is it to be this easy? Is there to be no struggle? My fingers are cold, all blood drained from them, but the chain is warm. I lift it over my head and it catches a strand of hair. I pull and it tugs and hurts; such a little pain. I press the silver to my cheek, whispering 'Goodbye'. I can't think of anything else to say, so I loop the chain over a twig and it twists around itself, then unwinds and hangs free.

Should I call his name? Surely he knows. I step back, slowly, slowly, my feet finding their own way across the grass, my eyes never leaving that tree and the glint of silver below the branch. The whole world is still, forgotten beyond this garden and the gentle mist. The heaviness of silence presses down on me like a mountain of emptiness as the waiting stretches on and on.

There!

Between the trees I see a ripple of light, as if the air itself were melting. I hold myself like a stone, afraid that even my breath may betray the moment. The air parts and he steps through — such an easy thing to do. He looks towards me, his eyes brimming with sadness and hope, and then to the tree and its strange fruit. And for a while he doesn't move. Then his voice. I hear it in my head, although I swear his lips don't move.

I had a little nut tree, nothing would it bear,
But a silver nutmeg...

He turns to me again, and smiles across the distance that separates us, raising his hand in readiness for mine. But I can see the doubt in his eyes. He knows. I shake my head. Then he turns again to the talisman. His fingers trace the line of the chain, then carefully, so very carefully, he lifts it with both hands and takes it from the branch.

He turns, holding the silver necklace out to me. A last temptation. Again I hear his voice.

The King of Spain's daughter came to visit me,
And all for the sake of ...

I shake my head, and this time, although I bite my lip, my voice seems to ring between us. But the sound is only the throbbing of my pulse. *Take it,* it says, *take it, take it.*

And he does.

He lifts the chain high above his head, and his neck arches back, his nostrils flaring like those of some wild creature. And, as the talisman comes to rest on his body, his shoulders flex and his arms stretch wide so that he stands as if on some high mountain crag, ready to take flight.

But one last time he turns to me and offers his hand.

Go, please go, I beg him in silence.

There is a moment that draws on and on. And then his voice in my mind.

I danced over water, I skipped over sea,
And all the birds in the air...

He moves backwards. The air parts around him, like the curtain of a waterfall

... couldn't catch ...

and he steps through

... me!

and is gone. And the silence of the morning crashes in around my ears and I am buried alive in it.

I stand watching the space where he has been, and it seems like forever, although it could be a moment or an hour. A light breeze stirs my hair and quivers the branches of that one tree. On that same twig the last leaf comes away and begins its slow, tumbling journey to the ground.

Before it reaches the earth, I turn and flee.

Swiftly across the lawn. I won't look back. Through the kitchen, the hall. I daren't stop. Out the front door. It bangs shut behind me, such a final, echoing sound that I know it will never open for me again. Into the car and the keys drop and I fumble for them and the engine turns and lurches forward and the wheel spins and mud flies like black rain.

I daren't drive like this. Rounding the bend, I pull into the kerb. Breath screams in my chest and my heart is pounding. I lean on the coolness of the steering wheel while the world slows to a gentler rhythm. A deep breath and I stretch my spine against the seat and turn and look back. The thatched roof is just visible between the trees where the old, familiar chimneys twist into the sky.

Is there something?

Yes.

A small dark thing, moving against the clouds. It circles high above the rooftops, then turns again, making a wider sweep.

A bird.

It is a bird that has no place in this stark, fen landscape. Its wingspan is too broad and splays out to catch the air; its eye is too bright, its beak too cruel. Unfaltering, it dips to swoop across my path, then banks, rising higher, cresting the wind, flying free.

And from its talon, a flashing blade of light, as if the sun catches something bright, something that spins and sparkles as he flies.

As if it were made of silver.